A
Heart Life

a novel

Patricia Yager
Delagrange

Dedication: For you, Allessandra

Other Books by Patricia Yager Delagrange

Passing Through Brandiss
Moon Over Alcatraz
Taken Away
Maddy's Phoenix
Mending Fences

MICHAEL

Present Day

Outsiders call Balmoral State Penitentiary the rich man's version of San Quentin. A prison for pussies, the guards say, as they shove us into our individual cells. No sharing cells in this place. Guess they're afraid we might find a way to smuggle in a shank on visiting day and kill our roomie.

Wikipedia describes Balmoral State Penitentiary, otherwise referred to as BSP, as a state penitentiary in California nicknamed "the vacation spot for white-collar criminals." Labeling BSP as a vacation spot is the most egregious offense of all. I don't have anything to compare it to, since this is the first time I've ever been in prison, in jail, in any place they send people who commit a crime. Immediately after sentencing, my attorney told me Balmoral would be an easy place for me to fit in.

My first feeling, after he said that, was indignant. I don't want to ever "fit in" in prison. I know what he means, though. So far, I haven't been beat up by any gang members. That's a good thing. Here at BSP, they separate the not-so-bad from the bad from the worst. I'm categorized as not-so-bad. Interesting, that.

First of all, I don't belong here. But isn't that what every prisoner says?

I didn't do it.

There's been a mistake.

You're confusing me with someone who looks just like me.

Now, let me reiterate. I don't belong here. I didn't say I didn't commit a crime. In prison, there are levels of severity of crimes. No, what I should say is, there are levels of acceptability of crimes, amongst prisoners as well as guards, referred to as the G's.

Not everyone has been sent here for a white-collar crime, though. California prisons are notoriously overcrowded. Prisoners are transferred from prison to prison. Here at BSP, we have some typical white-collar criminals who are businessmen or government professionals, people of high social status whose crimes include bribery, extortion, embezzlement, cyber crimes. They're at the top of the heap.

Then we have the guys who we (and I use that term loosely, since I've never felt a part of this place) consider the bottom-of-the-barrel criminals. These guys have committed major crimes like murder, rape, child molestation, kidnapping. These rapists, child molesters, pedophiles, and most of the kidnappers are considered the lowest of the low in BSP, the scum of the earth.

Sandwiched between the top of the heap and the bottom are the middle guys, the murderers who, for numerous and random reasons, are not considered despicable, depending on their victims and the reasons behind their crimes. Fortunately for me, I am not at the top, nor am I at the bottom. Theoretically, I fit in the middle. However, most of the guys here don't consider me a murderer either.

My attorney has taken almost my last dime at this point, but he's worth it if I can get out of this place early, which looks as if that might happen. According to him, since California just passed a law making assisted suicide legal, he swears he'll be able to have my sentence for involuntary manslaughter reduced to time served.

But he told me it's not a slam-dunk. While it has now become permissible for doctors to prescribe death-inducing medications, it's still taboo in the medical community, of which I am no longer a member, by the way. The court ripped away my privileges before I stepped through the prison doors. Additionally, my crime, if you're so inclined to call it that, isn't a classic case of what California terms "assisted suicide."

According to the new California law, a doctor must examine the patient, verify that s/he has an illness that will likely be terminal within six months, and determine that s/he's mentally competent. Those findings must be verified by a physician who isn't affiliated with the first physician.

The patient must then fill out and sign a form requesting the life-ending medication, and the signing must be witnessed by at least two other people. Once the prescription has been written, the patient can decide whether to fill it and when. California law requires the patient to then take the medication themselves. No one is allowed to administer it.

And there lies the rub in my case. Or several rubs, actually.

Heather didn't fill out and sign the form requesting the medication. Also, there were no witnesses. Additionally, my wife didn't fill the prescription then decide to take it on May 23, 2013. She was unable to administer the drug to herself. She couldn't even pick up a utensil to eat.

I administered the pentobarbital. Heather told me that's what she wanted. Well, she didn't ask for the pentobarbital, per se, but she told me at the end, when she could still talk, that she wanted to die. She begged me to help her before she got to the point where she was incapable of speaking or writing or puckering her lips to kiss me or move her arms to hug me. "If I get to that point, Michael, please promise me you'll help end my life. If you love me, you will."

So I made her a promise. She couldn't talk or write or kiss or hug. She was dying. She was practically dead. And she was suffering, terribly.

I just made her experience shorter.

LEENA

"Hey, Joy, could you come and set the table, please?"

My daughter's footsteps pound down the stairs. She sounds like a two-hundred-pound man with steel-toed boots. Joy measures five feet tall and weighs one hundred pounds, but her big, black, clunky shoes are indeed capable of irritatingly loud noise. However, she's nineteen and can wear whatever she wants. And do whatever she wants as well.

I've never tried to push her in any direction with regard to clothing, neither ultra-feminine nor businesslike nor high-fashion. Joy has her own style, though I'd be hard-pressed to define it. No matter the weather, it's long sleeves every day that come past her knuckles, sometimes to her fingertips. Her pants are usually Army camo or leggings. In her ears, she has what are called "gauges," which are holes that start out small then are enlarged step-by-step with earrings, until now she has a half-inch hole in each earlobe. Her septum is pierced as well, which has always reminded me of Elsie the cow, but I'll never tell Joy that. And last I heard, she's interested in having her nipples pierced. It's her body. What can I say?

"I thought I didn't have to come to dinner tonight," she says. "You said Karen's coming over."

I give her The Look, and she turns with a huff, mumbling under her breath, and walks to the kitchen.

"What're we having anyway?" she yells.

I enter the kitchen behind her, and she's gathering silverware out of the drawer. Her hands are covered in various colors of paint.

"Honey, why don't you wash your hands first?"

She sighs in an exaggerated fashion, dumps the knives and forks back in the drawer in a heap, sidesteps to the sink and washes her hands. She doesn't slide her shirt sleeves up, and by the time she's finished, her cuffs are soaking wet and the paint is still there and has permanently stained her shirt.

I don't want to pick on her, as she often calls it, so I say nothing. I'm happy she's engaged in an artistic endeavor and encourage it wholeheartedly. Money for the arts in schools has been dwindling for years, so I'm thrilled Joy's interested in something other than listening to music on her iPhone. I've seen many of her paintings, and I'm impressed. She has a flair for using pastels to create happy scenes through the brushstrokes spread across the canvas. Sunrises, sunsets, beach scenes, horses in green pastures. When I look at her art, I smile. Then I wonder how it is that Joy doesn't emanate the same mood and feelings that fly off her painted canvases. I would never call her ebullient. Ofttimes, the adjective morose is most descriptive.

While drying her hands with a towel, she looks at me and asks again, "What's for dinner?"

"Baked chicken casserole. You know the one with mushroom soup and bread crumbs with cheese on top."

She rolls her eyes. "What about me?"

Joy is picky about everything she eats and vows to turn Steven and me into vegetarians before she moves out. Since she's nineteen and in junior college, she doesn't have much time left to pull off a feat of such magnificent proportions. Although Steven's a doctor, he'll fight till the cows come home, literally, to prove that eating beef in moderation won't kill him. And so the argument goes.

I roll my eyes as well, mimicking her. "I made twice-baked potatoes. Your favorite. With broccoli and Gouda cheese with bacon bits on top."

Joy places her hands on her waist, arms akimbo. "I don't eat bacon."

"This bacon's made of soybeans, Joy. It's a recipe I found in the vegetarian cookbook you gave me for Christmas."

She stands in front of the cupboards, her long, straight, dark brown hair swaying just above her waist, looking through the glass doors at the plates and saucers and glasses.

"Joy, since when does Karen's arrival mean you're exempt from joining us for Sunday dinner? I thought you enjoyed Karen's company."

She turns her head in my direction, one eyebrow raised. "Will Daddy be here?"

I inhale deeply, then let it out as slowly as I can, while trying to come up with another plausible excuse for Steven's absence. I could make one up, but Joy would know. She has this special sense. She knows when I'm lying. It would be better if I just say nothing, then she can come up with her own hypothetical reason for why Steven can't be here—again. No matter what the reason, she's aware her father won't be joining us, and this is just a silly game we're playing.

"Oh, the silent treatment," she says. "Well, that could mean he's in surgery. But on a Sunday night? Hmmm. Even though they don't schedule surgeries on Sunday nights. So, that must mean it's an emergency, right? Oh, that's right, he's not on call this weekend." She pauses and stares me down. Seconds pass. "So where is he, Mom?"

I walk toward her, wanting to envelop her in a huge, all-encompassing mom-hug, but she's not having any of it.

"Don't," she says, placing both hands out to stop me from coming any closer. "No amount of babying me is going to change things."

"He said he'll be here if he can, honey."

She takes three plates, three saucers, and three glasses out of the cupboards, setting them on the counter. Her face is set in such a way that there's no expression whatsoever. It's as blank as a chalkboard that's just been erased with a wet sponge.

Dark brown bangs, iron-straight, hover above lighter brown eyebrows. Her green eyes reveal nothing. Wide lips, perfectly covered in a purple slash of lipstick, dip slightly at the edges. Her displeasure is obvious. Or is it sadness? I can no longer tell.

My daughter was close to her father. Until he was no longer here. It has nothing to do with Joy, however. Yes, she's morphed into the typical silent-most-of-the-time, moody, unaffectionate teenager, but only with me. Steven and Joy were the dynamic duo, making private jokes and subtle remarks only the two of them shared. Most of the time, I felt like the odd woman out. Yet I was happy they shared a bond. I was never close with my father. I envied Joy and Steven's relationship, but not in a green-eyed monster sort of way. I was grateful she had what I never experienced.

Then Steven's surgeries grew to unbelievably outrageous proportions compared to the time any human has available in a twenty-four-hour day. Concurrent with the rise in surgeries came the ballooning of Steven's reputation as the best of the best. And so it went. And so it goes still. He's just never home.

Joy doesn't turn to me to make up for the deficit in her father's attention. I try my best to integrate myself into her life, but to no avail. She's usually polite, but always with minimalist descriptions of her day at college and her personal life. Which leaves me standing on the doorstep of her emotional home, the door slammed shut in my face. But I haven't given up, and I never will. I continue to try.

However, it has become impossible for me to fill the gap of Steven's disappearance from our home life. The look on Joy's face when he graces us occasionally with his presence makes my heart crack—a sound so loud I can almost hear it inside my head. There's such hope and need and yes, joy, in Joy's face when her father's home. I want so much for Steven to see it, too. But he's blind to her need for him. And I can't imagine that ever changing.

For months, I continued to set the table for the three of us. Until it became obvious Sunday dinners were a thing of the past. Something I've endeavored to fill by inviting my best friend, Karen, as often as she's available.

"When's Karen gonna be here?" Joy glances down at the three sets of dishes and silverware. "Is she coming alone, or is she bringing that guy who came with her last time?"

"Alone. The time you're referring to was last year, honey. She's not been seeing him for ages."

She shrugs. "What a surprise. I don't think she's ever been with any guy for more than a month." She walks toward the dining room.

I follow her, grabbing the salt and pepper shakers on my way out. "She's still looking for that one special person."

Karen works at the same hospital as Steven, and being a surgical nurse keeps her busy. But she's never dated anyone she's met at St. John's. She says she doesn't believe in mixing work and romance. And most of the time, she's available to join us for dinner, occasionally introducing us to one of the men she's dating.

Her schedule is six a.m. to three p.m., Monday through Friday, and she loves her work, a big part of that due to the fact her hours are what one would call in the medical field pretty "normal." Whereas Steven's are out of control.

Joy stops next to the dining table. "Just like you found your one special person, Mom?"

"I guess you could say that." I take a step back, allowing Joy to pass as she sets the plates on the table.

She returns to the kitchen, and I walk behind her. She picks up the glasses, while I pull three cloth napkins out of the drawer.

"Your father and I have been together for a long time, Joy. I love him."

She returns to the dining room with me right on her heels.

"Seems to me you spend more time without him, considering he's your husband."

I fold each napkin in half, then place one on top of each plate. I'd love my marriage to be an example of what I want for my daughter. Sadly, I wouldn't want this life for Joy. I hope she finds someone she can share her life with in all the ways that count. Most of the time, I feel guilty for what she's not seeing between Steven and me. Public displays of affection in our home are sorely lacking.

"He's here as much as his schedule allows, Joy. He and I have talked about it, and he's trying to change."

She glances at me, and I can see, it's so damn obvious, that her eyes are shiny and unshed tears are about to spill over her eyelids. But, knowing her, she'll hold them back until she's out of my sight, unaware of all the times I've seen the makeup drooling down her face when she's standing in front of the mirror in the bathroom. She's unhappy, and I don't think it's her period or hormones. It's Steven.

I want so much to reach out to her, but she doesn't want my hug, no matter how much I want to surround her with my arms and squeeze her with all my might. Whether it's out of sympathy for her father's distancing himself from our little family or a gesture of pure mother love on my part, she wants none of it. It seems no matter how much I try, Joy rebuffs me at every turn. But I keep trying, hoping one day I'll be accepted, even if I'm a disappointing substitute for Steven.

I busy myself moving a vase of flowers from the sideboard to the middle of the dining table. Joy plunks down my mother's crystal glasses at each place setting, and I imagine one of them breaking into pieces each time it hits the mahogany table. I keep my mouth shut and breathe an inner sigh of relief when she finishes. I don't want to get on her bad side right before our guest arrives. Though Karen hasn't been considered "company" for years.

"Thanks for setting the table, honey."

Joy doesn't acknowledge me and walks up the stairs to her bedroom.

I sigh. Who said having young children is the hardest thing ever? In my opinion, as Joy grows older, dealing with her has become harder and harder. I'm still trying to break through the shell that keeps me from getting close to her.

And I'd like that to happen before she moves out, though she's never mentioned that. Where would she go? She has no job. She's a full-time student. And when she's not at college, she says she's studying in the library. I believe her, because she's made all A's in every single one of her classes so far.

"Dinner's in an hour," I yell to her backside. "I'll call you when it's ready."

"'Kay," she replies before slamming her bedroom door.

At that exact moment, the doorbell rings. It must be Karen. When I look through the side window facing the porch, Karen's standing there in all her glory.

I met Karen at a Christmas function at St. John's Hospital in San Francisco, back in the day when Steven's reputation was in its nascent phase. His rise to fame was quick, nearing meteoric. Perhaps five years ago, he rocketed to the status of the surgeon to call for those once-in-a-lifetime surgeries that only he can perform.

We were close, Steven and Karen and Joy and I. Back when Steven had time. The four of us went out to dinner together. Sometimes, Karen would even accompany us on our family vacations. Joy loved Karen, and Karen was a great "sitter" when Steven and I wanted alone time.

As Steven's career took off, my relationship with Karen blossomed. She was the girlfriend I hadn't had since I was in high school. We did everything together. Shopped. Went out to lunch, saw movies, plays, the opera. Bottom line, I spent Steven's money. I'd been a stay-at-home mom since I'd gotten pregnant with Joy and never looked back, as they say.

When you're married to a famous surgeon in the San Francisco Bay Area, there are quite a number of galas, dinners, and meetings that require your presence by his side. Enough to keep me very busy, along with serving on committees raising funds for childhood cancer, organ donation, after-chemo care, post-surgical rehabilitation. I gradually had less and less time for Karen as Steven became well-known, concurrent with Joy morphing into a teenager. But Karen often takes Steven's place at our family's Sunday dinner table, and she and I still meet up occasionally for "girl time."

Karen turns toward the window, sees me, and smiles. I understand why men always look two or three times when we're out together. But when I mention it, she always has a comeback.

"They're not looking at me, Leena. You're the one with the huge rack. I can hardly fill an A cup, for Christ sake."

I always laugh, feeling my usual red-hot blush burn up my throat into my cheeks and forehead.

"Leena, you're the one with the naturally wavy auburn hair, big boobs, and curvy little body. Dudes confuse you with what's-her-face. Except, you don't have the accent or the coloring. Sofia something or other. Vergara. Sofia Vergara. Without the Colombian touch."

And so goes our banter, back and forth, back and forth. But we love each other, BFFs all the way. The only thing we don't talk much about is my personal relationship with Steven, or our sexual relationship either. I've never felt comfortable doing so. Karen often works directly with my husband, for hours on end in the OR. Surgical nurses are the crux of any surgery. At least, that's the impression I have from the scuttlebutt at parties and social gatherings of staff from St. John's. From everyone I've ever spoken to, Karen has a fantastic and well-deserved reputation.

She is model-perfect. Perfect blonde hair to her

shoulders, straight and shiny, with not one split end to be seen. Makeup done with a light touch, just enough mascara to highlight her thick, long lashes. Smooth pinkish lipstick on her full lips. She weighs all of a hundred and fifteen pounds and works out at the gym, her biceps and forearms toned, her calves sleek and not too muscular. She has the face and body of someone you'd see on the red carpet at the Oscars. You just don't recall what movie you've seen her in.

I open the front door, and Karen pushes her way past me, headed straight for the kitchen.

"Brought a very expensive bottle of wine. Yesterday Steven performed the most beautiful orchidectomy I've ever had the pleasure of assisting on, and some old guy handed it to me today as a thank you gift."

Karen says all this while scrounging through the kitchen drawers, looking for a corkscrew. When she finds it, she points it in my direction, smiles, and begins screwing it into the top of the wine bottle like a pro. "I'm sure the patient was so excited his dick was still going to be functional, he failed to notice the year and thus the price of this bottle of wine he gave me in thanks for the outcome." Karen grabs two wineglasses from the cupboard, pours a tablespoon into one glass, swirls it around, sniffs near the edge of the glass, then glances up at me. "You're gonna love this shit. All because some old codger now has a new set of prosthetic balls."

I laugh. Karen's sense of humor borders on the edge of the gutter, but never quite drops over the curb into embarrassingly crude humor. At least in my opinion.

I grab the bottle and finish filling Karen's glass, then pour my own. "Then I guess we should consider ourselves lucky Steven is such a good surgeon."

"Good surgeon, she says." Karen rolls her eyes. "Your husband has the hands of God, is what the staff says. He can work miracles performing surgeries other doctors won't even touch."

"So I've heard," I say seriously. "His hands do indeed work miracles." I sigh, silently wishing those hands would occasionally work miracles on this body instead of his patients.

Karen lifts her eyebrows up and down several times. "Miracle hands, Leena. Or so I've heard."

I shake my head. "Not from my lips, you haven't. Is there something you're not telling me?"

Karen laughs out loud. More like a guffaw, but coming out of her slim little body, the word guffaw would give you the wrong impression. Her laugh is hearty and makes you want to join in, just for the hell of it.

"There's nothing I'm not telling you, Leena. How would I know anything about Steven's sex life? It doesn't take a rocket scientist to see how adept he is with his hands in surgery to extrapolate how he must be in bed. Am I right?"

I take a huge gulp of wine, choke, put the glass on the counter, and bend over, hands on my knees, coughing until I've cleared my airway.

Karen pats me on the back. "Are you all right? I'm sorry. I was just making a joke."

I nod, trying to catch my breath, still feeling as if I've swallowed something huge instead of a tablespoon or so of expensive red wine. After straightening up, I look her in the eyes. "I've never talked to you about my sex life with Steven. Or anyone else, for that matter. I'm not going to start now."

Karen shrugs. "You told me he was your first. And I'm not asking anyway. But, hey, Leena. It's not unusual to share that with your BFF, you know."

I glance at the ceiling, then return my gaze to hers. "I don't talk about what goes on behind closed doors. It's private, okay?"

"I know. I know. You've made that perfectly clear. It's not something you feel comfortable chatting about."

I cock an eyebrow. "Whereas some people have no qualms about telling it all."

Karen chuckles. "Sex was never taboo in my family. Then again, what would you expect when your daddy's a pimp and your momma's his hobby?" Her face instantly changes from having a good time and joking around to funereal.

I reach out and lay my hand on her forearm. "Let's not go there. It's all in the past. Look where you are today, no thanks to the two of them, right?"

Karen places her hand on top of mine, looks me in the eyes. "May they both rot in hell."

I nod. "Which I'm betting is where they both are right this moment."

She shakes her head like a dog that's just exited a lake. "All in the past, as you said." She grabs the wine bottle. "Let's go finish this thing."

"Hold on. I've made food to go with that wine."

"Isn't the wine supposed to go along with the food, Leena?"

"Yeeeesss," I add. "But why is the wine always finished and there's leftovers I have to put in the refrigerator for another night? That bottle won't have a drop left by the end of our meal."

"True dat," Karen says, then winks. "I learned that from one of our patients. Young kid from the hood. It's kind of cute, don'tcha think?"

"At our age?"

Karen shrugs. "Age is a number, Leena. Not a way of talking or behaving. I'm going to be like this until I'm laid in my casket."

"Over my dead body," I say, then laugh out loud.

Karen slaps at me, sets the wine bottle back on the counter. "Let me help you with dinner."

"No need. Everything's in the oven and will be ready in a few minutes."

"Where's Joy-girl?"

"In her bedroom, I suppose. Where else?" I let out a sigh.

She cocks her head. "Is she okay? You said she doesn't open up much."

I nod. "She doesn't tell me about her classes. She's rarely home. I assume she has a group of friends, but honestly, Karen, when I was her age, I had tons of girlfriends. Didn't you?"

"I did. I was in nursing school and was a very serious student, but we knew how to par-tay like the best of the guys in the frat houses."

"From what I can tell, friends are glaringly missing in her repertoire of people she mentions. When that happens. Which isn't often. And she never says anything about crushes. She has no posters of lead singers in bands on her bedroom walls. In fact, she never mentions boys at all."

Karen shrugs. "Maybe she's gay."

"I've often wondered that. But why would she hide it? I'm openly accepting of anyone's sexuality. I've spent most of my life in California."

"It's one thing to be accepting of gays outside the house. She may think if she told you she's a lesbian, that would hit a little too close to home."

"I see your point." I pause. "Sometimes I wonder if

Joy has had any friends since middle school, because that was the last time anyone came to our house."

"That is kind of weird. But I'm not a mom, so what would I know? Plus, in Joy's eyes, we're both old, Leena."

"Things are definitely not like they were when I was young, I'll give you that. She's glued to her cell phone like everyone else. It's possible she's texting her friends on Instagram or Snapchat."

Karen chuckles. "Virtual friends, I call them."

"Better than no friends at all, right? Though my personal jury is out on that one."

"Having real people for your pals is a helluva lot different than those found on the internet, Leena. When you really need someone to hold your hand or look you in the eye when you're down, where are those people?"

"On their phone or the computer."

"That's what I mean."

"And all that catfishing? That happens too frequently for my comfort. But that's just me."

I sigh, and Karen opens her arms.

I walk into them. "I love you, ya know that?" I say.

"BFFs forever."

Karen is the best person I have in my life right now. I know that sounds terrible, but when you have a husband who's never home and a daughter who misses her dad's presence so badly she won't talk to anyone else, well, you get my drift.

STEVEN

I glance at the ceiling of the OR and let out a whoosh of breath. "Dr. Arlington, would you do the honors and close, please?"

Dr. Arlington is so surprised, her raised eyebrows touch the bottom edge of her surgical cap.

I step back and look into her baby blues, almost indecipherable behind thick protective glasses.

Eyes wide, she says, "I'd be happy to, Dr. Coughlin."

I nod ever so slightly, turn, and walk out of the OR to the scrub room.

As I'm pulling off my surgical gloves, someone pats me on the back. I turn my head. "You're still one of the best surgical nurses around, Ms. Roberts."

"Nice the way you let Dr. Arlington close."

I tear off my surgical mask in one swift jerk, then throw it toward the open bin. "She deserves it. I can always tell the Stanfords from the Harvards."

Karen laughs.

That laugh would make most men cringe. But coming from someone so strikingly gorgeous…

"You're a prejudiced elitist, Dr. Coughlin."

I shrug. "My wife says the same thing."

Karen bumps my butt with her hip as she passes me

on her way to the women's locker room. I smile, shaking my head. She's a pistol. And she knows it.

After showering and dressing in street clothes, I head for The Drunken Ball—the upscale bar down the street from St. John's, frequented by almost all surgeons and nurses on staff at the hospital. There is a story behind the name. The man who bought and renovated the place is an oncologist's son. He was diagnosed with testicular cancer at an early age. His father, also his primary physician and oncologist, treated him. His son went into remission and to this day is cancer-free. He told me once that he wanted to celebrate his zest for life and thankfulness for being alive every single day. Hence, The Drunken Ball is open seven days a week until one in the morning.

The atmosphere is very noisy and very loud. Given the typical day of any of the people in this bar at this hour, the level of laughter and release of tension emanating from every table in the house is not surprising.

Reminds me of a bar I went to once that was an after-hours meeting place for cops. I could almost feel the pent-up tension, like steam coming out of every pore of every single cop in the bar, whether male or female. But if you think about what they see and do while on their beats, it's no wonder the atmosphere's that way. There's a need to let down their guard and let go, some way, somehow, whether by drinking too much to forget or screwing someone, anyone, before they explode.

Same with The Drunken Ball. We deal with death every single day of the week. I would say most times, I win. Very few times, I lose. That's what places me at the top of the heap. I wouldn't say I'm egotistical. The statistics are what they are, and they just so happen to be in my favor. I'm good. No, I'm great at what I do, and I seldom fail.

But at the same time, living up to my own image is daunting. I dare not fuck up. Not once. Or I could join the bigger heap at the bottom of the pile, and I've already been there, done that. I like where I am today, and I deserve all the kudos I get. It's been one of the hardest roads I've ever traveled, and I'm finally reaping all the benefits befitting a man of my caliber.

Call it what you will, I'm worth every dollar I get in my paycheck. When you hold so many people's lives in your hands for so many hours every day, what with the amount I pay in malpractice insurance every month for doing so, you bet I deserve what I make. You'd feel the same way in my shoes.

And the price I pay for my success comes not only in the dollars for malpractice insurance, but I owe a huge debt of gratitude for the silence of my colleagues about what they probably know of my personal life when I'm not at home.

Don't get me wrong. I love Leena. And I love Joy. I give them everything they may need or want, for being so understanding of the hours I work and the time I spend at St. John's. Many wives would have deserted my ship a long time ago. My daughter still speaks to me, even after all the plays I've missed and parent/teacher conferences where I was a no-show. So I gladly hand over the money I make to Leena and Joy and say, "You go, girls. Buy whatever makes you happy." I'm fine with it.

The way I look at it, I don't come home and bore them with the endless stories of life hanging on the edge of death at my workplace. I do enough of that at The Drunken Ball. My tales of sticky plaque and diseased hearts stay in the hospital and in this bar. I don't want to relive them over and over again at home. I don't think

Leena or Joy understands how difficult it is to function in that atmosphere, day in and day out, 24/7, 365. I keep that to myself.

When I'm home, which, granted, isn't often, I try to be there one hundred percent. Just me. Not as an employee of St. John's Hospital, but as the husband of Leena and the father of Joy. What they don't know about life and death at St. John's will not hurt them. Though, I admit, the number of hours I spend at home pales in comparison to the overwhelming amount of time I'm at the hospital… and other places.

And what goes on at The Drunken Ball is but a tiny slice of my personal life. And my family does not need to know about it. When I'm at the bar, I'm Dr. Steven Coughlin, surgeon. When I leave the bar and don't go straight home, I'm still Dr. Steven Coughlin, surgeon. But when I walk into my house in Pacific Heights in San Francisco, that's when I'm Steven or Dad—a husband and a father. And I'm all theirs.

The phrase "the truth will set you free" doesn't have anything to do with what I do outside my home. That truth would not set me free. It's a ball and chain I carry around my neck as penance for leading a life very few individuals are privy to. But it's only the smallest part of what's important to me. My family means everything, and I gladly wear that ball and chain of secrecy in exchange for having a family I love, who remain ignorant of my "other life."

"Steven, over here."

I look across the way-too-crowded room and see Arthur Pembroke, chief of surgery at St. John's. He's actually a complete incompetent asshole when it comes to running the surgical staff, all of whom have him wrapped around their fingers, not the other way around. But at the end of the day, when we all leave our white coats and green scrubs in the locker rooms, he's a funny guy. He tells the most off-color jokes I have ever heard, short of listening to Dave Chapelle on Netflix, but he makes me laugh until I can hardly stand it any longer.

In some sense, he saves me from myself, because without him, I gravitate to the sexiest female in the room, which often can be playing with fire. Until I know the person I'm talking to can keep quiet about my activities here and outside of here, I have to be careful. It's an unspoken rule that what happens at The Drunken Ball (or immediately after leaving the place) stays at The Drunken Ball. So I have to watch my p's and q's and totally trust those to whom I tell my p's and q's.

But I've developed an innate ability to weed out those who can't be trusted. It's usually single women who are the ones who talk too much. They have yet to refine the necessary sensitivity in the art of discretion. The married women know all about that. The single women need to be taught. The single women I do select have already learned the lessons, before I have anything to do with them outside the walls of this establishment.

I don't want to be the one to show them the ropes, so to speak. Let that come from someone else with the time and the interest to slog through the rules of behavior that come with frequenting this place. I just want to have a few drinks, let off some steam, and sometimes go straight home afterward.

And sometimes not.

LEENA

It's late the following Sunday. The bed dips on Steven's side. I'm having a hard time opening my eyes. I was sound asleep, dreaming of having sex with Denzel Washington. I wonder ofttimes where my dreams come from, what was I doing or watching or reading that would prompt such mental images. But not this time.

For some strange reason, Joy joined Karen and me for what inwardly I term "Sunday dinners without Dad." We watched Training Day, which is, in my opinion, one of the best feats of acting Mr. Washington has ever accomplished in his more-than-acclaimed life of fame. He gave his sidekick, Ethan Hawke, a joint laced with PCP, and Ethan was as high as a kite. Thus, I know where tonight's dream came from.

Joy walked into the room, after insisting on doing the dishes (what the hell?), and asked if we minded if she joined us.

I glanced at Karen, who immediately scrunched farther into her end of the couch and patted the middle. I was sitting at the other end.

"This place has your name on it," Karen said with a smile.

Joy was acting a bit timid, and this was indeed unusual behavior. She never likes any movie I'm interested in. If it's not showing on Netflix, it's essentially worthless.

"Certainly," I said. "Come sit near me. I'm going to make some popcorn when it's half over."

"I can do that," Joy piped up.

I gave Karen the eye and shrugged. "Sure, if you want to, honey."

"Where's Dad?"

Karen's gaze didn't leave the television. I don't know if this was a loaded question or not. Joy knows Steven rarely, if ever, shows up for Sunday dinner. He used to. Back in the day. Before he became so sought after. "Comes with the territory," he'd said. "Guess so," I'd answered.

"He's at the hospital, Joy," I finally answered. "Why?"

"Just thought…" She shrugged. "I'd like to talk to both of you. You know… together."

My Mother Bear radar went up. I was on full alert. "I'm here. Do you want to talk now?"

Karen stood. "I'm really tired. I should go."

"No, don't," Joy interrupted. "It can wait. It's nothing urgent."

"Are you sure?" I asked.

At that point, Joy had been MIA for about a week. More than usual, that is. She's still moody, even though she's out of high school. But she's still a teenager. She's nineteen. So I worry about her. I worry about everything. Is she being introduced to drugs? Is she having sex? Is she having sex without protection? What does she want to do when she finishes her two years at junior college?

These are all subjects she does not want to talk about. In fact, she really doesn't want to talk about much of anything, ever. The days of her and Steven sharing are in the past. That leaves me with the ball in my court, and Joy doesn't want to play.

So her asking to talk to me and her father is a bit alarming.

"How about we get together tomorrow night?" I asked. "I'll see if your father's schedule is open. If not, perhaps the next night?"

Joy nodded, stood, and walked into the kitchen. "I'm going to make popcorn."

Karen and I looked at each other, and both of us frowned. Karen sat back down on her side of the couch, grabbed the remote, and rewound the movie to the place we were before Joy entered the room.

My stomach is tied in knots. Joy's behavior is not normal. And I wish it were normal for her to want to talk to me and her father, but it isn't. And that's sad.

Now I turn over and look at Steven as he slips under the sheets. Glancing at the clock next to the bed, I note it's two thirty in the morning. He's not on call. Was it a surgery gone wrong? Why would he be returning home so late?

Steven has another life. Not like some woo-woo, unearthly place he goes, like an alternate universe or something. I think his life at the hospital is so unlike anything I've ever experienced, nor will ever experience, that he withholds that part of himself from me. He doesn't share. No stories of surgeries and the outcomes. No gossipy tales of nurses and doctors having sex in broom closets, like you see on daytime soap operas.

He usually comes home late, which invariably wakes me up, hangs up his suit coat, kisses me hello, makes himself a drink at the minibar in the corner of our gigantic bedroom, then keeps me up watching TV for thirty minutes. He says it helps him wind down, watching reruns of Friends or Seinfeld. I try to stay awake while he tells me about another party or meeting I'm expected to attend with him. I always oblige. Frankly, I think they can be fun, but most of the time, they aren't. I meet the people Steven never talks to me about, see who he spends most of his life with.

It's not the type of marriage I envisioned. I'd say Steven and I are friends. With benefits. Though, to be sure, it's infrequent that I benefit from anything physical between us anymore. Almost always, it is he who reaps the benefits.

Steven slides over and cups my breast. I can feel his erection next to my thigh. I've grown to resent him when this happens. And it happens often. I guess I should be happy that he's coming to me for sex and not someone else. He's obviously getting satisfied at home, as opposed to in some broom closet at the hospital. At least, that's my theory.

Then why do I resent it? Well, it all comes down to sharing a bed with someone with whom you're not sharing much else. Like I said, our conversations are late at night. I'm half asleep. He's exhausted. We go to quite a few hospital affairs each month. That's when we spend the majority of our time together. We look like the perfect couple. But there's something missing. More like, there's a lot missing.

It's like the elephant in the room that he just doesn't see, no matter how many arguments we have over his absence. I tell him it's the mundane, everyday things that make a marriage: dinners together, coffee over breakfast, going to bed at the same time, talking after having sex. Those are all missing. The grit that makes a marriage real and whole. All the rest is frosting on the cake—the parties, the galas, the hospital festivities. The problem is, we have the frosting but not the actual cake.

So I turn over, and he kisses me. Steven knows how to make me feel good, though after so many years together, it's like a Beatles song. You never forget "I Wanna Hold Your Hand." The words just flow out of my mouth when I hear it on the radio. So we begin our old song that we've been singing since we've shared a bed. But there's nothing new, and frankly, what used to make me feel good has become boring. I rarely have an orgasm, but I fake it. It would take too much effort to change. The discussion would devolve into an argument, and it's so damn late, I'm tired. And so is he.

But this time, I stop, wrap my fingers gently around his wrist.

"What is it?" he asks.

"Joy wants to talk to us."

"And we need to discuss this now, Leena?"

I roll over onto my back and stare at the ceiling.

Steven huffs out a breath and rolls onto his back, too.

I turn my head to look at him. "I know this may seem like an odd time to bring this up, but when else are you around?"

Steven throws his arm across his forehead. "Here we go again."

I sit up and lean my back against the headboard. "I know this is what the life of a surgeon is like. We don't need to get into a discussion about your hours and all that. But it's gotten so much worse in the last few years—"

"They offered me the position as chief of surgery."

"What about Arthur Pembroke?"

"He's an inept asshole, and everyone knows it. The board is firing him. They want me."

"Oh. Wow."

"That's all you have to say? 'Oh, wow'?"

"I don't know what else to say, Steven. If I thought you were already a mere shadow of a husband, this means you'll disappear altogether."

"A shadow of a husband. What a nice thing to say."

"Steven, the only time I ever see you is when we're at some doctor or hospital function. And we both know it's expected. I can't not go."

"I didn't know you hated going. You can stop at any time."

"I don't hate going. I never said that. And I think you're being purposely obtuse."

"I'm not being obtuse, Leena. You don't enjoy going to the functions I'm obligated to attend, so I'll go alone."

"You're missing the point."

"I'm not missing anything. You don't enjoy eating fine food, drinking expensive wine, talking to the other wives who I thought were your friends. And along with all that are the clothes and the lunches out, tennis. You sure don't mind all the money flowing your way."

"It's not about the money," I shout.

"No need to raise your voice, Leena."

"I'm sorry, but you're not hearing me."

Steven crawls out of bed, leans over, and grabs his boxers and sits with his hands dangling between his knees. "Oh, I'm hearing you. Over and over again." He pauses.

I can almost feel him pulling away from me emotionally as well as physically, as if he's attached to a rope and he's being reeled in the opposite direction, out of my life.

"I've been chosen to participate in a very important upcoming surgery. I've accepted the position. It will require a tremendous amount of time for the next two or three months. Siamese twins. We're separating them. It's been quite a few years since the last one, and this surgery is particularly difficult, so this is a big deal for St. John's."

"That's amazing. And I know how much this means to you. I understand what it means for you to be the chief of surgery, too. But what I don't understand is why being a father and a husband always takes second place. That's what I can't swallow."

He stands up as if in slow motion, pulling his boxers up at the same time, then turns toward me.

"Any free time I have, Leena, I give to you, to this family, to Joy. I don't know what more you want from me. There are only so many hours in a day, and mine are all filled. I sleep four hours a night. I work all day. I come home whenever I'm free."

I shake my head.

"Is there something you want to say, Leena, or do I have to interpret your head shaking for what it appears to mean? You disagree."

"No, Steven, I don't disagree. There are only so many hours in a day. I'm not stupid. But I also know you have more free hours than you're willing to admit. And those hours are not spent with me or with your daughter."

"What are you implying?"

"You mentioned your colleagues' wives. My supposed friends. I wouldn't say I'm really close to any of them, but they do talk. And I listen. Their husbands come home for dinner. Their husbands spend time alone with them, outside of the requisite gatherings they attend. Their husbands know what's going on in the lives of their children. Why is that, Steven? Why are you any different?"

His face morphs into a perfect portrait of a man gone mad, eyes wide, mouth like a knife's slash below his nose, nostrils opening and closing with each breath, his face almost contorted into that of a man I don't recognize. "Yes, as a matter of fact, Leena, I am different. I'm different than all the rest of them." He gestures with his hand as if swatting a fly that is not there.

But I'm getting the impression the fly he's meaning to swat is me. And in that moment, I'm so frustrated that he doesn't get me. He doesn't get his daughter either. I jump out of bed, walk around to his side, and stand directly in front of him. "I'm sick of your excuses for being an absent husband and father. I feel as if I'm not even married any longer. And I'm definitely a single mother. I don't care about the fucking money, Steven. I care about us. I want a partner."

He squints at me. I can see his hands bunching into fists. "I apologize for being a good provider. For working so hard to give you anything and everything most women would die for—"

"Oh, I'm dying, all right, Steven, but not in the way you mean." I place my hand on my chest. "I'm dying inside. I'm lonely. I never wanted to feel this way. It's not what I thought my marriage would turn out to be."

"Oh-ho-ho," he says, smiling. "Sorry to disappoint you. I admit our lives would be different if I weren't so successful. But it's not as if we don't see each other, Leena."

"At all the gatherings and parties, yes, but I'm talking about alone time. Just you and me."

He says nothing.

I take in a huge breath, as if I'm preparing to dive into the deep end of our pool. "I shouldn't have to explain what it means to have a good relationship with my husband."

Silence.

"I swear to God, I'm so sick of having discussions

with myself. I wish I could talk to Karen. She's my best friend. But she works with you, so I don't."

"Wise move, Leena. Don't talk to Karen about our personal life."

"I said I don't. Will Karen be on this new surgical team?"

"No, she will not."

"Why not? She's one of the best surgical nurses at St. John's."

"That surgery will require so much preparation time, I guess Stephanie decided it's necessary to maintain a select few surgical nurses for all the ongoing surgeries we normally have. Plus, Karen's never assisted in a separation of Siamese twins." He shuts his eyes for a few seconds. When he opens them, he stares into mine. "I'm serious, Leena. Don't talk to people about our personal life. My personal life. It's inappropriate."

"Oh, for Christ sake, Steven. There's really nothing to talk about anyway. We, you and I, don't have a personal life together."

"What goes on inside our relationship should stay between us, Leena."

"You already said that. I'm not deaf. I heard you the first time. But, Steven… who am I supposed to talk to? You?"

"Yes, me."

"When?" I shout. "You're never here. Shit! No wonder I resort to writing—"

"Writing to whom?"

I pause. I'm teetering on a precipice off which I know I can't jump, so I dare not get too close to the edge. I take in another deep breath, calm down my stomach, which is roiling as if I'm about to vomit. "A journal. Writing in my journal."

"I didn't know you have a journal."

"It's not for anyone but me to read. It's hidden. And you're forgetting about our daughter, Steven."

"I didn't forget about our daughter."

"Which brings me to what opened up this can of worms to begin with. She wants to talk to both of us."

"About what?"

I sigh. "I don't know, but does it matter?"

"Well, is it something that can wait until I have some free time, or is it an emergency?" he asks, more than a little irritation in his voice.

Clearly, I'm asking him too many questions. He just wants to have sex and go to sleep. Now I've interrupted his entire night or his entire life. I'm not sure which.

"I get the impression she wants to talk to us as soon as possible, but that's just my take on it. I could be wrong."

"You don't know? You didn't ask? You're the one who spends so much time with her."

I shake my head. "We do not spend a lot of time together, Steven. She's pulled so far inside herself, she's like a turtle. Sometimes she'll stick her head out, but not that often. She's on her phone whenever she is around, but so are all the rest of the young people her age." I shrug. "It's pretty normal."

He sits on the bed and looks up at me. "Are you worried about her? Should I be worried about her?"

I sit next to him, place my hand on top of his, and squeeze.

He squeezes back.

"I hear things. From some of the wives who are real enough to open up a little and talk about more than who's marrying who in the UK."

"What things?"

"Some of the wives' kids' friends. For all I know, it's actually their own son or daughter, but they're too embarrassed to get that real with me. But they talk about depression, cutting, suicide attempts." I squeeze his hand again. "I'm scared, Steven. What if Joy's going through a bad time and doesn't have anyone to open up to but her parents? I mean, she doesn't seem to have any friends. None that come over to the house, that is."

He glances down at our clasped hands, then looks me in the eyes. "Talk to her. Ask when she wants to meet with us." He pauses, sighs. "I'll be there. Text me." He stands. "I've gotta go."

My entire body tenses. I feel as if I'm being squished in a vise. "You just got home."

He takes a brief look at the Rolex I bought him for our last anniversary. "It's three thirty. I've got a meeting at four a.m. The Siamese twins I told you about."

"It's starting already?"

He remains silent.

I guess I shouldn't have noted that it's months before the actual surgery, and his life is already changing. Our lives are already changing.

"I'll talk to her today," I say.

"Thank you."

I stand and move to within a foot in front of him.

He looks down at me.

His eyes are hooded. He looks exhausted, and his day hasn't even begun. Suddenly, I have a surge of emotion toward this man. He's a hard worker, a good provider, as they say. But I need him in ways he seems incapable of fulfilling any longer.

And what he doesn't know is, I'm sharing my emotions and feelings with someone I'll never meet.

MICHAEL

It's five thirty a.m., and I still, after five years, get an adrenaline rush at this time of the morning. This is when my day used to begin at the hospital. I would see patients until noon in my office, located on the first floor of the hospital, perhaps take a short lunch break, but most times not. Then I'd visit post-surgery patients, accompanied by a small cadre of young residents following excitedly behind me.

I used to love that inner blooming inside my chest, when I'd see that one (there's usually one who stands out from the rest) who "gets it." Who possesses that special quality that will make him or her a fantastic diagnostician, something so absolutely and unequivocally necessary in diagnosing diseases and malfunctions of the heart. Then, hopefully, that same person will have the hands and the skills to perform the delicate and time-consuming and tedious maneuvers necessary to fix cardiac problems.

Those days are gone for me, though my attorney keeps telling me that, with the changes in California law, I just might be able to get back my medical license. To be able to practice medicine again would be a miracle I hardly dare to dream about, though at times like this, when I can see the tiny patch of blue sky through the bars of my cell, I allow my hope to peek through the dark regions of my soul that have been dead since I entered this place.

Hope. Something all too absent in prison. They've transferred in a lot of "lifers" since I entered. They may not be on death row, but they're going to die before they ever see a day when they might be up for parole. There have already been ten guys who've passed away of sickness or old age, only months or weeks before their parole hearing. In my opinion, they were past hope. And without that, there's nothing to keep you alive here.

Unless, perhaps, visitors. And I have none. All that could even come close to having someone visit me are the letters I receive from a woman who wrote an anonymous letter to any prisoner hopeful enough to grab it from the short stack of envelopes that arrive from PrisonersNeedFriendsToo, an organization founded on the principle that with hope there can be progress, and with progress there can be model behavior, and with model behavior sometimes comes an early parole.

I selected a pink envelope a year ago. It had one sheet of light green stationery and was signed with an A. Which only served to remind me of Heather. Her favorite television show, which we watched together every day until the day she drew her last and final breath, was Pretty Little Liars. I don't know if they ever discovered who the hell A was. Sometimes, they led us to believe it was one of the main female characters, then it was some guy messing with their heads. Heather and I didn't care. It made for interesting speculation and fun for both of us during the worst time of our lives.

When I read my first letter from A, I thought I found my soul mate, even though she couldn't visit me. I have no visitors. To my colleagues who I thought were my friends, I am the plague incarnate. To Heather's mom and dad, I am the devil in an orange jumpsuit. To only one,

one of Heather's friends, I am the Angel of Death. That friend knew Heather wanted the Angel of Death to visit at the end. That one friend still sends me an occasional card. But she and her husband moved to New York, so once again, no visitors for me.

So the letters from A mean a lot.

"Casspi. Letter."

I sit up so fast, the blood rushes to my head. Breakfast is still on the horizon at eight a.m., and I'm starving. For years, I got up at four a.m., took a run, then went home, showered, drank a smoothie, and was at the hospital by five thirty to finish paperwork. So at eight o'clock in the morning, I'm famished.

The guard waves an envelope at me. I've never seen this G before, since they change their shifts every few months. I heard the reasoning behind that is so none of the prisoners becomes "pals" with any of the male G's (and one female G), who wield most of the power in this place. Changing the floors that the G's supervise makes for less camaraderie with the prisoners, and hence no possibility for special treatment and/or smuggling anything that could be used to help us hurt one another or ourselves.

Though we all know the G's know, we can make a mean and deadly shank from a piece of paper. But I've never learned how, and I don't want to learn. If there's a possibility I don't have to spend my entire ten-year sentence in this hole, I'm going to be a model prisoner.

He slips the pink envelope through the bars, and it goes flying onto the floor. I instantly bend over and pick it up, wipe it off, and smile. A hasn't written in several weeks. Her letters arrive erratically. I haven't been able to figure out a rhyme or reason for why they come when they do. I guess it depends on what's going on in her life, which is way more than anything happening in mine. It's so mundane in here, sometimes I feel like I'll go insane.

But going ballistic will surely get me a few days in solitary. Some guys don't have the mental fortitude to last through more than a few hours of pitch black, stifling air, little space, total confinement, with food you can't eat and bugs you can't see. I'll keep my screaming to a low roar with my head inside my ratty pillow with no pillowcase.

I have a special ritual, I guess you'd call it, that I perform when I receive a letter from A. I wash my hands, so they're almost as sanitary as they'd have to be before slipping on surgical gloves. Then I put my pillow behind my back on what passes for a bed in this place. In reality, it's a piece of what seems like canvas that covers a piece of too-soft foam surrounded by plastic. You can tell it's plastic by the noise it makes, sort of like a crackle, when you put any pressure on it. I've learned to fall asleep by keeping utterly still, but I wake up a million times each night, every time I turn over and the plastic crinkles. It's tiring and annoying.

I lean my back on the pillow and hold up the letter so I can read the address: Mr. Michael Casspi, Balmoral State Penitentiary, Glen Ellen, California 95442. I looked up Glen Ellen in the library once. Last population count: 784. Located in the Sonoma Valley, about an hour and a half from San Francisco. My old hometown.

The return address is cut out, and the envelope has been opened and the contents thoroughly read. But months ago, once, I was able to decipher the bottom edges of the city of the return address. There was definitely a "San" and the second word began with an "F" and had eight letters. So A resides where I once called home.

No telling exactly what area she lives in. Could be we were neighbors, though that's probably not the case.

Letters are screened. Sometimes entire sentences are blacked out. I have no idea where she or her husband is employed. She has a daughter.

All this is peripheral, though. It's what she reveals about herself that counts. Her letters are never boring. She's smart, seems educated, has problems like all of us. She talks of marital difficulties, though not specific enough for me to offer advice. She's a bit more forthcoming about her daughter, though her daughter's behavior appears typical of teenagers.

There's no way she's allowed to visit me, since I don't know her full name, and the prisoner is the person who requests the visitor. Plus, Balmoral's computer system isn't fully integrated with the PrisonersNeedFriendsToo website. Though they tell us it should be up and running soon, they've been saying that for months. Until that time, information shared between prisoners and anonymous writers from PrisonersNeedFriendsToo is limited, hence visiting is prohibited so far.

I slip my finger through the hole where her return address once was, acting as if I'm actually "opening" her letter, since it's already been opened and read. If there are any offensive words or sexual innuendo, it is scratched out. If there is anything written about where she lives, it is scratched out as well. She doesn't seem the type to include swear words or sexual innuendo. She knows the rules, and she's never slipped. Her letters are free of deletions of any kind.

I extricate the pastel green piece of five-inch by seven-inch stationery and instantly recognize A's handwriting.

Dear Michael,

I'm sorry I haven't written in two weeks. Actually it's been two weeks and two days. I apologize and hope you do not take offense at my infrequent missives.

I enjoy our communication, but I've made that clear to you on numerous occasions. I miss having someone to talk to, and you have become that person. But I don't want to burden you with my problems, and I certainly don't expect you to solve them for me. They're my responsibility, and one day, perhaps soon, I will act.

How have you been? That seems an inane question because, by the time you receive this, if you've been ill, you're already better. But I ask it anyway because I think about you often. Our friendship is a light in my dark hours, which are all too plentiful.

I am well. The flu that has hit us hard here in the Bay Area…

I would have expected those two words to be deleted, but they are not—a mistake on someone's part, obviously.

… but no one in my family has succumbed. I try to get out and exercise, be alone for awhile.

I know what you're thinking right now. Why would I need any more alone time than I already have, because I'm always complaining about needing conversational stimulation. You'd think being married would give me that. But, as I've told you so often, it is sorely lacking.

Today when I was looking at the view of the island…

Could she be talking about Alcatraz here? Another mistake that should perhaps have been deleted?

… I was thinking about you. How alone you must feel in a prison cell with no one to talk to, though you've explained the reasoning behind not having to share a cell in Balmoral and the need for safety first. I would imagine the few hours you are allowed to exercise in the yard do not allow for much stimulating conversation. And I complain about the lack of conversation in my household? You should resent me for even mentioning it. And I apologize for being insensitive.

But I have no one to talk to about my daughter. It's hard having a teenager. Actually, it's hard being a teenager. I remember only too well my own mood swings, hating anyone over thirty, especially my parents. Smoking in the park at night. Running from the cops who obviously could see the lit tips of our Salem Lights. Acting oblivious to the fact we were putting cancerous tar particles in our lungs.

I was never one to take drugs, though all my peers indulged. Sometimes to excess. In fact, one of my best friends (on Facebook we call her Dead Betty — a name she would have thought hysterically funny if she was alive) was in a car accident at age eighteen. She and nine of her friends were in the back of a van, and they were traveling up from LA.

Another mistake on the part of the people reading this letter?

They hit another car head on. Betty was the only one who did not survive. Everyone else walked away with bruises and/or a few broken bones. She was in surgery for ten hours while the surgeons tried to reattach her leg. She died on the operating table.

After that happened, I swore I would never do drugs—ever. The driver of the van was high on I don't know what, and it cost the life of my dear friend. Betty was airlifted to UC San Francisco…

Ha! Another blooper.

… where one of the best surgeons couldn't save her. It was so sad.

That is one of the few experiences that stands out in my mind when I recall my teenage years. There were so many in my group of friends who needed the escape from reality that can only be found in illegal drugs or alcohol. You probably already know marijuana will soon be legal in California. Will you be allowed to partake? Will it be illegal if you're in a state penitentiary? I'm not sure whether Balmoral is or is not a federal prison. I should know that. Sorry. I should just Google it right now, but I'm too involved in writing to walk over to my computer. Isn't that the height of American laziness!

I just reread my letter, and I sure do go every which way but logical in my communication. I was talking about my daughter and ended up talking about Dead Betty. What is wrong with me? I'm so tired. I didn't sleep well last night. It's still hard, after so many years of sleeping with my husband, to find myself alone most nights. And when he does come home, like he did last night, often we argue.

But here I go again, right? Being insensitive to your situation. You are alone. Sometimes this house feels like a jail cell, too. But I'm betting mine is better decorated! Sick joke? Just thought I'd try to make you laugh. Though, how would I know if you're laughing right now?

You've never told me, though I've asked numerous times, what did you do before you went to prison? If you don't feel comfortable telling me, then just tell me so, and I'll quit hounding you. Isn't that a funny phrase, "hounding you"? I believe it refers to the hounds chasing the fox or some other animal in England, right? Is England even called England anymore? Isn't it now just referred to as the UK? Do you know?

I just heard my daughter come in. I have to hide this letter, and I will send it to you tomorrow. I hope you are well, my friend. And I look forward to your next letter. Take care.

Fondly,
A

JOY

"Which philosopher found that he could not doubt that he himself existed, as he was the one doing the doubting in the first place? In Latin, the language in which this philosopher wrote, the phrase is cogito, ergo sum. Which means?" Miss Vargas scans the small class of forty students before meeting my gaze. "Joy?"

A wave of heat crawls up my neck to my face. At the same time, I'm so angry for blushing, I want to scratch my own eyes out… or scratch the inside of my wrist with a razor blade. But it's still so raw from last time, I better not, in case it bleeds through my shirt. Then Mom'll know, and that'll open a can of worms, as she's always saying.

Chuckling surrounds me, and it's obvious everyone notices my beet-red face. I want to crawl under the chair, except I'm too fat.

"I think, therefore I am," I say, sort of under my breath. I swear, if I have to repeat myself, I'm gonna run outta the classroom. But I've done that before and found it more humiliating the next day when I returned. So I keep my butt in my chair and wait for the laughter to subside.

Miss Vargas smiles at me. "You're correct, Joy. And the class assignment for the week is to read the first ten chapters of Principles of Philosophy, which Descartes wrote when?" She turns left then right, searching for a hand. She stops and looks me in the eye, then lifts one brow.

"1644," I mutter. Why, oh, why, can't I speak up in class like everyone else? Maybe 'cause I'm not like everyone else. Yeah, all of us here were born with a frickin' silver spoon in our mouths, but that doesn't mean we have to act like assholes. Which is how everyone acts with me. I don't know why everybody in my class has selected me as the scapegoat for their remarks and smirks. This isn't grammar school, and it damn well isn't high school. We're in college. Granted, it's junior college, but what's with the put-downs and sideways looks?

"The sixteenth century, then?" Miss Vargas asks the class. "Burton?"

Burton's one of the best-looking guys I've ever seen at this school. Hands down, Josh Duhamel in Transformers. He takes a quick glance my way, and I mouth, "Seventeenth."

Burton jerks his head in Ms. Vargas' direction and says, "Seventeenth century, Ms. Vargas," then he grins.

"See you tomorrow," Ms. Vargas says and starts gathering up her paperwork.

I stand and try to cover my face with my hair. I take after my mother in that department, with my long, dark hair, but mine comes almost to my waist, and it's brown. Mom's is just past her shoulders and auburn. Plus, hers is way prettier than mine. Mine's straight and limp, like a freaking board. Hers is wavy with a lot of body.

I never put my hair up in a ponytail, because then I can't use it as a shield for my face 'cause I'm constantly embarrassed when people say shit to me. Honestly, I truly believed the bullying would stop once I made it to junior college. But junior college has been a continuation of my life in high school, since I was fourteen. And I am so, so sick of it. You'd think I would have learned to stand up for myself, but I'm weak.

Just like my mom.

But that's a totally different story. It's so damn obvious Daddy isn't home because he's probably having an affair, and Mom is just so totally oblivious. She went to college, and she's so damn smart in a lotta ways. Why is she so dumb about her own husband? Lots of the kids here have moms and dads who are surgeons or partners in firms like Price Waterhouse. I hear things. Their fathers all come home for dinner most nights. I hear them talking about vacations with their parents and how their parents do stuff on date-night this and date-night that.

Daddy always says he's got a meeting, or he's in surgery. But one time, right after I got my driver's license, so I musta been sixteen, I took the keys to my mom's Mercedes and followed Daddy when he thought he was being all sly and shit. He left the house at two thirty in the morning. He wasn't on call, because I heard him tell Mom he wasn't. And they don't schedule surgeries in the middle of the night.

So I followed him to this bar called The Drunken Ball. Daddy turned his Porsche into the parking lot next to a dark BMW, opened his door, turned, and opened the driver's side door of the BMW. And out steps this woman. Drop-dead gorgeous. Long legs, makeup that looks professionally applied, a short, clingy black dress, and her boobs are practically falling out of the top of her stretchy, scoop-neck top.

Daddy reaches for her hand, and she grasps it, and he pulls her out of the driver's seat. They kiss, and it's so long and drawn out I'm wondering how long I can stand to watch before I spill my guts all over the floor of Mom's

Mercedes. Which I know I better not do, 'cause there's no way I can clean it up before I get back home. Follow Charlie's car wash is closed, and I can't hose it down in our front yard.

They finally stop giving each other mouth-to-mouth resuscitation and walk hand in hand into The Drunken Ball, and I immediately drive home, sick to my stomach that Mom's getting the shaft from Daddy. I've looked up to him my entire life. Now I think he's a lying, cheating asshat, and I don't want to ever talk to him again. But that's easy, because he's never home anyway.

Whoever the woman is, she's the type of chick who steals other women's husbands. I never want to be that woman. So I guess I'm glad I'm not pretty. But Mom's pretty. In fact, she's beautiful. People say I have her green eyes and her cheekbones. But that's about where the two of us looking alike stops.

I'm fat. I know I am. Mom's always telling me I have an incorrect body image and that I have a great figure. She also says I take after her, that I'm curvy. I think she just says that stuff to make me feel better. I hate myself for eating so much. I can't help it. When I eat, I feel like I'm in control of my life. I can't control anything else in my life, but I sure as shit can control what I put in my mouth.

And what I decide I don't want inside me anymore. If Mom found out I was sticking my finger down my throat to yak after I eat lunch and dinner, she'd be so mad. She'd tell Daddy, who'd go ballistic. Then she'd ground me forever. Then what the hell would I do? She'd take away my phone and my computer, and then I wouldn't have anything to do but eat. Then gack.

I've never felt good about being me. I just want to be normal like everyone else. But no one likes me the way I am. So I really don't like me either. And when I act like everyone else, they make fun of me anyway.

I look like a freaking marshmallow with clothes on. I don't know how to stop eating. I'm always so hungry. Food is like the only friend I've ever had, but I know that doesn't make any sense, because after I eat, I feel guilty and wanna gack.

I can't dress like everyone else either. I can't wear clingy tops and tight jeans. When I've done that in the past, the guys looked at me and whispered, and I know they're talking shit about me and how fat I am. Like a fucking freak. When I go to the cafeteria or walk by the restaurants near the junior college, I see my classmates scarfing down burgers and fries. They're not fat. There's obviously something wrong with me.

Mom and Daddy told me when I was in grammar school that my baby fat would disappear. They said the same thing for the first two years of high school, too. Mom always tells me to eat healthier, like carrots and celery and smoothies. No one in high school brings that shit for lunch. They used to look at me like I was a human form of an elephant. The few times Mom made me bring a cucumber sandwich and carrot sticks, everyone talked behind their hands when I walked by them.

Daddy always says, "I'm damned if I do and damned if I don't." Now I know what he means, because if I eat, I get fat and people look at me, and if I don't eat, they still make fun of me. It doesn't matter what the hell I do. No one likes me. But what do I expect? I don't like me either. Fuck.

I make it to the doorway of the classroom, and just as I'm about to step through the doorway, Burton exits, too. Well, that sure ain't gonna happen. We can't both fit through the damn doorway. Hey, Burton, here comes Dumbo. So I stop, take a step back, and let him pass.

Burton steps through first, then turns and faces me. "Thanks for the help, Joy."

I can't believe he even remembers my name. I know Ms. Vargas calls me Joy, but that hasn't stopped everyone else I've ever been around from forgetting my name. The entire four years of high school, there were people who called me Jo or Jehosaphat with a laugh. Now that I'm in college, where there's about twenty thousand students, no one knows who I am now either.

"You're welcome," I reply and look at the ground for a second before walking out the door. I scurry across the quad to the car lot, where I'm parked. Where I know there are candy bars and that pink popcorn shit that comes in a clear cellophane wrap in the glove box.

I grab a Twix and stuff the entire two sticks in my mouth, one right after the other. I catch a glimpse of myself in the rearview mirror, and my cheeks look like a squirrel that's saving up for winter. I close my eyes and feel tears dripping down my face, off my chin, onto my baggy camo pants.

That's when I reach into my purse, unzip the side zipper, and feel the tiny plastic box with the blade inside. I take it out and set the edge next to the two vertical veins on my wrist. I push down, hard, and slide the blade up to my elbow, pressing until little droplets of blood ooze out of my pinkish white skin.

I sigh.

I can feel okay for a while.

But, really, I don't wanna be here anymore.

What the hell for?

LEENA

"What do you mean you can't come home?" I ask Steven.

He just called to tell me he can't meet with Joy this evening, to talk to her about whatever it is she has on her mind.

"I knew you'd do this," I say. "You used to be a man of your word. At least, that's what you always said about yourself. But now? That's a bunch of bullshit."

"Stephanie called a meeting about the Siamese twins I told you about. I don't have a choice. I have to attend. You know I do." He sighs loudly. "I didn't plan this, Leena. Can't we make it another night?"

"You're the one who said tonight was a good night for you. What am I supposed to tell Joy?"

"The truth," he shouts.

I pull the phone away from my ear. His voice is so loud, it vibrates through my brain. "Just as you always tell the truth, Steven?"

"Oh, my God, what is that supposed to mean? Must you always talk doublespeak? Just say what you want to say and be done with it."

I sigh, rein in my anger... for Joy's sake. "What would be a better day, Steven, so I can tell her something? So she won't feel like we're not totally blowing her off."

There's silence on his end, and I know what he's

going to say. He knows, and I know, that I'm not going to like it.

I calm myself by breathing in through my nose and out through my mouth, like I do when I'm meditating. However, it's not going to help the three of us get together, no matter how many deep breaths I take. I may as well stick my head in a bucket of water and then take a deep breath. Who would care? Not Steven. Joy doesn't talk to me, so maybe she doesn't give a shit either.

But Michael does. He cares. Oh, what a sorry state of affairs this is.

"I understand you have a busy schedule. But Joy needs us. I just have this funny feeling something's wrong."

"What do you mean by wrong? Is it about some boy she has a crush on? Is it school related? What?"

"When was the last time you had a real, one-on-one talk with your daughter?"

"When have you?"

"At least I try, Steven. That's better than I can say for you. She feels you ignore her, that you don't have time for her." I pause, and he says nothing. "Is she wrong?"

He huffs.

I can see his face in my mind's eye. He has a way of looking at me that makes me feel stupid, as if what I'm saying is idiotic.

"For God's sake, I don't have time for this, Leena. I have to go. I'm walking into a meeting right now, as a matter of fact, and I don't have time to argue with you."

"I thought we were having a discussion."

"Okay," he says, lowering his voice. "I'm outside the door leading into a conference room full of people. Can we please discuss Joy and her need to speak with us when I get home tonight?"

"So you want me to stay up until two or three in the morning to discuss when you will have time to meet with our daughter? Aren't you on call this week? We are not going to have a meeting with Joy while you're on call. You know damn well someone will phone you the minute we sit down to talk. Also, I thought maybe we'd have dinner together, just the three of us, and talk over our meal. When was the last time the three of us were in the same room together?"

"If you want me to give you a date when I'm not on call, I'll try my best to be there. But it's still a tentative date, because Stephanie calls meetings on the spur of the moment, and I can't predict that."

"So what are you saying?" I pause, allowing him time to think. Then I realize I don't need any more time. "You know what? Just forget about it. I'll talk to Joy myself. She won't be happy about it, but if that's the best you can do—give me a date that will probably change anyway—well, that's just not good enough. I'll handle it myself, like I always do."

"Oh, so now the martyr side of you comes out. I hate it when you do that."

"You and she used to be so close, and now you barely talk to each other. Can you imagine how that makes her feel, Steven? I've tried to talk to her many times. It's as if there's a wall between her and me. It seems I do nothing but irritate the shit out of her. It's like she takes it out on me that you're no longer available for her."

"So everything's my fault? I'm working my ass off to give her everything she wants. Joy can transfer to Stanford when she's finished with her general-ed credits at the junior college, which is something she told me she really, really wanted, by the way. And I'm still the bad guy?"

"We're going round and round, like we always do. Let me just say one more thing, then I'll let you go to your meeting. Joy needs you. You're not available. And when you are, she's not home. But what do you expect? She's nineteen years old. I need you, too, Steven. But I'm a big girl and I can take your rejection. She cannot." I pause, take a breath. "I think she's cutting."

"Cutting classes? But why would—"

"No, Steven. I think she's cutting her body. With a blade. I saw blood on the cuff of her blouse last week. Unless she has another explanation. I'm pulling this out of my hat right now, but it makes sense. Remember how she denied the bullying the school told us about, back when she was in high school? Frankly, I think it's still going on."

"Not in college, Leena. You've got to be kidding me."

"I wouldn't joke about something like this, and yes, I'm talking about right now, at the junior college. I've read about it. And I've read about cutting, too. I think Joy's depressed. That's why I don't want to put off this meeting. What if she's suicidal?"

"For God's sake, Leena, you always take everything to the extreme. And you're such a pessimist."

"I'm a pessimist? What the hell are you talking about? You know what? We're getting nowhere with this conversation, and I'm ending it. I'll talk to Joy tonight and tell you what happens whenever I see you. Which may be, oh… next week sometime? Unless you wake me up when you get home at two or three in the morning, when you're not on call." I hang up the phone.

All our conversations devolve into misunderstandings and blaming each other. He doesn't have my back, and I cannot have his. I don't know where he is most of the time.

I'm beginning to wonder if I'd be better off if I were a pessimist. I used to believe everything Steven told me. But it's becoming glaringly obvious, I've been a fool. He can't possibly have meetings that last until two and three in the morning. But I turn over, have sex with him, keep my mouth shut.

Does he have another life I know nothing about? Am I purposely not putting the pieces of this puzzle together to create a picture I don't want to see? If my marriage was portrayed in a Lifetime movie, I'd be shouting at the woman on the TV, "What the hell's wrong with you, you dumb bitch? Your husband's having an affair. He's leading a double life. Jesus! Get a clue."

Then again, if I'm honest with myself, I'm leading a double life as well.

I reach into my desk, into the very back, and grab the box of pastel green stationery, along with a pink envelope.

I sit in my favorite chair and begin to write…

Dear Michael…

STEVEN

The meetings regarding the twins, David and Billy Parthas, are excruciatingly long, involved, highly technical, medically challenging, and draining beyond belief. We plan to have twenty-five surgeons, fifteen anesthesiologists, and fifty surgical nurses on our team. Luckily, I'm just one of the surgeons involved and not the head surgeon, who has responsibility for planning and executing the twins' separation. The surgery itself could take up to twelve hours or longer and is scheduled for two, maybe three, months from now, depending on whether we meet the organizational deadlines Dr. Stephanie Yates drew up.

I exit the conference room at ten o'clock in the evening and breathe a sigh of relief. I could leave and put this behind me for at least the next few hours. I'm tired physically, but mentally, my mind's going at full speed. I need a distraction. And I know exactly where I'm headed. As we all exit the meeting, bunched together in the slender hallway, mumblings and laughter echo off the walls. Everyone's headed for The Drunken Ball for some well-earned but short-lived R&R.

And I'm not about to miss it. I need to let go of the constant swirl of ideas and plans concerning the twins' separation. I can't leave that at the hospital door. But with a few drinks and a lot of distraction, I can put it at the back of my mind and relax for a while.

I wait for an elevator headed for the basement garage and join several colleagues I don't know very well. We nod at each other, and the ride down five floors is silent. Several surgical nurses are plastered against the back wall of the elevator, and I turn and smile at them.

One of the nurses raises an eyebrow, and I respond in kind—our secret acknowledgment that tonight will be "ours." Whether from across a room or hallway or an office, the eyebrow lift conveys our agreement for "hooking up," as Joy calls it. My generation has other ways of describing what I plan to do after having a couple of Scotches on the rocks. I look forward to relaxing for the first time in what seems like months but is actually only a week. But it's been one helluva week, what with the constant worry over the twins' surgery and the most recent arguments with Leena over our marital life and our daughter.

I click the key fob for my Porsche, throw my briefcase in the back, and slide into the soft leather seat, close the door and relish the absolute silence. I sigh. Why is it that I carry no guilt around, knowing how I'll pass this evening with someone other than my wife? I've rationalized it all in my head a million times. The coupling doesn't go any further than sexual relief. There's not much talk, but a helluva lot of action.

It's where I live out the fantasies that have lingered in my mind since I was a teenager. I am too uncomfortable to act them out with my wife. But I am hurting no one. Not the other women, nor Leena, nor Joy, and certainly not myself. It is total, one hundred percent sex. No strings, no future, no harm, no foul. I do not feel guilty. I walk away from my tiny blip of infidelity with a relaxed mind, ready to go back to work and give it my all, knowing I'm providing for my family so they can live a life they would otherwise never experience. And I love my work. And I love my wife and daughter.

But Leena is pushing more often and harder these days for a bigger slice of the pie that constitutes the number of hours I have in a day to spend outside of work. I keep in contact with her as much as possible through texts about my meetings. I don't have a set schedule, and even then it constantly changes based on surprise surgeries, abrupt rescheduling of meetings, unexpected visits from high-end donors. I often have to walk out of one important meeting to attend another the president of the hospital deems more crucial. And Leena knows all this, so most of my texts to her about my schedule are meaningless. It inevitably changes.

My life is not easy to keep organized, so it certainly makes it impossible for Leena to know where I am at any given time. But I am free from any constraints, and I've never felt I have a ball-and-chain wife. But recently, she's been extremely unhappy about my work hours, and that worries me. When Leena believes something needs fixing, she's relentless in her plans to mend the brokenness.

I pull at the tie constricting my throat and slide it away from my collar, breathing a sigh of relief. I feel better already. After driving out of the parking garage, I gun the engine and take a short ten-minute spin up and over the hills of San Francisco, enjoying the rumble of the Porsche's engine through the leather seat. I roll down the windows and breathe in the salt air that is this beautiful city. And I begin to relax. It's time to head to the bar to mingle and have a few drinks, before I can leave for "our hotel," where what happens at the St. Croix stays at the St. Croix. The staff is the epitome of discretion, which alleviates any worries about sneaking in and out or leaving any paper trail. It's all good.

Few parking spots remain available in the lot at The Drunken Ball, but I find one on the far edge, and the Porsche slides right next to her white Lexus, with only inches to spare on either side. The Drunken Ball is filled to capacity. Everyone from the meeting must have agreed en masse to come here tonight.

The bartender catches my eye, and within seconds, he slides a napkin in front of me, then places the Scotch glass on top and nods. I nod and pick up the glass, swirl the golden fluid round and round, before draining it in three long gulps. The head rush is quick, and my entire body responds, heat emanating from my face, down my throat to my limbs, into my stomach and groin. I let out a sigh.

My eyes rove over the crowd. Laughter and chatter fill the room. When I see her, I smile, and she rolls her eyes. Schmoozing isn't what's on either of our minds tonight, so I immediately order my second and final Scotch and swallow it quicker than the first. It's as if I've popped a couple of Xanax, the stress slipping from me like shedding a second skin. I catch her eye a second time and tilt my head toward the front door. She smiles, places her glass on the table, says a few words to her friends, then wends her way through the crowd.

After reversing the Porsche, I notice she's made it out of the bar quicker than I thought. She enters her Lexus, and I wait for her to follow me out of the parking lot. We ride in tandem, as if we're already coupled, to the St. Croix. We've done this so many times, we are both on autopilot.

I enter the hotel first. She waits five minutes, then meets me in front of the elevator, where we stand next to each other until we reach the top floor, where the views take my breath away. After sliding the key card into the door, I hold it open for her to follow me inside.

No words are spoken. We walk to the bed, undress ourselves, slide beneath the covers, then turn toward each other and smile. She'll do anything I ask, things Leena wouldn't like. Sometimes, even to me, it sounds as if I'm trying to rationalize my infidelity. Maybe I am. But I need this.

I love Leena. She's a good wife, and she tries to be a good mother. It's hard raising a teenager, and from what Leena tells me, Joy is still going through teenage angst. Being nineteen, that makes sense.

Do I care about this woman I'm sleeping with? Of course I do. But either of us can walk away at any time, no questions asked.

Much later, she turns over, and I know, even though it's still dark outside, she's watching me dress.

"Where are you going?" she says.

I bend down and squeeze her exposed breast, kiss her neck. "Gotta go home, run, take a shower, have breakfast. The usual."

She stretches. Her white breasts glow in the shaft of light from the moon coming through the curtains. She has a beautiful, taut body and is the most sexually savvy woman I've ever slept with. She knows how to pleasure me. That's understandable, since she admitted to me one night when she'd had too much to drink that she put herself through nursing school by working as an escort. She knows the ropes… very well. And being the recipient of that "hands-on" knowledge is amazing.

"Do you really have to leave?" she asks, and I detect a hint of a whine in those few words, which makes my antennae twitch in alert.

Grabbing my suit coat off the chair, I say, "You know I do."

She sits up, letting the sheet fall to the side, and looks up at me. I know that she knows what it does to me to see her naked. She stands and rubs up against me. She's practically purring, a low sexy rumble, while licking her lips, her tongue darting round and round, her hand encircling my erection, then squeezing in a pulsing fashion.

I push her away gently. "I don't have time. Please don't do this."

She huffs and sits back down on the bed. "You're always the one who leaves. Have you ever noticed that?"

"I need to be at my desk by six a.m. Why are you giving me grief?"

"Do you know how long we've been seeing each other?"

My breath catches in my throat. I can't believe what I'm hearing. We don't do much talking, she and I. And there's never been talk of "this" being a relationship of any kind. "I really don't have any idea. What does it matter?"

Her bottom lip sticks out a bit, reminding me of when Joy didn't get her way when she was a toddler. It irritated me then, and now, seeing it on the face of an adult, I find it even more irritating.

"I'm no more than a fuck buddy to you, aren't I? If your wife knew—"

This cannot be happening. I need to leave. I do not have time for this shit. I lean down, digging my fists into the bed, one on each side of her, boxing her in between my arms. I glare into her eyes. I am no more than five inches from her face. "Don't ever think this is more than it is. We have sex. We don't, quote unquote, share our lives. We hardly talk. You go your way, I go mine."

She's looking down at her lap, and I grab her chin between my thumb and forefinger, forcing her to look at me. Her eyes are wide and glassy. I can tell she's afraid of me. I have never raised my voice to her, and I'm not doing that now, but I don't need to raise my voice. It's obvious from my tone and my face, I am not fucking around.

"Do we understand each other?"

She nods.

"I said, do we understand each other?"

"Yes, I understand, Steven."

"And don't you ever threaten to tell my wife, because if you do, you'll regret it. And that's putting it mildly. You'll find yourself out of a job at St. John's and anywhere else in this city and beyond." I straighten up and grab my phone and keys and walk out the door.

In my business—and being a surgeon, let me tell you, is a business like no other—I need my wife. I need a smart, gorgeous, presentable woman on my arm when I attend a convention or a meeting or a Christmas party. But, I also need a fuck buddy—someone one step up from a prostitute, but I don't pay her for her services. She has fun. I have fun. And that's the end of it. I need what a fuck buddy can give me. I've had many of them, but I can find someone else. It doesn't have to be this one.

LEENA

I wish I could tell my only close friend about Michael, but I don't dare, in case somehow, though I don't know how, Karen slips, says something, and Steven finds out. He'd think I'm crazy, as well as dishonest and perhaps unfaithful. I've never been unfaithful to Steven, ever, and I will never be unfaithful to him. I just need some adult male conversation, and if I can't get that from him… well, God knows I've tried. So the way I look at it, he forced my hand.

I heard about PrisonersNeedFriendsToo from, believe it or not, my daughter's high school. Unfortunately, one of her fellow students was caught selling marijuana, and the police also found a gun in the trunk of his car. He was ready to graduate and eighteen years old, so they tried him as an adult. I recognized the boy, having met him at one of the parent/student/teacher conferences at Joy's high school. He and his mom and dad had the appointment after us (us minus Steven, naturally) where I met him. He seemed like a good kid, a bit reserved and shy, but polite, and we even had a conversation about his being in the church choir. So when I heard he was going to prison, I made it a point to find out how to contact him, so Joy could send him a letter or a Christmas card.

I was afraid for him being integrated into a prison community. I'd heard enough stories on the news and read articles about prisons—gangs, sexual assaults, and more. The PrisonersNeedFriendsToo website cited research that showed inmates who establish and maintain positive contacts outside of the prison walls are less likely to return to prison. In fact, they're less likely to return to crime and substance abuse and are more likely to find employment and remain productive members of society.

Joy and I got the young man's inmate number directly from his mother. Because Balmoral Penitentiary had just opened its doors and hadn't yet been fully coordinated with the PrisonersNeedFriendsToo website, the only details available were a prisoner's first name and whether he was interested in receiving correspondence from an outsider who wanted to be his pen pal. There was no other information yet about any prisoners, though those details had been promised soon.

I'm still waiting for Michael's information—what he's in prison for, the length of his sentence, his release date—all questions I have chosen not to continually ask him. I assume if and when he feels comfortable telling me, he will. I have no idea Michael's age, race, religion, nothing. But I enjoy telling him about my life in bits and pieces and have actually revealed quite a bit about my personal life. In turn, he tells me stories, some funny, others frightening, about his days in Balmoral. I check the website every now and again to see if Balmoral has completed the connection with PrisonersNeedFriendsToo, but it's been months, almost a year, and the system is still not fully up and running.

So it comes as a huge surprise when I log on to the Balmoral website and find the interconnection with PrisonersNeedFriendsToo has been completed. They've posted profiles, photos, contact information. The viewer is now able to select which prisoner s/he would like to correspond with, after viewing all of the prisoner's personal interests, goals, etc.

I look through numerous profiles and find only three men with the first name Michael. I peruse their personal information and find one individual who speaks only Spanish, so I'm able to rule him out as the Michael I've been corresponding with. The second man mentions being a "lifer," and Michael said once that he looks forward to being released one day.

I click on the third and last name of one Michael Casspi and take in a quick breath of surprise. He looks to be perhaps thirty-five or forty years old. His dark brown hair is styled in what I surmise is the requisite buzz cut. Caterpillar-long black eyebrows hover above wide, blue eyes. What I find unusual is the fact he's smiling. In all the other photos of the prisoners, the men are either frowning or looking quite frightening, or they appear beaten down and tired. This Michael, who I believe is the person I've been corresponding with, is very attractive and appears almost happy. I surmise that can't be true. He's in prison.

I skim down to the bottom of his profile. His release date is blank. Hmmmm. Any prisoner whose release date is within ninety days from now is allowed visitors. I'm wondering if "my" Michael fits into that category. I pause for a second, then go back up to the top to find out what crime he's committed. Suddenly, my stomach feels as if I've eaten two Ramiro & Sons mega bean and cheese burritos.

Involuntary manslaughter.

Then they must know his release date. How about never? I don't know the difference between murder and manslaughter, whether involuntary or voluntary, or even if there is much of a difference. I immediately Google "manslaughter versus murder" to find out. I've always found legalese highly confusing, but this definition appeals to my nonlegal brain:

Manslaughter is an unlawful killing that doesn't involve malice aforethought—intent to seriously harm or kill, or extreme, reckless disregard for life. The absence of malice aforethought means that manslaughter involves less moral blame than either first- or second-degree murder. Thus, while manslaughter is a serious crime, the punishment for it is generally less than that for murder.

The explanation goes on to say that voluntary manslaughter is often called a "heat of passion" crime that occurs when a person is either strongly provoked under circumstances that could similarly provoke a reasonable person, or kills in the heat of passion aroused by that provocation. For "heat of passion" to exist, the person must not have had sufficient time to "cool off" from the provocation. That the killing isn't considered first- or second-degree murder is a concession to human weakness. Killers who act in the heat of passion may kill intentionally, but the emotional context is a mitigating factor that reduces their moral blameworthiness.

Involuntary manslaughter often refers to unintentional homicide from criminally negligent or reckless conduct. It can also refer to an unintentional killing through commission of a crime other than a felony.

Granted, both of these definitions don't tell me what Michael has actually done, and I also know the crime committed can be reduced to a lesser crime if the district attorney bargains with the prisoner's attorney, based on certain evidence and circumstances. For all I know, Michael committed a worse crime than "involuntary manslaughter" and will be let out earlier than he would be normally, because something about his case allowed his charge to be reduced to a lesser crime. The law is open to various interpretations and negotiations that the public is never privy to.

But the fact remains, someone died at Michael's hands.

I snap my MacBook closed and stare out the window. Should I continue to write to him? Have I made a foolish decision to communicate with a killer? I thought Balmoral prisoners had committed white-collar crimes. Have I already put me and my family in jeopardy by sending letters to a murderer? If Michael's released, will he come to our home and want to be my friend? But wait! He doesn't know my first name. I've used only the letter A, because my legal name is Annaleena. No one calls me by my given name. I've gone by Leena since I was a child.

Have I ever told him where I live? No, I recall that the rules require that all return addresses are cut out of any letters sent to a prisoner, and all letters are read before they're handed over to the prisoner. He knows I'm married, though I've revealed being lonely. He also knows I have a daughter. But none of that is enough information to find out who I am and where I live.

I blow out a sigh of relief. The letters I wrote to Michael could have come from anywhere. I never wrote what city I live in, nor anything about our house or Joy's high school or that Steven's a surgeon and where he practices medicine.

My family and I are safe.

But wait! Something niggles at the back of my mind. When I signed up to write to a prisoner at BSP, I checked a box stating that, after the BSP and PrisonersNeedFriendsToo websites become totally integrated, the prisoner I am writing to would have access to my address. So I rented a post office box. That was something both BSP and PrisonersNeedFriendsToo encouraged anyway. But I cannot be sure I didn't accidentally write my physical address on the upper left-hand corner of my last letter instead of my post office box. BSP would normally have cut out the address, but did my last letter get through before or after the two websites were fully coordinated?

I stand, grab the keys for the Mercedes along with my purse, and head out the door. I need a shot of espresso and drive to Peet's Coffee down the street, even though all I want to do is go to bed and pull the covers over my head. I feel as if I could have dodged a bullet by being more diligent about writing my address on that last letter. Now I may have shot myself in the foot, along with my family. The idea that Michael knows where I live keeps yanking my internal chain.

Also, I need a post office box because I don't want Steven to find out I'm writing to Michael. Even though it's strictly platonic, and I'm not having an affair, I've still been doing something behind Steven's back, and Steven would definitely be angry if he discovered my secret. I feel there's nothing wrong with writing to Michael, but sharing that information with my husband would open up an argument Steven will always win. Therefore, I have no intention of telling him about my letters to a man in prison.

Steven has a streak of jealousy which manifests itself every time we're out together in a social setting, which is often. Driving home after any event morphs into a relentless inquisition. Who was that man you were talking to? Who were you standing next to at the buffet table? Non-stop questions about every conversation I have with anyone other than Steven himself.

Why would I be writing any man in the first place? If I have to prove to Steven it's platonic, the only way to do so would be to tell him Michael's in prison, and I didn't know anything about his background, or the crime he committed, until today. I admit I'm writing Michael because of everything that's lacking in my relationship with my husband. I admit it. I'm lonely. And Steven refuses to acknowledge or discuss the ramifications of his absence in my life. He believes that throwing money my way will make up for his lack of any effort to improve our marital relationship. And so it goes.

After standing in a short line at Peet's, I add five sugar packets to my caffè latte and drive to the post office. Now I'm suddenly exhausted from worrying, and I need to wake up. I have an organ-donation meeting this afternoon and have to be on top of my game. I'm making a presentation to the committee. After opening the post office box, I pull out a slender white envelope with no return address. It has to be from Michael. No one else knows about this post office box.

"Leena!"

I don't have to turn around to know it's Karen. Whom I have not told I have a post office box, nor that I'm writing a man in Balmoral Penitentiary. My God, what am I going to say?

I take a deep breath, my mind whirling, and look over my shoulder. My best friend is walking my way and will be at my side in seconds. I don't have any time to make up a story, but I damn well better do so anyway. Please God, give me some idea of what to say to her!

"Karen! Hi."

"What are you doing here?" she asks, her eyebrows bunched together.

"Buying stamps."

"Since when do you have a post office box?"

Think, dammit. Open your mouth, Leena, and say something. "It's for Steven."

She tilts her head, looking directly in my eyes. "Why would Steven need a post office box?"

I open my purse and stuff the envelope inside, giving me only two or three seconds to make up an explanation. "He wouldn't want anyone to know this, Karen, so can I rely on your discretion?"

She smiles. "Of course you can. It's not like he and I are best buds. I know we all used to do things together when I first met you and Joy was a baby, but that was a long time ago. I see him in surgery, but that's definitely not the forum for talking about personal things."

"Oh, I know." I nod. "I just don't want to embarrass him. You understand."

"Sooo?" She draws out the word like a lasso that's going to wrap around my neck and choke me if I don't tell her something believable.

"He suggested to me once that he should have a post office box after he gave his address to one of his patients. She wanted to write him a thank-you note. At least, that's what she told him at the time. In reality, she ended up being almost like a stalker. She had a crush on him. I mean, she was in her teens, but she wouldn't stop sending him letters. She showed up at our door, and it was near impossible to get through to her that her behavior was inappropriate. Naturally, after that happened, when patients say they want to thank him for saving their lives or whatever, he gives them a business card with this post office address." I shrug.

"Future crises averted," Karen says. "I get it. Wise move."

"But don't tell him I told you. He felt like a fool at

the time for giving out his family's address. I mean, you never know, right? People can be crazy."

Karen laughs and grasps my hand. "Let's go have coffee or something. I traded shifts and don't have to be at the hospital for another couple of hours."

"I can't, Karen. I'm sorry. I have to prepare for an organ-donor meeting today. I'm giving a presentation."

"Ahh," she whines. "Are you avoiding me?"

"No, of course not. I really do have a presentation to make. You can read about it in the St. John's bulletin."

She laughs. "Of course I believe you, silly. Then let's make a date for the future. Right now." She fumbles around in her purse and brings out her phone, then glances up at me. "When do you want to meet?"

I close and lock the post office box, then grab my phone out of my purse. "I can do this Friday. How's that?"

"Perf!" she says. "It's a date. You can tell me everything you and Steven and Joy have been doing."

"And you can tell me about your latest crush." I smile.

"I don't have crushes. That's such a teenage thing, Leena."

"Okay, forgive me. You can tell me all about the latest hottie you're trying to get into bed."

She guffaws, literally, and I laugh along with her.

"I never should have told you about Robert. You'll throw that in my face forever," she says.

"And Troy and Peter and, let me see, Dan. Oh, and Ashton and—"

"Stop it!" She covers her face with both hands. "Okay, I get it. But I've changed."

"Why?"

"What do you mean why? I've learned my lesson. I

want to get married and have kids. Just like you. And the clock is running."

"Your biological clock is ticking is what you mean."

"Whatever. I'm into finding someone who's serious about having a relationship." She gasps. "To be continued at our lunch date, okay? I just remembered something I have to do." She turns and practically runs out of the lobby of the post office, waving her hand in the air. "See ya, Leena."

"See you," I mumble, sighing in such relief that I feel as though I'm deflating like a balloon.

JOY

It's been awhile since I told Mom and Daddy I wanted to talk to them. I've decided that today is the day. I have no idea when Daddy'll be home, but if he's not, then tough shit. I'll just talk with Mom and to hell with him. He's the biggest part of my problem anyway, so maybe it'd be better if he's not there anyways.

After ditching my afternoon classes, I drive home, gearing up for what is to come, and after walking into the house, I see Mom's purse sitting on the dining room table with her keys thrown down next to it. The house is silent, and I call out for her, but she doesn't answer. I can't help noticing the white envelope sticking out of her purse. Did she get something in the mail that's made her upset and she's upstairs lying down? Did she find out somehow that Daddy's been cheating on her? I call out for her again and walk to the bottom of the stairs and yell for her. All I hear is the silence of the afternoon.

I reach out and slowly slide out the envelope from the side pocket of her purse.

And a memory blasts into my brain like I've been shot in the head.

I was about five years old. Mom and Daddy must have gone into the bedroom while I was taking a nap. Maybe they were taking an afternoon siesta, too.

I remember walking down the hallway toward their bedroom and seeing Daddy's suit jacket draped over the banister and Mom's bra on the carpet. At the time, I had no idea why they would get undressed in the hall when their bedroom door was so close and Mom always told me to pick up my clothes and put them away. Their bedroom door was closed, and I couldn't hear anything from where I stood.

So I tiptoed up to the door and placed my ear on the wood and pushed against it, to see if I could hear something. There was absolute silence. Then I heard, like, a grunting noise and Mom's voice, low and giddy, then Daddy's voice saying he loves it when she does something, but I couldn't hear what he said.

At the time, I didn't know what to do. I wanted to talk to them and ask when we were having dinner, but I had the weirdest feeling if I knocked on the door and interrupted them, I might get in trouble. So I stood there and stared at Daddy's pants. That's when I noticed the edge of something that looked like a photo sticking out of the inside pocket of his suit jacket. I remember thinking that pocket must be a special secret storage area for things Daddy wants to keep away from what he always calls "prying eyes," though I was never sure what he meant by that. I never pried open anything in my life. I always let Mom or Daddy open jars and things because it's too hard for me. My hands are too small.

I reached in the pocket of Daddy's jacket and grabbed the edge of the piece of paper, which was thicker than the paper I wrote on at school, and I pulled it out. It was one of those photos you see sometimes on the front of movie theaters. There was a woman who wore only a black lacy bra, with the biggest boobs I'd ever seen in my life, way bigger than my mom's breasts, which tells you something right there, 'cause she's got big-ass boobs. The woman was wearing a stringlike thing between her legs, which I didn't understand what it was for. It didn't cover her enough to keep her dry when she put on her clothes. It was too small. And she didn't have any hair down there, like Mom.

Then I looked closer, and underneath her was a man kneeling down, and it took me a few seconds to realize it was Daddy. He had his tongue stuck out toward where she didn't have any hair. And his other hand was wrapped around what, to me at the time, looked like the long thing he pees out of. But it didn't exactly look like the one he pees out of because it was huge and round and fat and was sticking straight up in the air. I remember thinking, why would Daddy want to go pee in front of some lady with no clothes on?

And why would he want someone to take a picture of that anyways? And why was the photo in his jacket pocket? Did he plan to show it to Mom? All this was going through my head when the door burst open and Daddy was standing there with nothing on, like in the picture, and that thing he pees with was sticking up in the air again, just like in the picture. And Mom was behind him, but she had on a long T-shirt, not some string and a bra.

Daddy yelled something like, "Holy shit," which was something I'd heard him say before. He grabbed my arm and pulled me to my bedroom and yelled for me to get in there and stay there until he told me to come out. I hadn't done anything wrong, so I was crying and crying.

But it wasn't until high school when I saw Daddy with that bimbo in the parking lot that the old memory of Daddy in the picture with that woman popped into my mind. Then I put two and two together and realized something.

My father has been cheating on my mom forever.

And I hate him for it.

He and I used to be so close, all through middle school. Until we no longer were. He got busier and busier at the hospital, and then in the last few years, he never comes home even after he should have left the hospital. He's probably doing the same thing he's always been doing, and I hate him.

He doesn't love me, or my mom either. He spends all his time with some bimbo, or bimbos plural, and doesn't talk to me anymore. And when he comes home, it's really late at night, and he thinks I don't hear him. But most nights I can't fall asleep until three in the morning. I toss and turn, and then, when I hear him walk up the stairs, I pray he'll come to my door and ask me how I've been and what's been going on. But that never happens.

He always goes straight to his bedroom door, because I hear the click of the doorknob when he turns it. Then he closes it, and it makes a different clicking sound. Right after that, sometimes I hear them talking, but I don't know who's saying what. Then sometimes the grunting and sighing starts. I know what my parents are doing, and I don't blame them. It's what couples do. But I know damn well he's doing it with women who aren't my mom.

And I hate him for it.

And I hate that I don't mean enough to him to stay home instead of fucking around. Mom and I have dinner together some nights, but I don't have anything to say. What I really wanna say is, Your husband is cheating on you and has been for most of your marriage. But it's not my place. She should feel it, know it somehow, by the way he acts or the things he doesn't say, just like in the movies. My mom isn't stupid, so how can she not know?

Unless she doesn't wanna know. And I sure as hell am not gonna be the one to tell her. If she's chosen to believe all the shit Daddy tells her about loving her and being so busy he doesn't get home until two or three in the morning, then fine. Let her dream. Maybe reality is too hard for her to accept. Everyone has their dreams. God knows I did.

Until I didn't. And now I don't know what it would feel like to have a dream. To want something that could really come true. When I was a sophomore in high school, I started blowing out my birthday candles with the wish that Daddy would love me like he used to. But he's no different than the people at my high school and now at college.

No one loves me. I guess Mom does. But she doesn't hug me like she did when I was a kid. But, hey, I usually run the other way when she tries to anyway, 'cause I feel like she's trying too hard. Or maybe she and Daddy both feel the same way about me. Maybe all the kids at school and college are right. I'm a worthless piece of shit.

And now, not only do I hate Daddy, I hate myself.

I push the envelope back into Mom's purse.

I don't wanna know who it's from.

LEENA

"Joy!" I shout a little too loudly. Did she just finish reading the letter from Michael, or is she just now taking it out of my purse? I can only hope it's the latter.

Joy jumps back, as if the white envelope is a rattler, and turns toward me as I'm walking down the stairs.

"Where have you been?" she asks, stuffing her hand into the front pocket of her jeans.

"Did you need something?"

Joy opens her mouth, looking like a fish out of water. "Uh, no. I found that envelope on the floor and stuck it back in your purse."

I look into her eyes and see that she couldn't possibly have read the letter. Otherwise, she wouldn't be looking so normal.

"How was school?"

Joy shrugs. "All right. I'm not so sure junior college is where I should be."

"Why's that? You could probably apply for your sophomore year at Stanford and forget about finishing up at the jc."

Joy shakes her head, not looking me in the eyes, but rather to the side of me. I don't know if she's upset or bored or just doesn't want to talk to me, which has been the case for most of the last three or four years. I can't remember when she became so morose and quiet and more to herself than she's ever been. She'd been a pretty gregarious child, always talking and laughing and playing with a bevy of friends from around the neighborhood as well as from school.

After she entered middle school, kids came around less and Joy played by herself more and more. Once she entered high school, she spent most of her time in her bedroom with the door closed, and whenever I knocked, she didn't answer. When I'd open the door, she'd have her headphones in and her computer snuggled in her lap. If she didn't look up, I'd back out of the room. If she noticed me, I'd ask her what was up with her day, and I always got the same answer. Nothing much.

It's only recently that I noticed blood on the cuff of one of her long-sleeved shirts. It looked as if she'd tried to wash it off herself with bleach. The chlorine had eaten through the material on the cuff, but some bits of the edges still had bright red stains on them. I sniffed it, but all I could detect was the overpowering odor of bleach.

She'd taken to wearing long-sleeved garments continuously, whether it was cold or hot outside. It reminded me of Diane Keaton in Something's Gotta Give. Jack Nicholson asks, "What's with the turtlenecks? It's the middle of summer." Diane Keaton replies, "Why do you care what I wear?" He says, "Just curious," to which she replies, "I like them. I've always liked them. I'm just a turtleneck kinda gal."

"Joy?"

"Mmm?"

"What do you mean when you say you're not sure the junior college is where you should be right now? What do you want to do?"

Joy glances at me, and our eyes connect. She looks as if she's going to cry. Just as she did when she was a toddler, her mouth gets tight, like a slash in the middle of her face, and her eyes squint.

I reach out toward her and open my fingers. "Come over here. Let's sit down in the front room where it's comfortable."

She doesn't grasp my hand, so I turn, and she follows me into the front room. I sit on the couch and pat the cushion next to me. Joy sits much farther away, in the corner of the couch, and slides her knees up against her chest, then surrounds her shins with her arms. She reminds me again of a turtle retracting into its shell.

"You said the other day you wanted to talk to your father and me. He'll be in meetings. I don't know if he mentioned it, but St. John's is going to be performing a surgery to separate Siamese twin toddlers. It's been several years since the last one, and he's on the surgical team. It takes literally months to prepare for something like that. The meetings get called at all times of the day, with no notice. We can either wait for him to join us, though I don't know when that will be. Or I can play the part of both parents and you can just talk to me instead." I smile.

She doesn't smile back.

I scooch toward her and reach out and grasp her hand dangling next to her calf. It's cold and clammy. "Are you feeling okay?"

"I'm fine."

She's staring at her knees, which are practically touching her chin, she's in such a balled-up position.

I let go of her hand and tip her chin in my direction. "You can tell me anything, Joy. I won't be mad. If you don't want to go to the jc any longer, that's okay. If you want to take time off school, get a job, that's fine, too. I know you feel closer to your father than you do to me, but he's not here right now. I am. And I want to listen. I love you."

Tears begin to pour from her eyes, down her cheeks, dripping off her chin onto her shirt, which, again, is a long-sleeved cotton T-shirt that covers her from neck to knuckles.

"No judging, Joy. I promise not to judge you. Whatever you say, I can handle it." I pause, thinking of the typical teenage problems, wondering which one she's dealing with. "Are you having relationship problems?"

She lets out a rough, "Ha!" followed by, "As if."

"Well, I don't know what you do with your free time. Perhaps you're seeing someone now, but you don't want to bring him home. I was your age once. I know that's hard to fathom, and my mom used to tell me the same thing. And I looked at her the same way you're looking at me now. Like you wish I'd shut the hell up and go away."

I watch her tears fall, wishing I could make them stop, because for Joy to cry in front of me is so unusual and so out of the realm of normalcy, it's got to be something really bad that's hurting her so much that she would open herself like this to me.

"I'm glad Daddy's… I mean, that Dad's not here. I… I need to talk to somebody, but I don't know what to do."

"You mean, you want to see a counselor or a therapist or someone? Or can you tell me what's bothering you? Joy, I'll do anything to help you. And I'm here for you. Some people tell me I'm a great listener."

She looks at the ceiling, and the tears drip toward her ears, then fall off the tips of her lobes onto the back of the couch.

"You know that movie with Bruce Willis and that little boy? The movie that everyone's seen that's pretty famous? It's kinda old, though—"

"The Sixth Sense with M. Night Shyamalan as the director? The young boy, Haley Joel Osment, whispers, 'Sometimes I see dead people.' That one?"

She nods, then turns her head toward me and looks in my eyes.

My heart hammers in my chest. All I can think is, how long has this been going on? Is she really telling me she actually sees dead people? Does my little girl need to see a psychiatrist? Is this why none of her friends come over? Does she even have any friends? Is this because her father is gone all the time, and I allow her to sit in her room all night long after school, doing God knows what on her computer with her damn headphones smashed into her ears, listening to that weird music they play these days?

"Do you see dead people sometimes, too, Joy?"

She laughs, but it's not the laugh you hear when she thinks something is funny. It's a hollow sound, as if it's coming from deep within her chest, a chest that's all curved into her knees, which are pressed so tightly into her breasts, I can't see how she can breathe.

"No, I don't see dead people, Mom."

"All right. That's a good thing." I pause, not knowing what she's talking about yet. I'm afraid to interrupt her, because I feel she's on the cusp of telling me something important. She's going to reveal why she wanted to talk to Steven and me, and I don't want to break her train of thought.

"Um, yeah, Mom, I guess it's a good thing I don't see dead people. But sometimes I wanna be one of 'em."

"I don't understand, Joy. You want to be one of the

people like—" A whooshing sound suddenly pops into my head. It's happened before, when I've been caught by surprise, or when Steven didn't come home one night years ago, and he wouldn't answer my pages, and the hospital didn't know where he was. My head feels like there's a waterfall inside, or I have the worst case of tinnitus ever. I curl my arm around Joy's shoulders. "Are you saying you want to die, honey?"

She nods.

The whooshing sound gets worse. I have to be the strong one in this scenario. My daughter has just announced she's suicidal, and it doesn't matter one whit how I physically feel. I am not the center of the world right now. Joy is.

I take in a breath and hold it for a count of two, then let it out slowly, and the rhythm of my heart slows. I can do this, I tell myself. Because I have no choice. "Oh, Joy." I am trying so hard not to cry, but I feel that sting in my eyes when I tear up, and I blink and blink to hold them back. Inner strength is what's called for right now, and I have that. I know I do. And I will not cry. Save that for later, Leena.

"Have you ever tried to hurt yourself?" I wonder if she will admit to cutting herself, or if I'll have to tell her about the blood I saw on her shirt cuff.

She nods, not saying a word.

When I glance down, she's staring at her hands, fiddling with her fingernails. Her bottom lip is trembling.

In all my life, I never thought I'd be in this position. My daughter is telling me she doesn't want to live, and I can't think of a goddamn thing to say to make her feel otherwise. What's happening in my mind is what happened when another car hit my car and I was ejected from the front seat because I wasn't wearing a seat belt.

The cliché phrase "your life passes before your eyes" happened to me. But this time, it's Joy's life, not mine.

I see her in the mirror the nurse is holding in front of my widespread legs just when Joy's tiny head crowns at the opening of my vagina. I see blood and a white cheesy substance, then a forehead, then a nose, and then a teeny mouth. Suddenly, the rest of her body slips out into Dr. Farraday's hands, and behind the mask, I can tell the doctor's smiling, because the sides of his eyes crinkle. He tells me it's a girl, and she's a beauty.

I see Joy taking her first steps, that moment when she lets go of the glass table with her slobbery fingers and waddles into my outstretched arms, her eyes focused one hundred percent on my face, drool dripping down her chin. And when she makes it all the way to my chest, she's smiling and laughing, and I'm crying while I kiss her sweet-smelling head.

All this happens in a matter of seconds now, and I want so much to not be daydreaming, because I have to say something to Joy. I need to help my daughter, and dammit, I don't know how. I am inept. I am a failure. Because my daughter wants to die, and that isn't right.

I haven't read about teenage depression. Yes, I've seen TV commercials about teen suicide as I left the room to get a snack. I didn't pay much attention to them. Teen suicide didn't have anything to do with my life. I didn't have to watch them.

Now I wish I did.

"Have you been cutting yourself?"

There's silence for at least a minute or two. I think, if she felt comfortable enough nodding that she's tried to hurt herself, then she'll eventually admit what she's done. But if she's having a hard time, which is pretty darn obvious, then perhaps I should help her out.

"I noticed blood on the cuff of your shirt a while back, but I didn't think anything of it."

She nods again, and I'm wondering if she's ever going to tell me what she's thinking. I need some help. I can't read her nineteen-year-old mind, and I can't remember where my mind was when I was nineteen either. I am useless.

Joy takes a big, shuddering breath. "Sometimes I just feel like nothing." She pauses and rubs at the skin above her wrist.

As she does so, her shirt rides up a bit, and I can see scars, white and ropy-looking. I avert my gaze, because it just makes me want to cry. My baby is in pain. I don't speak, because I want her to talk to me at her own pace, and I feel she's about to say more than she has.

She coughs and swallows, and she's still crying. This must be so hard for her to say aloud to another person. And I get the impression I'm the only person she's talked to about this. She doesn't appear to have any close friends, but I could be wrong. She's been MIA around here for several years, and I don't know much about her life.

"Most of the time, I just feel nothing. Like I am nothing. Like if I wasn't here, no one would fucking notice." Her head jerks up, and she whispers, "Sorry, Mom."

I laugh and squeeze her shoulders, bringing her closer to me. "I think I can handle the fact my daughter has a potty mouth, Joy. I swore up a storm when I was your age."

Her lips curve up a tad bit at the edges. "Can't picture it."

"No kid pictures their parent either swearing or having sex."

She wriggles her shoulders, more of a shudder, I think, and says, "Please don't let's have the sex talk, Mom. And definitely not about your sex life. Gack!"

And I'm thinking, boy, could I make an inappropriate comment right now like, What sex life, Joy? But I'd never do that. If a consensual slam-bam-thank-you-ma'am can be considered a sex life, then I'm guessing I have one. But Steven and I haven't had anything I'd call "making love" in years. Is that when people say, The thrill is gone?

"Joy, your father and I love you, and I can't believe you don't know that if you weren't with us, we'd be devastated." My voice begins to tremble, but I continue. If anything, I have to prove to her somehow that I wouldn't want to live without her. I won't live without her. I can't live without her. "You mean everything to me, Joy. And I don't expect you to understand that, because you aren't a parent, but you have to trust me on this, baby. I can't let you die."

"I'm nothing but a freaking disappointment to myself and especially to you and Daddy. I couldn't get into Stanford or Cal with my high-school grades, so I had to go to a junior college. Now I can't cut it there either. I'm flunking out. I just got my midterm grades, and I got three D's and one F. I'm a fucking failure. I can't do anything right."

"Honey, I had no idea you weren't passing your classes. When I ask you how things are going at college, you always say everything's fine."

"I hear you and Daddy fighting about how he's never around and how he used to spend a lot of time with me. I know you guys aren't happy together. I can see it, Mom."

"Your father's a pretty famous surgeon, Joy, and he's now the chief of surgery at the hospital. And I probably didn't tell you that he's been selected to participate in a surgery to separate Siamese twins. That alone will require hours and hours of his time. Along with that comes so much responsibility and a ton of work. There are only so many hours in a day, and unfortunately, that means he and I don't spend much time alone together, and neither do you and he. I wish we could go back to when life was less hectic, but we can't. I'm proud of your father, that he's gone so far in his career. I just wish he… I don't know… I guess I wish he'd cut back on something. I don't know what, but something so he'd be around more for you and me. But you don't have to worry about your father and my relationship, Joy."

"That's not what I meant." She shrugs. "If I wasn't around," she shakes her head slowly side to side, "maybe you'd probably be divorced. But you won't because of me. Both of you would be happier if you weren't together, but you won't leave, and neither will he, because you have a kid. So if I wasn't here, both of you would be happier. I know it's true, but neither of you will admit it."

I take Joy by the shoulders and turn her toward me, look straight in her eyes. "Your father and I will work out whatever problems we have, Joy, and it doesn't have anything to do with you. Do I think he should be home more? Yes, I do. But he just can't do that right now. I don't think he had a clue how much time he'd be spending at the hospital after he became so in demand. He's such an excellent surgeon, everyone wants him, and I'm proud of that. He's an amazing surgeon, and of course he'll be the one they call when they need someone of his caliber and expertise.

"So in a way, I feel guilty complaining about it, but I miss him. That's what it really comes down to, Joy. He and I aren't staying together just because we have a daughter. He and I will work out our problems. Yes, he and I have arguments about the fact he doesn't spend time with you. I don't want him to lose out on the few years left to spend with you while you're living here at home. Once you move out, you'll have a life of your own, and I know one day he'll regret he didn't take advantage of that. And you and I have never been as close as you and your father. But I've tried to get close to you, Joy. But you push me away, and I can't be a substitute for your father, though I've tried."

Joy shrugs. "I guess I feel like Daddy threw me away for his work. And he threw you away, too." The tears continue to slide down her cheeks, and she sniffs, wipes her nose with her sleeve. "I don't mean to reject you, but… I don't know, at least you get to see him after he comes home at night. I hear you guys talking and stuff. I guess I resent the fact that you at least get a little of his time. But I get… well, I get nothing. So I kinda take it out on you, I guess. Which is totally fucked up, Mom. And I'm sorry. But shit, he never talks to me. I don't see him hardly ever. Why can't you do something about it? Why can't you fix it? Make it like it used to be?"

My stomach muscles tighten, and I'm gritting my teeth. This discussion makes me so angry, I want to scream. My daughter's in pain, and I'm useless. Mostly, I blame Steven for this. But I don't know how to change it, to make it better. It's been hard for me to swallow the reality of his situation, and now I find out my daughter can't either. It's just too much to swallow, and she shouldn't have to anyway.

It's up to us as parents to be there for her, and it's obvious Steven's failed in that endeavor. And so have I, because I didn't insist Joy be around enough, or pester her to accompany me, or ask her to join me in sharing something she and I would enjoy doing together, like going to the movies or a concert. Why is hindsight often more clear than what's staring you right in the face right now?

It all sounds so simple. I should have been stronger. I should have come right out and told her I wanted to spend more time with her. And when I felt rejected by her absence, I should have spoken up, told her I missed spending time with her, not shrugged it off as typical teenage behavior. Looking back, I took the easy way out. Not dealing with the problem was easier than facing it head on, fighting for what I really wanted—to be with my daughter in spite of her preference for Steven's company. I took the easy road, and where has it gotten me?

Here I am, facing my daughter who doesn't think we care if she lives or dies, and she's cutting herself to ease her pain. The pain Steven and I caused her by our neglect.

Not only am I going to talk to Steven about this, we as a family need to see a therapist, get some help to fix this problem. But will Steven go? I think Joy will. And I definitely believe we need help.

"Joy, would you be open to seeing a therapist? Either alone or as a family? I want to fix this, help you feel better about your life, work things out so you're happy again. Like you were when you were younger, before your father became glued to the hospital, and I felt I was such a poor substitute for him, so I didn't try hard enough to take his place."

Her eyelids droop, and she looks as if she's falling asleep.

"Joy? Did you hear me?"

She nods. "Yeah, I heard you. But Daddy's not gonna change, Mom. You know it as well as I do. His job is what it is. I get that. I have to learn to accept that his work is more important to him than either of us. And you're just doing this because you feel obligated to try and make me happy. But you can't do that. You can't change Daddy, and you can't change the situation, and you're not gonna be able to change how I feel either." She stands and looks as if talking is over, and she's going to walk away.

I grasp her forearm. "We can't leave things like this, Joy. We haven't resolved a damn thing."

"It can't be resolved. You can't fix me. You can't fix Daddy. I always knew I couldn't fix him. You've argued enough with him to try to fix it. You can't. And ya know what? I realize I can't fix me either." She shakes off my hand and runs for the front door.

"Joy!" I shout, running after her. I trip over a pair of my shoes as I round the corner of the couch and fall flat on my face, push myself up, begin to take a step, and realize I've smashed my knee. I scream out in pain and look up to see Joy's back as she exits through the front door. I crawl to the nearest chair, and as I try to stand, I hear the engine of Joy's car roar to life, then the squeal of the tires as she skids away from the curb. The sound of the engine lessens to a distant hum, until I hear only the ticking of the clock in the kitchen.

She's gone. And I can't be sure she isn't traveling down a path of total and utter destruction.

STEVEN

The sun is shining through the hotel curtains, warming my face. Her backside snuggles against my stomach and groin, and instantly, my erection presses against her butt.

I twist to my left and reach for my phone on the bedside table, press the button. "Shit!"

"What's wrong?" she asks, running her fingernails down my back.

I stand and grab my clothes draped over the chair, stuff my legs into my pants. "Leena's been calling me for hours. My phone must be on silent."

"Is it important?"

My fingers fumble with the buttons on my shirt. "She texted me something about Joy leaving the house, then left me a voice mail. I've gotta go."

"Are you sure? Why don't you listen to her voice-mail message and call her back?" She sits up and lets the sheet fall to her lap. Once again, she knows the moment I get a glance at her breasts, I almost always acquiesce and return to bed.

"Not this time," I growl. "Leena's never done this, so it must be serious." I press the voice-mail then speaker buttons before sitting on the edge of the bed to put on my shoes. "Shh."

Joy and I had a talk today.

Leena's crying, and my gut tightens.

You know, the talk she wanted to have with both of us? She's depressed and said she wants to die.

Leena's voice hitches, and she begins to wail.

Steven. I think she's suicidal, and she—

Leena pauses, coughs, takes a deep breath, then continues.

She left the house, really upset. I don't know where she's going. She won't answer her cell. I called 911, and I was put on fucking hold. After five minutes, I hung up. You have to come home, Steven. I don't know what to do.

"I'll see you tomorrow," I say, grab my suit jacket and tie, and run to the hotel door.

"But, Steven—"

I slam the door behind me. Doesn't she understand I have a daughter who's in trouble? That she really is not that important? Sure, the sex is great. She knows that's what we're in this thing for. Sex.

The elevator descends like it's free-falling to the first floor, and my stomach plummets. I'm starving, but now I don't have time to stop for anything. As I step off the elevator, I text Leena. I'm on my way home.

I make it there in less than ten minutes, and Leena opens the door before I reach the porch. She flings herself into my arms, and I drop my briefcase and hug her close.

"You have no idea where she went?" I ask.

Leena shakes her head against my chest, and I feel the wetness of her tears on my shirt.

"What did she say? She wants to kill herself? What—"

Leena pulls back and looks me in the eyes. "She was trying to explain how she feels useless. That if she wasn't around, we wouldn't even care. She thinks she's the reason you and I argue about how you're never home.

That if she wasn't around for us to argue about her, then we'd get a divorce and both be happier."

"That's ridiculous." I pick up my briefcase and walk into the house. Leena follows me.

I immediately grab a bottle of my finest whiskey and pour myself a drink. She's watching me, and I raise my eyebrows. She nods, and I pour her one as well, then hand it to her.

We walk to the front room, and I sit in my favorite overstuffed chair. She settles on the couch across from me.

"What about her friends? Did you call them?"

Leena rolls her eyes. "Steven," she says, then looks at me. "She doesn't have any friends. Actually, I think she's been bullied for years, but I have no proof of that. She's not very talkative. She's kind of introverted. And that all started—" She pauses.

I clench my teeth so hard, my temples hurt. "I know what you're going to say. When I started working more. Because I'm never home." I pause. "Hold on. I saved the police commissioner's life. He owes me. I'll call him. Tell him about Joy, what we know or better yet, what we don't know. I'm sure he'll bend over backwards to find her."

She smiles. "That's a great idea. Thank you."

I grab my phone out of my pocket, and head for my office down the hallway, closing the door behind me.

When I return, she stands abruptly, eyes wide. "Well?"

"Now we wait."

She plops back down on the couch. "What I was saying before—"

I let out a breath. "I know. I know. I'm never home."

"Well, it's the truth. I'm just telling you what Joy said. And dammit, I stood up for you, Steven. I told her that because of your reputation you're asked to do surgeries, because you're the best. That you have to be at the hospital even more because of that. I explained you're the chief of surgery, and you have the Siamese twins' separation coming up. Dammit, I'm proud of you, and I bet she is, too. But there comes a time when the ramifications of your actions are staring you in the face, and who the hell is going to tell you to look at them but me, Steven?"

She covers her face with her hands, takes a deep breath, drops her hands, and stares at me. "Your hours come with the territory, so to speak. I get that. But the truth is, it's affecting your personal life and the lives of your family to the point where your daughter feels worthless and wants to kill herself. And here it is, the middle of the day, and you and I are home having a discussion about what we're going to do and how we're going to find our little girl. When's it going to stop?

"You have to step up and do something, because the status quo isn't working any longer. You know it, and I know it. And it may be the death of our daughter." She stands, and tears flow down her cheeks. "And I swear to God, Steven, if she kills herself over this, we're through. Because I know you can change your work situation, and if you don't, then I guess you've chosen your work over this family. And I can't accept that." She reaches out with a shaky hand and grasps the glass of whiskey and downs it in one gulp.

I can hear myself breathing, it's so quiet in the house at this time of day. I'm never here to notice, and that should tell me something. I look at my wife and realize I don't notice many things. Even though she's crying, she's a strikingly beautiful woman. So what am I doing being unfaithful? If I forget the fact our sex life is a bit too tame for my liking, Leena is exactly the type of woman I'm attracted to. She's incredibly smart, well-educated, a great conversationalist, sexy as hell. But because of my diverse sexual proclivities, I feel the need to sleep with other women.

Is that fair to her? What if the proverbial shoe were on the other foot? Would I care? The thought makes my teeth clench, and I realize I'm basically a sexist son of a bitch who, if I found out Leena was sleeping with another man, would probably kill him with my bare hands. I don't own a gun, but if I had one, I can't say I wouldn't use it. What does that make me? Have I turned into some kind of wacko?

I drain my own glass, sit down next to her and put my arm across her shoulders. "I'll change. I promise."

She shakes her head. "We'll see if you'll change, Steven. Right now, at this very moment, that's not important. Right now, I want Joy back. Here. At home." She turns toward me, tilts her head. "What're you thinking?"

"That it's partly my fault Joy's missing. And I get that."

She reaches out and grasps my hands in hers. "She misses you. I miss you. Your job has taken control of all our lives and changed all of us. We're really not a family any longer. And I want us to be a family again. Like back in the day, you know? But Joy has other problems. It's not all you. At least, it doesn't seem like it. She has little, if any, self-esteem, but it goes further than this house. Her peers have a lot of influence in this scenario. She's still being bullied. In junior college!"

"You've tried to tell me, Leena. Time after time. And I hope to God Joy hasn't done anything drastic, because I couldn't live with myself if she has. The guilt would kill me." I feel beaten down, crushed. And the look on Leena's face tells me I should feel exactly that way.

LEENA

I can already feel the waiting driving me nuts. My mind keeps going round and round with what-if's, until I'm dizzy. I tell Steven I need to go to the bathroom then head up to our bedroom. I glance at my purse, knowing Michael's latest letter is safely hidden in the zippered side compartment. But I have to hide it with the other letters. Though I ask myself often, why am I saving them? I feel guilty reading them over and over, as I ofttimes do. My intention was to discard all of them once I discovered Michael's in Balmoral for involuntary manslaughter.

I don't know what I surmised he was in prison for before I knew. I guess I thought perhaps some type of white-collar crime, like embezzlement. I should have been smarter. They transfer small-time criminals to prisons comprised mainly of murderers and rapists and gangs all the time.

I hear Steven downstairs, snatch the letter out of my purse and head to the bathroom. Anything to take my mind off the gruesome scenarios I keep conjuring, if Joy isn't found soon. I'm going crazy with worry, and I feel useless just sitting downstairs waiting for the phone to ring. I lock the bathroom door behind me, and sit on the sink counter to read it again.

Dear Leena,

Balmoral is now completely coordinated with the PrisonersNeedFriendsToo website, so now I have your real name and your address, so you must have given permission when you signed up to communicate with a prisoner, otherwise they wouldn't be able to reveal that information. Now my letters no longer need to be addressed by the G's, which slows the time of their arrival by almost a week. Not that that makes any difference. It's not as if I'm going to show up at your doorstep bearing a bouquet of roses and a box of Godiva chocolates! Though I'd like to, in thanks for your friendship over all these months.

We've gotten to know each other well, Leena. But I also know that you have no idea why I'm in prison. I never told you, and you've been polite enough not to ask. But now you'll be able to look at the website and see that I'm in Balmoral for involuntary manslaughter. To most people, it sounds like I'm a murderer or a serial killer. That couldn't be further from the truth.

I am not a murderer, Leena.

I know they say almost all prisoners swear they're innocent of the crimes for which they've been found guilty. Thousands of prisoners can't possibly be innocent. But in my particular situation (I know, I know, you're saying to yourself, you're the exception to the rule, right, Michael?), I did nothing wrong. And I'd do the same thing again, if I was in the same situation.

Let me explain. At least if you've read this far,

I'm hoping you'll continue, because I hope you'll understand why I did what I did.

It all began when Heather and I had just celebrated our tenth wedding anniversary. We were happy and still very much in love. Heather was a pediatric surgeon. She loved kids. We were planning on having at least two children. We decided it was time for both of us to cut back on our hours at the hospital in order to start our family.

Yes, "our" hours. I, too, am a surgeon. Was a surgeon. A cardiac surgeon. Heather and I met at St. John's Hospital in San Francisco. I was a very sought-after surgeon and had a thriving practice. I participated in one of the first Siamese-twins separations in California. The two girls shared one heart. I had to leave the heart in one of the little girls and perform a heart transplant on the other in order to save both of them. I miss that more than anything. As I'm sure you can guess, I was stripped of my medical license the moment I was convicted. But all that happened five years ago.

I know you're wondering what crime I committed. In my opinion, and the opinion of many other people (proven by the fact California has now changed the law), I didn't commit any crime at all.

Heather was unable to get pregnant. After nine months, we went to an ob/gyn, and when they did an abdominal ultrasound, they found she had cancer—a very invasive type of cancer that had wrapped itself around every organ in her abdominal cavity and was impossible to surgically remove, no matter whether she had chemo to shrink it or not.

Slowly but surely, it was squeezing her other organs, closing them off until they would cease to function.

They gave her a month to two months to live.

We were both devastated. We had so many dreams yet to fulfill. It was next to impossible to accept the diagnosis. We didn't even have time to go through the stage of denial. Within days of the diagnosis, Heather's organs started to shut down. She was on very high doses of painkillers, and they helped for a week, then didn't. Heather was in excruciating pain.

I was a doctor. It was in my power to take her pain away. She was going to die. There was nothing they, or I, could do but ease her pain. And then even that was taken out of our hands, because the drugs no longer worked. And as a physician, my job is to heal, to stop the pain if possible, and I felt like a failure.

I don't know if you've ever been in such a position. I hope not. It's my job to take care of my family. And Heather and I were our own little family. When I realized I couldn't do a damn thing to help her, I couldn't accept that.

I'm a doctor. I live, eat, and breathe the Hippocratic oath—first do no harm, meaning do whatever it is in my power to help my patient survive an illness and feel better. And I wasn't doing anything of the sort. By keeping Heather alive, I was hurting her. She was in pain, and nothing could take that pain away. I was doing her more harm by helping to keep her alive. I couldn't live with that. I was going against everything I'd ever tried to do for my patients—helping them. I wasn't helping Heather one whit.

Also, it was in my power to take her pain away. I believed it was my obligation as a doctor to help her die a wee bit earlier than was expected, perhaps a week or two. And because I was a cardiac surgeon, I had access to more lethal drugs than your typical doctor. Pentobarbital was my drug of choice, and I had a connection. I was very close to a doctor in the federal prison system, specifically death row and executions. That's where I obtained the pentobarbital.

When Heather was still able to speak (the pain was so bad, she often couldn't concentrate enough to form a sentence), she asked if I could help her die, but in a way that I wouldn't get into trouble. At that point, I knew what I had to do and screw the system. I lied to her. The first lie I'd ever told my wife—ever. I said I could get the drug at the hospital easily (lie) and that I wouldn't get in trouble because there was no way to detect the drug in her system (another lie). She believed me, as she always did. So we planned her death.

Unlike the new law in California, which allows the patient to put themselves to death while they're able to physically do so, in Heather's case, she was so weak, she communicated most times with her baby finger. I'd ask her a question, and she'd move her baby finger left to right to mean "no" and up and down to indicate "yes."

Even if California had already passed the Death With Dignity Law back then, the parameters are ridiculously restrictive. Patients must be capable of taking the medication themselves, without assistance. Heather couldn't do that. Two licensed physicians must verify the patient's eligibility, including their mental competency (ability to make their own health care decisions), diagnosis, and prognosis. Heather could barely talk. The patient must make two oral requests in person, at least fifteen days apart. A written request must be witnessed by two people, one of whom is not an heir. In Heather's case, meeting the requirements of this law would have been utterly impossible. She was going to die before the fifteen days needed between requests, and she couldn't make an "oral" request, because she couldn't talk. So she wouldn't have qualified anyway.

So I told her I'd get the drug and administer it, whenever she wanted. She indicated the next day was her preference, and I made it happen. We had a farewell dinner. Well, I had a farewell dinner. Heather hadn't eaten in a week. We watched her favorite movie, Just Friends, with Ryan Reynolds. She lay in the bed, and I sat in bed right next to her. I ate her favorite meal—grilled asparagus, a baked potato covered in butter, and a piece of grilled chicken. She wanted one of us to taste her final meal.

When the final credits rolled for Just Friends, with Ryan Reynolds lip-syncing the song "I Swear," I looked over and Heather was grimacing in pain. I asked her if she thought it was time, and she moved her pinkie finger up and down. I asked her if I could kiss her, and she opened her eyes and once again moved her pinkie up and down.

I will never, ever forget the last moments of her life. I've been at many patients' bedsides during their final moments, but they weren't my wife. And I could not cry. Heather didn't want me to be sad. When she was lucid, which was weeks ago, we'd talked about it. She wanted me to go on. She made me promise I'd find someone else and marry again. And I promised her I would. I would have done anything for Heather.

So I did.

I filled the syringe with ten milligrams of pentobarbital and put the syringe on the side table. I sat next to her and kissed her, looked into her glazed eyes and told her how much happiness she'd given me and how much I loved her and that I'd love her until the day I died. I knew she loved me, too. We had been on a honeymoon for our entire marriage.

I asked if she thought it was time, and she moved her pinkie up and down once again. I kissed her again, vowed my eternal love again, carefully inserted the syringe into the vein in her arm, and slowly depressed the plunger, until the syringe was empty.

Heather stopped breathing within seconds. The ten milligrams ensured her death, and it was so.

I sat next to her for an hour before calling 911. When the paramedics arrived, they easily figured out what happened. I didn't hide the syringe. I knew what would come.

I was arrested within two days, waited months for a trial, was convicted of involuntary manslaughter, and sent to the only prison that had room at the time—Balmoral State Penitentiary.

Where I fell in love with a woman who I have never met nor seen in a photograph nor spoken to. Will you visit me, A? I know your name now. It's Annaleena, and you like to be called Leena.

"Are you okay, Leena?"
I jump so abruptly, I slide off the tile counter. My foot slips, and I fall to the floor.
"I'm okay, Steven," I answer. "I'll be right out."

STEVEN

When I enter the kitchen, cell phone in hand, Leena is sitting at the table, tears pouring down her cheeks. She turns in my direction, eyes wide and slashed with tiny red lines from crying for hours.

"They found her," I say.

Leena gasps, and when our eyes meet, my heart clenches, anticipating her reaction. "The police found her on the Golden Gate Bridge."

She covers her face with both hands. "We've been staring at that bridge all afternoon, and she was right there the whole time?"

"He said she was standing on the other side of the rail, on some sort of steel platform, as if looking out at the view. When one of the officers approached her, the moment she turned and saw him, she screamed at him to get back or she'd jump."

Leena lets out a huge sob, and I sit beside her and curve my arm around her shoulders, bringing her to my chest, where she lays her face against my neck and cries. Her warm tears drip down the opening of my shirt. I know it's been hard for her these past few years, with my absence and Joy's obvious resentment of my "abandoning" her. At the time, I thought that, as a teenager, she wouldn't miss the closeness we had. I guess I was wrong. No, I won't try to absolve myself of any wrongdoing. I was totally wrong, no doubt about it. I messed up. Royally.

"What stopped her?" Leena says, leaning back to look at me.

"That particular officer was brought in because he's dealt with a few what they call jumpers. After about twenty minutes, Joy pushed away from the railing and allowed the officer to help her get to a safe place."

"We owe him. Big-time, Steven."

"I know. Rest assured, I'll do something special for him. I promise you that."

"When will she be home? Can we go pick her up, or are they going to drop her off here?"

I take her by the shoulders and look into her eyes. "Neither. She'll have to spend at least seventy-two hours in the psychiatric hospital."

Leena's eyes fill again with tears, and her lower lip quivers. "Can we visit her?"

"Yes. But it's late, and Mark, the police commissioner, told me it would be best to wait until tomorrow."

"Where is she?"

"She'll be taken to one of the best facilities in San Francisco. UCSF Langley Porter Mental Health Clinic. Mark said she'll see the best of the best and for us not to worry. Joy's safe."

"For now, Steven." She sighs. "What're we going to do?"

"I would surmise she'll stay the requisite seventy-two hours. During that short stay, we'll visit her. Mark said her doctor there will arrange for a family meeting, then when she's released, I'll find her the best psychiatrist in the city."

Leena nods, staring at her hands, now folded in her lap. "That's good. That's really good," she whispers.

We wrap each other in a hug and hold on, almost for dear life. Why is it that it takes something this drastic to bring people together? After I phoned the police commissioner, Leena and I sat next to each other on the couch, her head on my shoulder, gazing out at the stunning view of the Golden Gate Bridge. We didn't talk much, but it was the most time we'd spent together in years. Most of our time together is spent at hospital functions, schmoozing other wealthy people, hoping to bring in more donations to St. John's Hospital. Sometimes, Leena and I played doubles tennis with another surgeon from the hospital and his girlfriend, then we enjoyed an outdoor lunch on the deck with them. But our time alone together was fairly nonexistent.

For the first time in a long time, not only were we alone, but we didn't have to make small talk. We were so exhausted that we both nodded off for a couple of minutes as the sunlight warmed our faces, then waned to a dull shade of gold along the hardwood floor.

We talked about Joy and her depression. I'd once again promised to start immediately reducing my hours at the hospital with the caveat that it would take some time to accomplish. I decided to resign as chief of surgery and, once the Siamese twins' separation was completed, to pull back on my surgical rounds, allowing some of the newer surgeons the opportunities always handed to me.

I take hold of her hand. "She'll be all right, Leena. She's safe. She'll be home in a few days."

She turns her whole body in my direction, folds her legs, and stares at me. "We don't know anything of the sort. You're just trying to placate me. We don't know if she's going to be okay. We don't know if she'll try this again. We don't know shit."

"I've seen my share of psych patients, especially during my rotation at SF General. Believe me, they'll put Joy on an antidepressant, and with counseling, I believe she'll get through this."

"If you say so."

"Why are you being this way? She's only nineteen years old. She has plenty of time to change and grow and learn."

"And while that's happening, she still won't have a father at home to help her get through this."

"I told you, Leena, I promise to cut back on my hours, resign as chief of surgery. What more do you want me to do? Quit working?"

"Of course not. I'm just saying all that will take months. You said yourself the meetings for the Siamese twins' separation will be at least for the next two months, and that's if everything goes perfectly, no glitches or unforeseen problems."

I let out a deep breath. "There's nothing more I can do. It's unfortunate this has happened right now, but I will fix it. It's just going to take time."

Her face reddens, and she stands abruptly and looks down at me. "It's unfortunate that this has happened? Are you fucking kidding me? Should it have happened at a more convenient time for you? Perhaps Joy should have waited until after the twins are separated? This unfortunate event, as you call it, shouldn't have happened at all," she shouts.

I stand and face her, my fists clenched at my sides. I'm already mad enough at myself for being an absent father, and she knows it. I don't need her to pound me over the head with it again and again. I already know. I've admitted it over and over during our discussions this afternoon.

"Don't blame me for literally everything that's gone wrong in Joy's world, Leena. She's a teenager. Ever heard of teen angst? I'm sure I've played a big part in her depression and low self-esteem, but I bet there are things you've done to make her feel like shit as well."

"You're right. I have. I left her alone, thinking; hey, she's a teenager, she needs her space. In reality, she needed me to force her to talk to me about her life and her problems. But I didn't do that. I thought she was handling her life, just as I did at her age. And I was wrong. Totally wrong."

"So you fuckcd up, too, Leena. It's not all on me!"

"No, it isn't. But you're a huge part of it. She told me as much."

"For God's sake, can we stop this blame game? We're both at fault. Me more than you. But we have to pull together now. Show a united front for our daughter. And unfortunately, until my schedule changes, you'll be the parent who's around the most. But that'll change."

"So you say." She walks away and drops down onto the couch and crosses her arms over her chest and tucks her legs underneath her, like an athlete jumping into a bobsled at an Olympic luge event.

"I'm doing the best I can, Leena. Cut me a little slack until I can get through this work schedule at the hospital. Can you do that for me?"

She lets out a short burst of laughter. "Oh, sure. I'll do anything for you, Steven. Just as I always have."

I walk toward her, our eyes locked in a stare. "What does that mean?"

"You know what it means. Remember something. You've not only been an absent father for Joy. You've been an absent husband. And for the record, I'm tired of the slam-bam-thank-you-ma'am sex that seems to be your preference for years now. You come home, and I feel like a highly paid whore. You get what you want, and in return, I get to live in a beautiful house in Pacific Heights, drive a gorgeous Mercedes, and enjoy the company of your colleagues at the functions I always accompany you to."

"I never knew that's how you felt about our lives. I wasn't aware all the money I make is such a burden."

"It is what it is, Steven. And it's been like this for years. I'm almost used to it."

"But not quite, right? Ready to call it quits, Leena?"

"I've thought of it. Often. I have my ways of dealing with it."

"What're you talking about?"

She stands and walks to the window and stares out at the lights beginning to make their way onto the scene that is San Francisco at twilight. "Forget I even said anything. It's just… I've been missing you for years." She shrugs. "I thought I'd just get used to it. But honestly, our marriage needed to change a long time ago."

"You never said anything."

She laughs out loud. "As if you don't know that our marriage is not the best in the world."

"I know marriage is a hard road to travel. And I realize now how my hours at the hospital have affected Joy and… and you. I'm sorry, Leena. I hope it's not too late to fix this. I believe it isn't."

She turns around, and her eyes slowly lift to meet mine. "I really don't know, Steven." She lets out a shuddering breath. "I just don't know."

JOY

I didn't sleep at all last night. After the paramedics brought me to the hospital, I had to have an intake interview with a psychiatrist, which was totally dumb. He asked me all these questions about how often I have thoughts about killing myself, why I chose to jump off the Golden Gate Bridge, do I self-harm, and if so, what methods do I use. Jesus Christ on a stick. I'm not gonna frickin' spill my guts to somebody I've never met and I'll never see again in my whole life. Shit!

It was hard enough admitting to Mom that I cut myself. Then telling her how I feel about Daddy. It's embarrassing. I don't need to be close to my father. I'm a big girl. I shouldn't need to be dependent on Mommy and Daddy, for God's sake. What's wrong with me? I don't hear any of the other girls at school talk about being friends with their moms or dads. I am so weird. And I hate being weird. And I don't know how I got so weird.

And now, everyone's gonna find out I went to this frickin' loony bin, and I'll be more of a freak than I already am. I can't do anything right. I can't make Daddy be interested in me. I push Mom away 'cause I'm jealous that she gets the little bit of attention Daddy gives anyone in our house. Who the hell is jealous of their own mother? They're married. They're supposed to spend time together. No teenager spends a bunch of time with their parents.

I can't even be a normal daughter. That I need my daddy makes me sound like a damn baby. I'm just not normal. I have no friends. No one likes me. But, damn, I don't even like myself. So what do I expect?

I feel like I have no father. I'm not close to my mom. I don't have friends. So what the hell do I have? I feel like a nothing. It's like my life is a big black hole. I don't have a future. That looks like a black hole, too. I'm flunking out of school. Another black fucking hole. My parents want me to go to frickin' Stanford, and no way can I get in there. Talk about a giant disappointment. Hell, I'm a disappointment to myself.

I give up. What's the use of anything? I cut myself because then I feel pain. Better than feeling nothing. Which is how I feel every single minute of every single day. If I wasn't here, Mom and Daddy wouldn't fight. He sure as hell wouldn't miss me. They could get a divorce and marry someone else, and then they'd both be happy.

I'm so tired of feeling like a nothing. When I looked over the side of the bridge, it was like I was looking at my life. It was scary and dark and cold, and the water was so, so far away. It was like it was calling to me. Like it was asking me to join it. I know that sounds weird, but it's like the water wanted me. And I wanted to go. I still want to go.

The doctor wants to put me on psycho meds. He says they'll make me feel better. How the hell does he know some pill is gonna make me happy? That's a bunch of bullshit. Who believes that crap? If everybody could take some "happy pill," we'd all be walking around with smiles on our faces, singing, "Because I'm happy," with Pharrell.

It took hours before they finally finished with me and all their frickin' questions and poking me in the arm, taking blood outta me, and weighing me. Which is totally another story, 'cause I'm fat no matter what the frickin' scale says.

A hundred and one pounds, the nurse told me! That's bullshit. Then they put me in a room with a bed and a closet and nothing else. I'm allowed to wear the same stuff nurses and doctors wear. I think they're called scrubs, but the ones for us psycho people are yellow. We also have to wear these slipper things with sticky bottoms. And they finally let me go to sleep after I swallowed two pills, and the nurse made me stick out my tongue, then she looked down my throat and under my tongue to make sure I swallowed 'em. The bed's not like mine at home, and I can't sleep. The doctor told me I have to stay here for seventy-two hours, then they'll evaluate me and see if I can go home.

Mom and Daddy are coming to visit between six and seven thirty. I don't wanna talk about my feelings and shit. We just go round and round and don't get anywhere anyway, so what's the use? It's all a bunch of crap.

And what else is bullshit is, I can't be honest about how I'm mad at Daddy because I saw him with that other woman years ago. I know he's probably sleeping with other women. I can't ruin their marriage by saying something in front of Mom. Then they'll both hate me for making them get a divorce. I have to fake it and pretend I'm a dumb shit and that I don't know anything. I wanna scream and I can't. Sometimes, I scream into my pillow at night at home, but I'm afraid they're gonna hear me in here. Then they'll keep me here longer than seventy-two hours.

I have to fake the funk. Say what they wanna hear, so I can get the hell outta this place. I need to go home and figure out another plan. It doesn't scare me to jump off the bridge. It scares me if I have to live like this. I hate my life. I hate myself. That's what I'm scared of—living like this forever. No one lives like this and enjoys life. It's awful and scary.

And I want it to stop.

LEENA

I've decided to visit Michael. After reading his last letter, my fears he might be a serial killer or sadistic maniac have flown out the window. I'd be lying to myself that my anger at Steven doesn't have anything to do with my wanting to visit Michael. I'm trying my best not to blame him for Joy's depression and suicide attempt.

When I heard the words come out of Steven's mouth that they found Joy on the Golden Gate Bridge, looking down at the torrid bay waters, I thought my heart would burst out of my chest. It hurt to breathe or walk or do anything.

I clung to Steven like he was a lifeboat in my own personal churning waters. I listened to his apologies for not being around. I heard the words come out of his mouth that he would cut back on his hours. I nodded when he said he'd resign as chief of surgery. I acted as if I believed him when he said after the Siamese twins' separation, he would be home more often. I played along with his promises and declarations of sorrow and blame.

But I don't believe him. I've heard it all before. I remember several years ago when he and I were asked to play doubles tennis with another surgeon and his then-girlfriend (now wife). I can't remember her name. I'll call her Barbie. Barbie is a buxom blonde who must have had tons of plastic surgery. She has huge boobs that she squeezed into a low-cut, stretchy top, pouty lips that are too full to be natural, a flat-as-a-board belly with a gold belly button ring, and the tight booty of a teenager.

Barbie's boyfriend, the surgeon, who is twenty years her senior, knew nothing about tennis at the time. He didn't know love from an ace. And neither did Barbie. And somehow (duh) it landed on Steven's shoulders (the poor guy) to teach her the ropes. While the surgeon friend and I took a break to get something to drink, because it was hotter than heck outside, Steven took full, and I mean full, advantage of teaching Barbie the ins and outs of tennis. His groin was pressed so tightly against Barbie's ass, I thought he was dry-humping her.

I was silent on the drive home from the club. Then I couldn't hold it in any longer, and I told Steven exactly how foolish I felt while the surgeon boyfriend and I watched Steven and Barbie on the tennis court, practically having sex. Steven argued and denied and refused to admit anything was going on. However, when I told him the truth meant everything to me, and I'd forgive his behavior if he'd just own up to his actions, he admitted he might have gone a bit too far invading Barbie's "personal space," that he'd had a little too much to drink and wouldn't normally have acted in such a fashion.

But even then, he was lying. He hadn't had anything to drink besides some Gatorade before we strolled onto the tennis court. So his denying and lying and subsequent admission of guilt meant nothing. It was all smoke and mirrors. He'd been flirting and touching Barbie inappropriately. I knew it, and he knew it. And he took me for a fool, which pissed me off.

I could have forgiven him if he'd come right out and told me the truth—that he found her attractive and was flirting with her. I understand that he's constantly under an extreme amount of stress and that exercise is one way of alleviating that stress. But the type of exercise on his mind on that court with Barbie is limited to our bed, in our house, with me.

Do I think he's had affairs over the years since he's become so well-known in the medical community? I've never heard any rumors from other surgeons' wives. No gossip has ever reached my ears that Steven's fooling around. So, should I take his behavior with Barbie as a one-off? His words sounded so sincere and heartfelt, I brushed it to the side and went forward. Little did I know at the time, going forward meant Steven spends even less time at home and comes home at ungodly hours of the night with valid excuses for being at the hospital.

But now, when I think about all those hours unaccounted for, well… He says he's in meetings or he's delayed, always due to some work matter. And I believed him. Every. Single. Time.

I've been a fool, I think. But I'm not sure.

I keep busy with committee meetings and luncheons and try to accept the situation. I've tried to engage Joy in joining me on the weekends for an occasional movie or dinner in or out, but she's rarely interested. I didn't realize that all this time she's been going through her own personal turmoil concerning her father's abandonment.

With this mind-set, I write Michael a short letter, telling him I'm interested in visiting him at Balmoral State Penitentiary, then drop it off at the post office. I'm rationalizing my response to his invitation as a harmless gesture of kindness on my part, but deep down inside my soul, I know exactly what I'm doing. I want to meet the man I've been having a pen-pal relationship with for months. I want to see what he looks like in person. And now that I know he was a cardiac surgeon who worked at the same hospital as Steven and participated in one of the Siamese twin surgeries as well, I feel as if it was meant to be. Wait! What if Michael and Steven both assisted in that very same surgery? That would be unbelievable.

I want to find out how I'll feel when I'm with Michael. He intrigues me in his letters. He sounds bright, funny, savvy. After I read his wife Heather's story, my heart went out to him for what a difficult and unenviable situation he must have been in when his wife begged him to help her die.

If I weren't married, I'd want him to ask me out on a date. But I am married. It should make a difference to me that my marital position suggests my response to his invitation to visit him should have been an unequivocal no.

Instead, I accepted. Now my heart's pounding in anticipation of seeing him. I'm not fooling anyone, least of all myself, by answering his letter with an acceptance to visit. I know what I'm doing. I want to see if there's a connection.

I already have a pretty good idea. If my heart's thumping erratically now, how will I feel when I meet him for the first time?

But should I visit Michael now? In the middle of our family crisis? To be honest, I need this. And it will only take a couple of hours out of my day. I can't just sit at home, wondering when or if Joy will ever feel better, if the treatment will work, if she'll be depressed for the rest of her life, attempting to kill herself over and over until she succeeds. I need something, or should I say someone, to make me feel better. I'm not going to get that from Steven, but I'm hoping a short visit with Michael will raise my spirits, since I'm emotionally devastated about Joy. I need emotional strength to carry on, and I won't get that from Steven.

But I'm betting Michael's just the person to help me out with that.

MICHAEL

Certain privileges exist for those with an impending release date. I just found out I have six weeks remaining in Balmoral. Therefore, I'm allowed one extra visiting day a month. I wrote Leena, asking if she'll drive an hour from San Francisco to Balmoral in Glen Ellen today. A short note arrived several days ago, announcing she'll be here this morning at ten a.m.

I wasn't sure she'd come. Not after I declared my love for her in my last letter. I debated whether I should tell her in a letter. At the time, a judgment hadn't been made by the parole board, and I'd already mailed the letter. Then I was summoned to the warden's office. I thought I'd given Leena plenty of time to think about her response. Now she's on her way, and I have no idea what she's thinking. I've been pacing from the barred window to the cell door, a total of exactly eight feet, back and forth, for two hours.

I couldn't sleep last night, though I haven't had a good night's sleep in this place since the day I entered. For five long years, I've tossed and turned every single night, averaging perhaps two or three hours of sleep a night. How much REM sleep I get is limited, and it affects my mood. I began running laps the day after my first night here, hoping it would help me relax, think, look forward to the future.

But it's been hard to keep a positive attitude when I'm surrounded by some of the most morose, negative, mean-spirited, violent psychopaths I've ever encountered. I've been able to distance myself from the small group of rival gang members since the guards appear to be more savvy about the existence of those types of individuals than I expected. Generally, the gang members are broken apart and placed in different sections of the prison where interaction between them is impossible.

By rotating the guards' shifts for different inmate activities—for work details, exercise, and eating—there's more peaceful coexistence than in other prisons. Or so I've been told. Thus, the guards don't get a chance to become chummy with any prisoners, thus staving off any added animosity between inmates.

Balmoral appears to be an experimental environment in the system, and I consider myself extremely lucky to have been placed here. I never thought I'd ever say it, but I'm happy I was sent to Balmoral instead of some of the other prisons where my attorney assumed I'd be placed. Thank God for overcrowding!

Leena's letters uplift my spirits immensely. I am so grateful, I sometimes wonder what I'll say to convince her that falling in love with her via letters is not a result of my thankfulness to her for communicating with a convict. Yes, I'm appreciative of her interest and kindness, but I don't feel beholden to her. I haven't fallen in love with her because I feel indebted to her for seeming to care about me.

Leena has shown me through her letters that not only does she have an empty marriage and she's lonely, but her heart is broken. I believe I can fix that. I made Heather happy. She told me so until the day of her death. I'm a good doctor. It's in my nature to fix people. Not that I think Leena is broken. But I think she's worth fighting for to bring her the happiness she's worthy of having. She's never told me what her husband does for a living, and it really doesn't matter. He's neglectful and unappreciative when it comes to everything she does for him.

She's told me about some of the mandatory social obligations required of her as his wife, but as far as the man's familial obligations? It appears he's been neglecting Leena and her daughter for years as his rise in the company he works for demands more and more of his time. At what point does a man take note of the fact his wife can't possibly be happy in such an empty marriage? She has a kind heart, and that appears on each page of her letters. She loves her family. She loves her daughter. But I get the distinct feeling she wants more from her marriage. And who can blame her?

My rumination has gotten me nowhere. If anything, I'm in more of an agitated state than I've ever been inside these four walls. I should never have reread all her letters yesterday in anticipation of her arrival today. It has done nothing to calm my nerves, and I don't want to come off as too needy for an answer to my declaration of love during the half hour we'll have together.

I glance at the clock on the wall outside my cell door. It's eight thirty in the morning. And I've been awake since one thirty. Yet, I'm not exhausted. I'm so amped, I feel as if I've drunk three cups of espresso—another one of the many things I'd taken for granted before entering this lovely establishment. The coffee here tastes so awful as to be impotable. Naturally, a prison doesn't serve croissants, bagels with cream cheese, sliced turkey sandwiches on sourdough rolls, grilled salmon, flan.

I've gotten to the point, since learning my release date, that I spend an inordinate amount of time dreaming of eating, drinking, sleeping on a soft bed, watching HBO, and perhaps having sex. But I'm not a man who's ever fooled around on his wife nor hired a woman for sex. And I've wondered for weeks now about Leena's husband's fidelity. If the man's never around, comes home at all hours of the night because his meetings extend later than expected, then he's probably not faithful. And Leena is worthy of so much more than a cheating husband.

Now it's nine forty-five in the morning, and I have a pounding headache. My muscles are so tense, I'm running in place to loosen my limbs and clear my head. I rinse my face with cool water, then take deep breaths while looking at the minuscule slice of sky through the bars of my window. At once, I hear the guard walking down the corridor.

It's ten o'clock.

LEENA

Once I exit the US 101 north freeway onto California 37 east toward Napa, the drive to Glen Ellen is pleasantly empty of traffic, and the weather gauge in the car says it's seventy degrees outside. I pass directly through the small town whose population is 784 and is known for numerous famous restaurants, especially considering its size.

I drive twenty-five miles per hour past the Glen Ellen Star, Yeti Restaurant, Aventine, the Glen Ellen Inn, the Wolf House. Because Glen Ellen is located in wine country and is part of the Sonoma Valley, vast portions of land are home to vineyards and wineries such as B.R. Cohn, the Benziger Family Winery, the Mayo Family Winery, and Valley of the Moon. After I drive past the Quarryhill Botanical Garden, the hill crests, and off in the distance I see the inevitable chain-link fence topped with barbed wire that surrounds what must be Balmoral State Penitentiary, which looks to be seven or eight buildings set in a circle with large spaces of grass between the buildings and a center court, just as Michael described in his letters.

My mouth is so dry, I grab a stick of gum from my purse, then roll down all four windows to feel the wind through my hair, hoping to relax before stepping inside a prison for the first time in my life. I've never visited anyone in such a place. I'm so nervous, my teeth begin to chatter. I'm chewing gum so hard, my jaw hurts, but I have to do something to calm my nerves.

When I finally meet Michael, I don't want to look as crazy as I feel. I'm still not sure this is the best decision I've ever made in my life. But at the same time, I want to meet the man behind the touching, open, and sensitive letters I've been reading for months.

The requisite gate and guardhouse are situated far beyond the actual prison. After I show my California driver's license and Permission to Visit document, the guard waves me toward a parking lot, where another small guardhouse is located off to the side, and a second fence with barbed wire makes a circle around the prison grounds.

A guard escorts me to what appears to be the main doors to the Administration Building, where I fill out a short form, promising to abide by all the rules and regulations for all visitors to state penitentiaries. Then I walk through a full-body scanner and metal detector, the same as those employed in airports throughout the United States. After this, I'm escorted by another guard to a room with windows along one side. It's bright, and the walls are painted a pale green. Plastic vases of flowers stand on each of seven round tables, set about ten feet apart in a straight line down the middle of the room.

I'm told I can sit anywhere I wish, and I select a table about a third of the way from the only other door leading into the room, which I expect is where Michael will enter. I'm told it will be a few minutes before he'll arrive.

I've already spit out my gum, and my mouth is again as dry as a desert. I can't stop shaking my leg, and I hate the fact I'm so nervous. Perhaps a married woman shouldn't be visiting the man she's been writing to without her husband's knowledge. Or am I shaken up over Michael's declaration of love? Or is it bothering me I don't know how I feel about him? If he's expecting me to say those words to him today, that's never going to happen. I'd be a fool to do so.

I hear a click and look up to see a man entering the room dressed in an orange jumpsuit. He's more good-looking than the photo on the website, like someone who'd play the part of the handsome young prisoner in a Lifetime movie. His hair is dark brown and cut fairly short, but it has a slight wave to it, making him look less like what I'd picture a convict would look like. He has a dark, thick mustache above full lips, a chiseled square chin.

But what strikes me most are his eyes. They're a piercing blue and are so focused on my own eyes, it's as if an invisible laser beam stretches from his eyes to mine as he walks in a straight line to where I'm sitting. His stare never breaks with mine as he sits across from me and smiles.

My stomach curls into itself like a rock has settled in the center of my abdomen. My lips tremble, and for some unknown reason, I feel I might burst into tears. I never expected Michael to look like this. I anticipated someone pretty rough around the edges, arms covered in tattoos, who'd swagger to the table and check me out like a piece of meat. Though his letters would never indicate any of this, in the back of my mind, I have a stereotype of what a prisoner looks and acts like.

And Michael looks nothing like that.

"Hello, Leena."

His voice is deep and—okay, I admit it—sexy as hell. It's the voice of an actor, like James Earl Jones, but not quite as deep.

My face feels hot. I've imagined this scene hundreds of times since making the decision to visit Michael. Yet, here I am… tongue-tied.

"Hello, Michael," I whisper.

There are several seconds of silence, then he smiles and reaches his hand across the table, palm facing outward like a stop sign. This takes me by surprise since I assumed we would not be allowed to have any physical contact. However, we're the only ones in the room besides the guard. Perhaps the guard doesn't care. I take a quick glance over my shoulder, and indeed, the guard is staring out the window.

I tentatively place my hand on top of Michael's and watch, mesmerized, as he interlaces our fingers and squeezes lightly. I'm staring at our hands, and he squeezes again, and I look up into his eyes.

"I've dreamed of this day," he says.

"I've thought about it as well." To my ears, I sound like a robot. I am so far out of my comfort zone, I feel like someone other than myself. As if I'm looking down at a woman I know who isn't me.

"I know this is awkward," he says. "It must be horribly uncomfortable for you, driving to visit someone you've never met, in a state prison, no less. Not exactly the type of venue to which you're accustomed, Leena. For that, I apologize."

I shake my head. "There's no need to apologize. I read your letter. I understand why you're here." I can't stop staring into his eyes. I now understand the meaning of the word spellbound. My eyes are completely transfixed by his, as if their blueness is the ocean, and I've come from miles away to see the beauty of it.

"I'm not asking you to understand, Leena. Many

people don't. Assisted suicide is an extraordinarily controversial subject. You may think I'm a monster."

"I don't."

"Really? If you were in my place, would you help your husband meet his Maker, sooner rather than later? With all the ramifications that go with that?"

"I haven't tried to put myself in your position. I mean, as far as Steven and I are concerned. But I do think it's wrong to allow people to suffer who are going to die soon anyway. It seems cruel."

"Steven?" He raises his eyebrows. "You've never told me his name."

"Your wife's name was Heather."

"Yes, it was." He looks down at our clasped hands. "The last time I held a woman's hand, it was Heather's."

I try to pull my hand away, but he won't let go.

"I don't want to make you sad," I say.

"It's not like that, Leena. When I think of Heather, I try to recall the good times. When we went to the beach or to one of our favorite restaurants." He stares at our hands. "I don't look at you and think of Heather." He glances up, and our eyes connect, like the laser beam I thought of before. "So… it's Steven."

"Yes, my husband's name is Steven."

"And your last name is Coughlin. Is that right?"

I nod. "What's your last name?"

He laughs out loud. A hearty laugh. He sounds like he's having a good time at a party, and I smile. I think of prisons as depressing institutions and wonder how often prisoners laugh, have a good time, smile.

"What's so funny?" I ask.

"We sound like two people at one of those get-to-know-you venues, where they go from table to table, one at a time, and introduce themselves and have exactly five minutes to determine if they want to go on a date with the person or not."

I smile. "Yes, I've heard about those. As if you can learn much at all in five minutes."

"Casspi. I used to be Dr. Michael Casspi. Now I'm just Michael Casspi. They stripped me of my title immediately after I was sentenced. I don't think it will be possible to get it back either. Unless my attorney finds a loophole in the new California law."

"I was blown away when I read in your letter that you're a doctor. What are the chances you and my husband are both in the same profession and working at the same hospital? I think being a doctor is unlike any other profession. It's not as if you can leave it at the door when you exit the hospital. It follows you everywhere. It's part of who you are, and it's almost impossible to turn off the fact you're a surgeon. It's like a snake. It twines itself into every aspect of your life."

He's frowning. And his eyebrows are so bunched together by the time I've quit talking, they've almost become a unibrow.

"I'm sorry if I've offended you, Michael. I didn't mean to. It's just—"

"Not at all. I can read between the lines of your letters, Leena. From what you wrote, you don't seem happy. But I didn't know your husband's a surgeon. Your loneliness seems to stem from his inability to leave his professional life at the hospital, and it's caused problems due to his lack of free time for you… and your daughter. What's her name?"

"Joy. She's nineteen."

"You mentioned she's attending the local junior college before heading off to Stanford, is it?"

I suck in my lips to keep from crying. "That's probably not going to happen."

"Why not? Is she not getting the necessary grades to transfer?"

"It's not that. She's…"

Michael takes my other hand in his and looks me in the eyes. We are so close, I can feel the warmth emanating from his body. His hands are almost hot to the touch, and the heat travels through my fingers to my wrists and then some.

"She's in a psychiatric hospital for a few days. I—"

"Depression?"

"How'd you know?"

"Professional guess."

"I know some of her feelings stem from typical teenage angst, but I'm not letting Steven off the hook. She and her father were very close up until his surgical expertise took a meteoric rise, after he participated in one of the most well-publicized Siamese-twins separation in history. After that, he just fell off the map at home. We never see him."

His eyes shift to the side of me. For the first time, he isn't deeply involved in what I'm saying.

"Michael? You look odd. Did I say something to upset you?"

He slowly shakes his head, side to side several times, before he stops and looks me straight in the eyes. "Steven Coughlin. The Steven Coughlin at St. John's Hospital in San Francisco?"

"Yes, that's Steven. You wrote that you and Heather met at St. John's. However, I don't know if your time there coincided with Steven practicing at St. John's or not."

"Yes, I know your husband."

"Are you serious?"

He nods, and the look on his face is very serious. Gone is the smile and the intense staring into my eyes. He's now looking at the ceiling, lips thin and straight.

"At the time of that particular Siamese-twin surgery at St. John's, there were, of course, many meetings to prepare for the separation. And many evenings afterward at a bar around the corner to let off steam, to talk, and whatnot."

"I've never been to a bar with Steven. We've dined out at many restaurants, but we've never gone to a bar. I can't believe you two know each other."

He pulls his hands away from mine and stares at the table.

"What's wrong, Michael? I don't understand what happened just now. It's as if you're a thousand miles away."

His eyes lift to mine, and he folds his arms over his chest. "Were you married to Steven at the time of the separation surgery involving twin girls with only one heart? I think their names were Eva and Ivana, from Russia."

"Yes." I nod. "Of course. That's how I know so much about it. And, like I said, that's when Steven started pulling away, soon after the surgery was so very successful."

"So you've been married for quite a few years now, if Joy's nineteen. Some couples don't marry until they've lived together for a while, or they wait until they've had their first child."

"Steven and I were a bit more traditional. What with our parents still alive at the time, plus, we'd been dating for several years. We knew we were headed toward marriage almost from the beginning. You know how you just know?"

"As a matter of fact, I do. That's how it was for Heather and me. Love at first sight. Such a cliché, but true. For us anyway."

"Why are you frowning? Is there something I said about me or Steven or the surgery?"

"It's a small world, isn't it?"

"Yes, it is. But something's wrong."

There's a chill in the air between his side of the table and mine, like an invisible cloud of cool air hovering between us.

He blinks several times, then leans forward and takes hold of my hands again. "He may have changed from way back then."

"What do you mean? There's something you're not saying."

"That wasn't you I saw him with at the bar after our meetings. The man who left that bar almost every night with a woman latched on to his arm. I'd have remembered you."

I shut my eyes and keep them shut, trying to swallow what he's just told me. Have I known this all along? Since that time on the tennis courts with Barbie? "That son of a bitch." I open my eyes, and Michael has slid from his side to my side. He surrounds my shoulders with his arm and brings me close.

"You and your daughter merit better than this, Leena. You know that, right?"

I begin to cry. It's now obvious—Steven's behavior on the tennis court years ago had not been a one-off. It's not as if he tells me where he goes and with whom after the supposed meetings he attends almost on a nightly basis. I am not a helicopter type of wife or mother.

Bottom line: I trusted him.

"It doesn't come as a total surprise," I admit. "There was a time, years ago, when he showed me a side of him I hadn't seen since he and I were dating. I know he's capable of being flirtatious, yes."

"But you never guessed he'd be unfaithful, am I right?"

I shrug, then grab for a tissue in my purse and dab my cheeks and nose. "Recently, I've allowed myself to entertain the idea." I pause, shaking my head. "I'm an idiot. A damn stupid fool for trusting him."

"This is not your fault. You're not the one who's playing around behind his back, coming home at all hours of the night, and ignoring your daughter. That's how he chooses to live his life. You've remained faithful." He pauses. "Or is this… this thing between us something you just… you've done before?"

I turn to face him, and our noses are inches apart. "I've never been unfaithful to Steven. My vows meant something to me then, and they do now."

"Even after what I just told you? Do you think I'm making this up for my own benefit?"

"Of course not. But I still want to confront him about it."

"You're going to tell him what I just told you?"

"No. I'm going to ask him about it. Tell him I heard it from another doctor's wife. See if he owns up to it." I raise a finger. "Or simply have him followed by a private investigator."

"That's a thought. That way, you won't have to take the word of an almost ex-con."

I stare into his eyes, feeling lost in them, wanting to be lost in them, especially after this conversation. "What do you mean by almost—"

"Six weeks," he interrupts. "That's how much longer I'll be in here. Six weeks."

"Six… weeks? Are you serious? How… when… I mean, what—"

"The parole board met and decided I'm eligible, me being a model prisoner and all that." He grins.

"Congratulations! Had I known, perhaps I would have brought you something. A cake or…"

He shakes his head and laughs. "Not allowed. You could hide a knife or explosives in a cake, Leena. That could be dangerous."

"Six weeks." I can't believe it. And the first thing on my mind is, I won't have to drive all the way to Glen Ellen to visit him. I grin back at him. "You must be so excited."

"I am. And I'm hoping I can see you again, Leena. Or…"

"Or what, Michael? What are you thinking?"

"If you confirm your husband's been cheating on you, will you try to work it out, or will it mean a divorce?"

Goose bumps pop out on my arms after he says the word divorce. Will there be a future for me and Michael? It's way too soon to tell. But at this point, I think Michael and I are at least friends. Perhaps friends is a first step toward a romantic relationship.

He grasps my hand, brings it to his lips, and kisses the backs of my knuckles.

I shiver, envisioning those same lips on my lips, my neck, my breasts.

He looks down at my arms. "You're shivering, Leena."

"It's not because I'm cold."

He slides a glance toward where the guard is standing. I follow his gaze. The guard's back is to us, and he's still intently staring out the window at a group of men playing a game of basketball.

Michael straddles the seat and faces me, opens his legs wide, and pulls himself closer toward me, then slips his hands slowly up my wrists to my forearms and pulls me forward. With his eyes never veering from mine, he brings his face closer and gently kisses me once. He pulls away, still looking into my eyes, then kisses me again. But this time, he closes his eyes and so do I.

He nips at my bottom lip, then kisses me once again, then again, then plays with my lips with his tongue. I open my mouth, and he deepens the kiss. I haven't been kissed like this in years. He's taking his time, lingering, exploring, bringing the kiss to a deeper level until we're French-kissing like teenagers, trying to catch our breath before we dive into another deep kiss, tongues entwined. His hands grasp the sides of my face and slide up into my hair, bringing our mouths closer. Our breathing escalates to a low moan, whether it's him or me, I don't know, and I don't care.

Suddenly, I hear someone clearing his throat and recall I'm in a prison. Michael and I are not a couple. What am I doing? I'm a married woman. But Steven has probably been cheating on me for years, so what does all this matter anyway?

We break apart abruptly, and Michael nods toward the guard and pulls his hands back to his sides.

"I love you, Leena," he whispers.

I'm crying. I'm not sure if it's because I think I've just found out my husband's probably been cheating on me for years, or am I crying tears of happiness because I think I could fall in love with Michael? And that exciting feeling of falling in love is just that. Exciting. I want to be loved. I need to be loved.

To think, I've spent so many years loving someone who doesn't keep that love close to his heart as he should. Because love is worth caring about and keeping safe. And right now, I feel as if I've wasted years on loving someone who took my love and discarded it, as if it's worth nothing.

And I have a gut feeling that I've found someone who will cherish my love and keep it safe.

And I had to go into a prison to find it.

STEVEN

"Good afternoon, Dr. Coughlin."

I nod to the head of surgical nursing while rushing through the lobby to the elevator.

"Wait! Dr. Coughlin!"

I almost don't turn around, but I recognize the voice. It's Dr. Stephanie Yates, head of the new Surgical Team Building Department at St. John's. If she wants to talk to me, then it has to do with the team she's put together for the Siamese-twins-separation surgery. She's a woman who doesn't know the meaning of synopsize. Therefore, there's no way in hell this will be a short conversation.

I stop and take a deep breath and am about to turn around when she scoots in front of me, blocking the path to my exit. I need to get into my car in the next five minutes in order to pick up Leena on our way to Langley Porter Mental Health Clinic.

I withhold my usual gracious smile and frown. "Good afternoon, Stephanie. I'm sorry, but I—"

She rests her hand on my forearm. "This won't take long, Steven. It's about David and Billy Parthas."

Of course it is. I nod. "Everything's flowing along as it should. We have a meeting tonight at six o'clock. I'll be there." I take a step to the side to go around her.

She doesn't remove her hand from my arm. Instead,

she lifts her chin and looks me straight in the eyes. "We need to talk, Steven. Before tonight's meeting."

I take a step back, and her hand slides off my arm. "I apologize for seeming rude, but I have a very important meeting and have to pick up my wife in," I stretch out my arm to glance at my wristwatch, "ten minutes. We have to be somewhere at three o'clock. Perhaps you and I can meet right before tonight's meeting and talk for a few minutes. I just don't have the time right now, Stephanie."

It's obvious she's made up her mind, because she doesn't budge. Rather, she moves in closer, her nostrils flaring. "Dr. Jordan from Stanford has agreed to join the team."

I shake my head. This is unbelievable. "We've been begging him for months to rearrange his schedule, and he waits until we're this far into our preparation to accept? You must have made him an offer he can't refuse."

She smirks. "We got him, Steven. That's all that's important right now. He's calling in ten minutes and needs to speak with you for just a second about your particular cardiac protocol for the separation."

It's more than obvious she's not backing down. Stephanie was the perfect choice of candidates for the position as head of the Surgical Team Building unit. She was relentless in her quest for hammering together the perfect team for the surgery, because she refuses to take no for an answer.

On top of that, she has connections with people who have money to throw at St. John's, especially because an operation of this kind places us on the radar of every news station in the country. We're already on the map, as she calls it, but now we're uniquely positioned as the hospital to conduct any future separation surgeries in the world.

I glance at the floor, trying to think of how I'm going to explain myself to not only Leena but to Joy. If this so-called few minutes with Dr. Jordan lasts any longer than five minutes at the most, I'm sure to be late. "All right. Let's go."

I follow her into the elevator, and she pushes the button for the top-floor offices where this phone conversation will take place. While in the elevator, I text Leena I've been unexpectedly held up and will meet her at Langley Porter in an hour. Leena and I have a meeting with Joy's psychiatrist at three thirty, then a family meeting with the psychiatrist and Joy at four, after which time we planned to visit with Joy until her dinner at five o'clock, giving me plenty of time to make the six o'clock team meeting at St. John's. That won't happen now.

Fifty minutes later, I'm in my car, headed for Langley Porter. By the time I get there, I've missed the parent meeting and the family meeting, and maybe I'll be able to talk to Joy for a few minutes before she goes to dinner.

After checking in at the front desk, I'm led to the front door of the psych ward, where they buzz me in. Leena and Joy are sitting in what appears to be a recreation room with couches lining the sides and windows all around. It's pleasant enough looking, but there's an air of silence that's missing in any other room meant for visiting and talking. I feel as if I'm attending a reception after a funeral.

Joy turns her head after Leena nods in my direction. But Leena doesn't stand to greet me, and she's not smiling. I know I'm not in either of their good graces, but there was nothing I could do. I curse my luck this had to happen today of all days.

I sit next to Joy and hug her from the side and kiss her on the cheek. "Hi, sweetie. Sorry I'm late, but—"

Joy wriggles out of my embrace and continues to look at her hands, clasped in her lap. "Never mind, Dad. It's been obvious for a long time now where I stand with you."

It doesn't miss my attention. This is the first time she hasn't called me Daddy, maybe ever. "You're the most important person in my life, Joy. You and your mom. It's just that I was—"

"I don't want to hear it," she says, raising her voice.

Several other parents and their kids turn in our direction, and I glance at Leena, who is also scowling. I shrug, and Leena rolls her eyes, then taps her wrist, indicating the time.

Joy stands. "I've gotta go to dinner."

Leena stands and hugs Joy. "I love you, honey. I'll see you tomorrow. Only one more day until they release you."

"Yay," Joy says in a monotone. "I'll get to go home. Yippee."

Leena pulls back, her hands clasping Joy's shoulders. "Remember what Dr. Peterson said. Your life is as good as you make it. Let's try. I'm willing to do anything to help you out. We'll take his suggestions and work toward you feeling better. Okay?"

Joy nods, then runs off in the opposite direction, away from both Leena and me. I stand and face Leena. It's as if an abyss has opened up between us. Missing the two meetings has placed me on one side and Leena on the other. And I don't know if it's even possible to meet in the middle, because the crevasse separating us makes it impossible for me to cross over to join her on the other side.

The expression that was the last straw comes to mind, and I don't know how I'm going to fix this. There are so many people pulling at me, needing my time and attention, there just isn't enough of me to go around. And that's not going to change until this separation surgery is over, so I'm looking at at least two more months, if we're on schedule, which ofttimes doesn't happen. There are an abundance of unforeseen changes that can and probably will pop up. Such as Dr. Jordan joining us. Already, he needs two additional weeks to join the team.

I'm screwed. And no matter how I explain it to Leena and Joy, it won't make a difference.

Leena silently crosses the room to the exit, and they buzz her out. I stand, watching her back, not knowing what to do. I stop by the desk, ask if I can speak with Joy's psychiatrist for just a few moments. I'm told he's left for the day. When I exit the building, Leena's car is no longer in the parking lot.

The meeting begins at six o'clock, and now I have time to go over my notes beforehand. But instead of returning home immediately, as I've promised my wife I'd do from now on, I head to the hotel instead. And if I don't plan to go home afterward, I don't think it will make a damn bit of difference.

LEENA

This night is going to be unusually interminable. Joy won't be coming home from her day of classes. Not that Joy stops to talk to me when she comes in, no matter what hour it is. But I always sigh with relief when my daughter returns at night. She isn't sleeping over at some guy's house, some guy I've never met because she never brings anyone home for me to meet anyway. Knowing she's safe and in her bedroom has always been something I count on each evening.

Little did I know the inner turmoil she's been going through for years. When I close my book and turn off the light every night, she's been only twenty feet away in her own room, fighting a depression so strong she drove to the Golden Gate Bridge with the plan to jump off.

I feel completely bereft, totally lacking in parental insight. I should have known. How could her moods have so escaped my notice? I thought she was fine. In my private meeting (since Steven didn't show up) with the psychiatrist, the doctor told me thousands of young people in their teens and older who live at home manifest no outward signs of sadness or upset. They are masters of deception. The typical guilt most parents feel as a result of suddenly discovering their son or daughter is self-harming, depressed, suicidal, or all of the above, is "normal," yet vastly misguided.

He said that parents often don't find out about their

son's or daughter's mental health problems until it has escalated to the point where she's a harm to herself, the police are called, then she's taken to a psychiatric hospital on what's called a 51/50, and held for seventy-two hours. I have a terrible headache, and I'm dizzy from the events of less than twenty-four hours ago. Discovering Joy fled the house to God knows where, finding out she was at the Golden Gate Bridge, then learning that she'd be spending seventy-two hours in a psychiatric hospital is all more than I ever expected.

The problem with Steven being an absent husband and father, and having spent the morning with Michael at Balmoral State Penitentiary, my life is splattered all over the place, like an abstract impressionism painting. But first things first, and the most important thing right now is getting Joy home, making sure she takes the antidepressant Dr. Peterson prescribed, and following all of the cautionary rules for living with a young person who is suicidal. My new reality? I'll be on suicide watch 24/7, until Joy is euphemistically "out of the woods."

And I'll be doing it alone. I don't have a job outside the home. My daughter was the center of my universe until she entered high school. Then I volunteered on hospital committees and accompanied Steven to social parties and out-of-town conferences. I also work at the San Francisco Doggie Doo-Gooders Shelter, my personal favorite. I let the rope I held so tightly to Joy go slack for the first time in her life after middle school, thinking that's what teenagers wanted.

I didn't ignore her, but I remembered how it felt to be a freshman in high school. I did not want my mom or dad serving on the hot lunch crew or volunteering for yard duty, watching over us while we hung out or ate lunch.

Joy has never been interested in sports, so I didn't have high school games to attend. I let go of her, allowed her to fly free, something she'd begged me for since middle school. I held tight to those parental reins until ninth grade, then I let go.

Now the ramifications of doing so have caught up with me. And her. Do I blame myself? No matter what Dr. Peterson says, I am at fault for not keeping closer tabs on my daughter. No one is going to convince me otherwise. Joy isn't old enough to be responsible for herself. So who was? I was. And I still am, to this day. Until she leaves this house, I am her caretaker.

It is my responsibility to guide her through life until, like a tiny fledgling, she's ready to fly away from home. Instead, I allowed the connections to Steven's life to become the center of my world. I swapped Joy for my committees and my volunteer work. And I was wrong to do so. I should have either done both or chosen Joy as my sole focus. She's my child. She cannot take care of herself. I am going to cut back on my volunteer work as well as accompanying Steven to his various and numerous hospital and social functions. I've made myself that promise. And I'm especially averse to continuing my role as Steven's trophy wife, if I find out he hasn't been faithful. Screw him.

I've now experienced the heartache of failure, and I will not let this happen again. The second time could be fatal for Joy, and I cannot let that happen. As far as Steven's role in Joy's life, he simply, as he says, doesn't have time right now. His promise to be here for me and for Joy in the future is yet to be known. But so far, in the few days since Joy's suicide attempt, Steven hasn't stepped up to the plate. Do I expect him to change overnight? No, I don't. But he has a way of talking himself out of any wrongdoing when it comes to time management. It's never his fault if he's late or a no-show at Joy's birthday parties or sleepovers or Sunday dinners or high school plays or even Joy's high school graduation. As Joy got older, Steven's practice got busier, and Joy and I were both put on the back burner in deference to Steven's professional integrity and specialization that bolted him into unexpected fame and, as he often reminded me, fortune as well.

When we could have spent money on family outings and vacations, the money was instead invested and grew and grew. We bought a house I never dreamed of even visiting, much less owning, with a pool. We bought my Mercedes, Steven's Porsche, Joy's Range Rover. Steven swapped material possessions for his presence as a show of how much he cared about us. And now, he and Joy and I are reaping the rotten fruit of that decision.

So, although I blame myself for not seeing Joy as the depressed and suicidal nineteen-year-old she's become, I blame Steven for pushing Joy down the road toward depression. He knew their relationship had changed drastically, commensurate with the rise in his professional responsibilities and fame. He let it happen, and so did I. We were negligent. In my opinion, we, as parents, both Steven and I, bear most of the blame for what has happened to Joy. Not that it makes me feel any better to share the blame. The end result is the same. Joy went to the Golden Gate Bridge to kill herself.

No way am I letting that happen a second time. A second attempt could be fatal. And what a waste that would be of a young life with so much promise.

MICHAEL

The BSP operator tried to call Leena on her cell phone for me a couple of times since Leena visited me. I think I may have come on too strong by not only declaring my love for her in a letter, but also my public display of affection during her visit. Also, it had to be tough for her to come to a state prison. My first months here were extraordinarily difficult. I didn't understand the unwritten rules of inmate conduct that had nothing to do with prison regulations.

I was fair game for anyone, due to my supposed "good looks" and "sexual appeal" and "male build." I felt like a walking target when I was being escorted to my cell for the first time. Now I understand how women feel when they walk down the street and guys yell, "Hey, baby, nice ass," out their car windows. It's shocking, humiliating, and I was scared to death.

Thank God, the fact I'd supposedly murdered my wife pushed me up the chain of to-be-feared-instead-of-messed-with guys in the cluster of cells where I was placed. There's an invisible level of acceptance that comes with the type of crime committed. Pedophiles are at the bottom of the pile. Many of the inmates here have families, and those who prey on kids are completely unaccepted and thus beaten, robbed of their possessions, the food stolen right off their plates. They're the scum of the prison's earth.

Murderers are feared by the thieves and embezzlers and white-collar criminals. So I had a leg up, so to speak, from the get-go. But my ability to run interference between sick or injured inmates and the infirmary doctors and nurses turned out to be much appreciated among the prisoners. When someone has an STD, and there are many, or has been sliced with a homemade shank, I have a direct line to the infirmary's personnel. And I have used my influence to buy myself peace in this place. But most of all, I'm left alone. No one tries to get at me in the yard or in the mess hall. It could be much, much worse, and I know it.

But the loneliness I've suffered since arriving is my worst enemy. I have too much time to think. About Heather, about our time together, about our home, our friends. Yes, I made enough money that I'm able to pay my attorney's fees. I still own our house. But none of our friends think I'm innocent. They agree with the court that I murdered Heather. They don't want anything to do with me. I understand why doctors and their wives, no matter which side they're on, don't want to associate with a murderer.

I'm in state prison. I spend my days surrounded by the lowest of the low in society. I wear an orange jumpsuit every day. I eat slop in the mess hall. For all anyone on the outside knows, I have a boyfriend on the inside who I'm having sex with on a regular basis. That's what I imagined when I came here. It has actually turned out not to be as bad as I thought it would be. But from the outside looking in, I understand why no one wants anything to do with me.

Now that I know there's a definitive end date to this experience, I'm so excited to get back to a normal life. But that's impossible. I won't be able to keep up with the house payments forever if I can't practice medicine. And no matter what machinations my attorney has gone through to overturn that part of the sentence, to date he hasn't been able to do so. Which means I'll never be a doctor again. And that's heart-wrenching.

Being a surgeon is different than, say, being an accountant or an insurance salesman. I saved lives. Every. Single. Day. Which, ironically enough, is why the judge and jury thought I committed such a heinous crime. I took a life. In their eyes, I went against everything they believe embodied a doctor. They could not see my side. The blinders were impossible to penetrate, no matter that my attorney railed and ranted about Heather's impending, torturous death. I was a surgeon, and thou shalt not kill.

But being a surgeon is what I am. It's who I am. It's how I think and breathe and act and love, all rolled into one human being, no matter what I'm doing. To be stripped of that privilege has been something I've thought about every single day I've been in here.

Did I not think about that before I gave Heather the shot of pentobarbital? Yes, I did. But I didn't really have much time to hypothesize what life would be as a regular, everyday person. I fell from being almost God-like to being the devil himself. And that scared the shit out of me. I don't know how to be anyone other than Dr. Michael Casspi, cardiac surgeon. And soon I'm going to find out exactly what it feels like to be just Michael Casspi. With no Dr. in front of my name, no place to work, no friends, no colleagues, no future.

And no wife.

Which brings me right around to Leena. Did I do or say something to turn her away? I told Leena my release date. Maybe she's forgotten. They finally put that information on PrisonersNeedFriendsToo, so that doesn't make sense. She can easily find out. Maybe I'm being completely ridiculous and anxious over nothing. It hasn't been that many days since she was sitting right in front of me. But time moves slowly in prison. What seems like days turns out to be hours. And that's exactly what's happening to me now. I have to back off. Give Leena space to process what transpired between us at the table in the visiting room. Hell, I need time to think about it.

But she kissed me back. I didn't plan that. There was such passion, too. I felt her loneliness and need and, yes, I thought she might well be in love with me, too. But she didn't say the words. Why? I don't know. Perhaps she's not in love with me and doesn't want to ruin her life. What do I have to offer her in comparison to her husband, the famous surgeon Dr. Steven Coughlin of St. John's Hospital in San Francisco?

What I do know is, I won't stop loving her until I've seen her one last time. I want to know what I did wrong, or if it's simply the fact I can't offer her anything but my love, and the rest is too important for her to leave behind. I don't picture her as that type of woman, but we've known each other only through letters and one visit in person.

She is so beautiful with that long, wavy hair, those big green eyes, and such a curvy body. I've been in Balmoral for five years, and I've never seen any female guard or visitor who looks like Leena. I saw very few woman outside prison who are as beautiful as she. And she's beautiful inside as well, which is what I find so attractive. That is why I'm in love with her.

I could find someone to have sex with when I'm out of this place. But sex was never the reason I was in love with Heather either, and it's not the reason I'm in love with Leena. What I can see and feel are Leena's qualities that affect me deep inside my heart. She's caring and empathetic and nurturing and giving and humble and smart. There's nothing I don't love about her.

I can only hope there's some reason, unbeknown to me, why she's not answering her cell phone. I'll just wait. She's become too important to give up. It'll take more than not answering her phone to stop me.

LEENA

The night looms ahead of me like a long, black tunnel. I try to read a new book by Jodi Picoult, and after the first chapter, I have no idea the names of the characters or what they're doing. I can't focus. I turn on one of my favorite TV shows, 9-1-1, and after fifteen minutes, I don't have a clue what they're doing under a freeway with nine cars piled on top of each other.

I peruse every cupboard and the inside of the refrigerator for something to eat. Nothing appeals to me. I don't drink alcohol very often and never that much. I walk to the minibar in the front room and scan various liquor bottles, but the thought of pouring myself a drink while alone makes me sad as well as nauseated.

There have been many nights when Steven doesn't come home then claims he's doing research in the hospital or a meeting ran so late he just slept at the hospital instead of driving home. Joy comes home every night. So to have an entire evening stretch out in front of me with no one returning to the house makes me antsy.

I could go to a bar and have a drink, but I've never done that, even when I was single, and I don't want to appear hard up for company or just a plain loser. I've never gone to the movies alone either, for fear people will look at me and wonder why I'm there by myself. I don't feel like going for a walk. It's something I've never done before.

What I used to do, since I was a teenager and learned to drive, was take long drives through Oakland, the city where I grew up. I'd get into my VW Karmann Ghia and race through the hills, stopping to look at the view of San Francisco, the Oakland Bay Bridge, and the Golden Gate Bridge, if it was a clear night.

After I moved to San Francisco, after Steven and I were married, I quit my job as the administrative assistant to the man I'd been working for for four years. He was an Asian entrepreneur who dabbled in many different industries in China. His luck for turning dead-end companies in Beijing into money-making conglomerates was legend. But I'd had enough of sitting behind a desk on a computer, so when Steven suggested I quit my job and help him out with administrative duties at St. John's Hospital, I jumped at the chance.

Then I had Joy and was busy being a stay-at-home mom, until I had enough time to accompany Steven to all the events that come along with being a surgeon. When his fame hit the fan, my job morphed into making sure I was seen plastered to his side, holding tightly to his arm, at the many and various functions to which he was obliged to attend. And I was expected to be there as, well, the trophy wife.

See, everyone? I'm a famous surgeon and I have a beautiful wife whose job it is to make me look good, play doubles tennis with me and my surgeon friends, drink fine wine, and mostly sit and make inane conversation with other doctors' wives, while I bask in the glory of being me.

Still, there were many nights, especially during the last year, before the team was formed for the separation of the Siamese twins, when I had nothing to do while Steven was at the hospital. I'd hop in the Mercedes and drive through the streets of San Francisco, getting to know the good districts from the bad, the safe from the scary, the cold and foggy from the cool and crystal clear. I'd drive up the steepest hills I could find and navigate my way to nowhere. In the process, I discovered every nook and cranny in a city the size of San Francisco, which is seven miles wide and seven miles long.

Tonight is one of those nights, especially since I know that the moment Joy returns home, it will be me, not Steven, who will be housebound with her until the antidepressants kick in, which could take up to six weeks. I'll be on suicide watch, sitting in front of the TV with Joy, or not. But I'll be home more than usual, without the option of getting out of the house whenever I feel the urge.

With that thought in mind, I grab the keys to my Mercedes and back out of the garage, headed for nowhere. We live in Pacific Heights, a district of San Francisco described in the monthly Chamber of Commerce magazine as "a posh residential enclave known for its architecturally significant homes, including the opulent Spreckels Mansion (as in Spreckels Sugar) and the 1886 Haas-Lilienthal house, a Queen Anne Victorian that's open to the public." There are a pair of grassy hilltop parks, Lafayette and Alta Plaza, and the Lyon Street Stairs that provide sweeping views of the bay. Fillmore Street is a lively hub with high-end fashion boutiques and cafés.

Although I could stop anywhere in my own neighborhood and stroll around and eat or window-shop, tonight I want to put down the convertible top and let my hair blow in the breeze while trying my best to clear my mind of all thoughts, as my meditation instructor told me years ago. I drive up and down some of the steepest hills in the city and see the most breathtaking views in the world. Though I've seen it all hundreds of times, the beauty never ceases to calm and amaze me.

I could almost be happy, if not for the niggling sorrow of seeing Joy in the hospital, picturing her standing at the railing of the Golden Gate Bridge, along with the never-ending mental video of Steven arriving late to visit Joy at Langley Porter and hearing the same old excuse that he couldn't leave an important meeting (again).

And suddenly, without consciously knowing it, I'm driving past St. John's Hospital.

The incident years ago with "Barbie" at the tennis court (with Steven trying to teach her how to play) is never far from my mind. Every late night, every missed Sunday dinner, every excuse, although the same, are constant, living in my mind like a latent cancer that's metastasized into a tumor, poisoning my thoughts.

I can't get it out of my head that Steven might be cheating on me. Especially after what Michael told me about seeing Steven with someone who was not me on his arm years ago. Years ago? Shivers run up my arms, and it isn't from the cool evening air. I decide I'll play detective. My efforts might turn out to be fruitless. Or not. But I'll know soon enough. I have nothing else to do tonight.

I have a pass that enables me to park in the basement lot for hospital staff. I drive up and down the aisles until I find Steven's Porsche, then park in an empty spot in the corner near a huge concrete column. My Mercedes is black and won't draw anyone's attention, especially Steven's. The lot is filled with vehicles like mine, so I'm not worried about being noticed.

It's a rarity for me to experience such silence. At this time of night in a parking structure below ground level, the quiet is almost deafening. My ears are ringing, as if I've been to a rock concert. I don't turn on any music, but rather enjoy the quietude. I roll down my window halfway in order to hear footsteps. The elevator leading to the garage is about fifty feet away.

I'm finding it hard not to doze off. With everything that's been happening recently, I haven't gotten a good night's sleep in days. What with my argument with Steven, Joy's dramatic sojourn to the Golden Gate Bridge, and my visit with Michael, I'm mentally and physically exhausted.

When I hear the tap-tap of shoes on concrete, I jerk awake, not realizing I've fallen asleep. It's Steven. He walks to his car, alone, then drives right in front of me toward an exit. I should have thought beforehand of the direction he'd take, and I slump down in the seat. He doesn't see me, thank God, because I have no excuse at the ready for being here.

I wait until he's driving up the slight grade toward the exit to follow him. He turns right, out of the parking lot, and heads down the street. It's easy to follow him at a discreet distance. There are very few cars on the road at the moment. After driving down the same street for three miles, he turns left, a quick right, then makes his way under the valet portico at the St. Croix.

The St. Croix? It's an impressive, high-class hotel catering to the rich and famous. Of course, this would be the venue of choice for Steven since he's both. Rich and famous, that is. He exits his Porsche, tips the valet, then walks nonchalantly into the lobby. He's been here before. It's written all over his demeanor—the casual way he walks, the content look on his face. This is nothing new. I know him. I can tell.

I park on the street with a perfect view of the curved driveway, the portico, and the lobby. After shutting off the engine, I lower the seat and slouch down as far as I can, pull up the edges of my collar to cover the sides of my face and my chin… and wait.

The seconds slowly tick by, until eleven minutes have passed. Then a white Lexus pulls under the portico. I do not believe it. This cannot be happening.

It's Karen.

My best friend, Karen?

Is this a coincidence? She enters the lobby, but that's as far as I can see from here. She's not dressed in her usual blue hospital scrubs. She's wearing a Dolce & Gabbana black dress that fits her slim figure beautifully, along with what looks like Manolo Blahnik spike heels. Her hair is down, unlike when she's at the hospital. She looks fantastic.

For all I know, she and Steven are meeting someone at the bar for a drink. I have no idea. He and I have not seen each other much, as usual, and our last conversation was an argument. We never talk about what he does on a daily basis. Our paths don't cross often enough to keep close tabs on our whereabouts. Perhaps they're meeting each other at the bar, just the two of them. They're friends. She's been a part of our lives for years. I'm sure they share coffee and lunches often while working together.

Or… Karen's meeting someone other than Steven, and it's totally coincidental that she's at the St. Croix at the same time as my husband. But tonight, at the exact same time? "Really, Leena?" I whisper. Who am I kidding? Certainly not myself. Let's get real here.

Should I go inside? Sneak into the bar, see what they're doing? But I'm sure they'll have an excuse. Maybe she wants to talk to Steven about the man she's meeting afterward on a date, and she wants Steven's opinion about him. Steven and Karen are obviously not having sex in the bar.

Maybe they're not in the bar! Maybe they took a room for the evening, and if so, whose name would it be under? I pay all the bills, and I've never seen a charge on Steven's credit card for the St. Croix. But if they're indeed meeting here for a sexual tryst, Steven could be paying cash. Or it might be under Karen's name. That would solve any problems with my finding out by looking at receipts, right?

My head is pounding. I have to either shit or get off the pot, as they say. I either need to go into the bar and look for them or ask at the front desk if there's a Steven Coughlin or a Karen Roberts registered as guests. Either one of them could be using a different name, however.

This is ridiculous. I start the engine and pull into traffic. I'm going home. This juvenile spying game is just that. A teenage game. I refuse to lower myself to playing. If I want to know, I'm going to ask. So as I'm driving away from the St. Croix, I pull out my phone and call Karen, knowing she won't pick up. And she doesn't. I leave a message, asking if she'd like to go to lunch or dinner tomorrow.

I plan to come right out and ask her what's going on, after telling her what I've just seen. Oh, my God, this is so like a Lifetime movie. I can only hope that, after all is said and done, there's a happily ever after to this story.

MICHAEL

I try phoning Leena again, and when the BSP operator tells me she's accepted the call, I'm ecstatic. I don't want to come off as desperate, so I calm myself by focusing on what I'm going to say and level my voice to a quiet and contained tone.

"Leena?"

"Michael. How are you?"

"Fine, thank you. You sound out of breath. What's going on? Out for a run this late in the evening?"

"I could tell you it's the best time of day for a run because of the cool air against my skin and the stars in the clear sky." She pauses.

"But that's not what's happening?"

She lets out a shuddering breath, and I brace myself for the inevitable. She's going to tell me she can't do this. She's not the type to go behind her husband's back and see another man. She doesn't want a divorce because her daughter is having a rough time of it, and it would be irresponsible of her to disrupt Joy's life right now. She's decided to work out whatever problems she's having with Steven. This is goodbye.

"I think Steven might be having an affair. With my best friend."

This comes right out of left field. It's nothing like

what I expected. I sigh with relief, then realize this is not the time to be happy over Leena's troubles. Though I feel a zing of pleasure that it's not me with whom she's having a problem. But the conversation isn't over. I mustn't get ahead of myself.

"Are you sure? How do you know this?"

"I'm kind of embarrassed to say I followed him to the St. Croix. While I waited in my car outside to see if he was meeting someone, Karen, my BFF, drove up, looking like a million bucks, and entered the hotel not more than eleven minutes later."

"There could be a reason behind their meeting, though, right? Perhaps—"

"I've already thought of all the supposed reasons they may have been there. Perhaps it was a fluke that she was there at the same time he was. Or perhaps both of them were meeting up with someone they both know. But the way she was dressed and the timing? I don't believe it was coincidental. It was planned. They've known each other for years. And Karen's a beautiful, sexy woman."

I hear her stifle a sob. I don't blame her. Even though her relationship with her husband appears to have problems, it doesn't mean she doesn't love him. And love hurts.

"Don't jump to conclusions, Leena. Deal with the facts."

"I am going to deal with the facts, as soon as I know them. I left a voice mail on Karen's phone after she got to the St. Croix. I knew she wouldn't answer anyway. I'm waiting to see when she'll phone back."

"That sounds like a better way to deal with it. Do you think she'll tell you the truth?"

"I think she'll be so surprised to hear that I saw both of them there, she won't have time to make up a story.

Hopefully, I'll blindside her. Maybe I'll be able to tell by the look on her face, or maybe she'll laugh with embarrassment. Or she may deny it too vociferously? She always said she'd never mess around with anyone she works with at the hospital. But, I guess there's a possibility she'll own up to it right away. God knows, Michael. I'm not sure I'll be able to read her at all. I left a message, asking her to dinner or lunch tomorrow. Oh, crap!"

"What's wrong?"

"I have to pick up Joy the day after tomorrow. She's staying an extra day. They want to monitor how she does on the medication. She's never taken antidepressants before. When she arrives home, I won't feel comfortable leaving her. Not until I know, or she tells me, the medication is working. So if Karen can't have lunch or dinner tomorrow, I don't know when I'll have time alone with her."

"Fingers crossed. So Joy won't be returning to school?"

"We haven't decided whether she'll be taking time off from college. She needs to make friends, though, be a part of the college community. I mean, what will she do at home?"

"Too much free time isn't good for people suffering from depression. It allows them endless hours for their minds to go over and over what's making them depressed and how much they hate being depressed. They go round and round in a vicious and dangerous cycle. She should keep busy. And college is the perfect venue. Plus, I'm betting they have groups on campus for people dealing with depression. At least, they do at the university level. I'm not sure about junior college."

"I agree with you. And I checked. They don't have anything at the jc, but they do have a group through our health insurance that meets not too far from our house in a beautiful old church, in one of the conference rooms. I'm going to encourage her to join. She doesn't really have any hobbies besides painting to keep her occupied, and she quit painting weeks ago. Said she can't concentrate. She no longer feels inspired… by life."

"And she doesn't have any close friends?"

"Not that I know of. When we were talking to the psychiatrist together, she said she keeps to herself mostly. When people talk to her, she shies away from them. She thinks she's a freak. Her self-esteem is as low as it gets. Ever since Steven, in her words, dumped her, she feels worthless. I think she wonders why anyone would be interested in being her friend in the first place. She actually said—"

Her voice hitches. This is obviously hard for her to talk about. But I'm glad she's opening up, because I don't think she's doing that with her husband, though I can't be sure. I haven't asked her.

"I'm here for you, Leena. You can tell me anything."

She sighs. "Thank you. I think I know that, Michael."

"Did Joy say anything else you feel comfortable telling me?"

There's a pause, then she says, "I do feel comfortable telling you… anything really, Michael. Joy doesn't think Steven or I really love her. In her words, why would we? She thinks she's worthless, so why would we feel any differently? It was heartbreaking to hear her say those words. I wanted to cry, but I forced myself to keep cool. I told her how much she means to both me and her father. But actions speak louder than words."

"You told me Steven isn't around much, but you are. So does she feel the same about you?"

"I'm not around that much either, Michael. I always looked at Joy's behavior as her acting like a typical teenager. Always sequestered in her bedroom. On her phone. Texting. On social media. I'd drop by her bedroom and try to talk to her, and I could tell I was interrupting her, disrupting what she was doing. And, of course, I spend a good deal of time with Steven at all the endless hospital functions and parties that come with being a famous surgeon's wife. Dinners to drum up donations for St. John's. I also do a lot of volunteering, as I've told you in my letters. I haven't been around for Joy, and I take the blame for the way she feels. It's partly my fault. And Steven's as well."

"Okay. I'm not going to lecture you about the fact that most parents blame themselves for their kids' mental health problems. Kids live busy lives. Parents are involved in their own lives, too. Especially when you're talking about someone who's nineteen, Leena. She's not in middle school or even high school. Kids her age are normally very independent. Or they've moved out of the house already, for God's sake. Did Joy tell you when her depression and suicidality started?"

"She revealed she was depressed when she was eleven years old. In middle school. It escalated after Steven went MIA and I got busy with joining him at all of his functions. But that happened when Joy was in high school. But I, or we, didn't know, Michael. We had no clue she was depressed when she was eleven. Eleven? My God, that just breaks my heart."

"There's nothing wrong with you having a life of your own, Leena, especially when she was in high school, and even middle school, for that matter. From everything you've told me, you were there for her when she was younger. When she was depressed, you were still a stay-at-home mom, right?"

"Yes, that's true. But I should have known, Michael." Now she's crying. "I should have known."

I want to crawl through the phone and hug her. "I'm not a psychiatrist, but I did six months of intense rotation in a psychiatric hospital. The juvenile ward. This was before I discovered cardiac surgery was what I wanted to do. Young people can act like they're having the time of their lives. They laugh and joke and smile and seem to be at the top of their game. Then when they're alone, their depression rears its ugly head, and they self-harm, have suicidal thoughts. That's what's going on in the inside, but most of the time, they don't reveal that to anyone on the outside. Which is why even their friends have no idea.

"Then after some of these kids kill themselves, their friends are the first to say they had no clue. These depressed kids spend the majority of their time with their friends, and their friends had no idea? Leena, the parents don't know. Most of the time, they just simply don't know. And you're a good parent, from everything I've gleaned through your letters. You're loving and attentive. Then Joy became a teenager and was typically more independent, so you backed off. That's completely normal and what any parent would do."

"Excuse me a moment, Michael."

I hear her step away from the phone and blow her nose. For some reason, that makes me miss having a partner so much. I want to be right there with her, drying her tears.

I hear a beep on the phone, meaning my time is up, and Leena comes back on the line.

"I have to go. My time is up. Can I see you one more time before I get out of here?"

"I don't know right now, Michael. Everything's up in the air. And my life is in such turmoil."

"I know. Steven, Joy, Karen. I totally understand. Think about it. Write me if you can."

"I promise I will. And Michael?"

"Yes?"

"I… I…" She pauses.

The line beeps again, meaning I have fifteen seconds to wrap up our conversation.

"I love you," she says.

The connection drops.

And my stomach drops.

I smile.

She loves me.

LEENA

Joy has agreed with Dr. Peterson's suggestion to stay in the hospital an extra day. Now that she's nineteen, she's voluntarily admitted herself into Langley Porter, so I'm happy she's concurred with the doctor. I think it would be better as well, especially since she initially had a bad stomach reaction to the Prozac and Abilify.

She sees Dr. Peterson once a day for about thirty minutes, which isn't enough to make too much progress in therapy. However, Steven gave me the name of a renowned psychiatrist in San Francisco, Dr. Darryl Simbulan. I made an appointment for her so she can continue the appropriate medication and concurrent therapy when she's released from Langley Porter.

Karen returned my phone call, and we've agreed to meet in Golden Gate Park for a picnic lunch. My day is totally free, since Joy won't be coming home until tomorrow. The weather's been hovering in the mid-sixties, and Karen's bringing blankets, pillows, napkins, plates, and glasses. I'm picking up deli sandwiches, potato salad, and drinks. We've done this several times in the past when we wanted to be able to laugh as loud as we want and talk as long as we want without the restrictions of a restaurant and the typical crowds in San Francisco. Karen has the day off, and we're meeting at twelve thirty. That'll give us plenty of time to talk. About everything.

After I park, I see Karen waving. She's sitting in one of those half-chaise-lounge chairs that sits on the ground. Her long legs are stuck out in front of her on the grass, her pink-painted toenails wiggling hello as well. She has such a great sense of humor. I'll miss having her around… if everything turns out to be true. I'm hoping beyond hope it's all a coincidental occurrence and that Steven has been true blue. Then again, after what Michael told me about seeing Steven with someone on his arm back in the day, hoping he's been true blue is a non sequitur. I guess I simply want to know how low he's stooped, if he's been screwing my best friend.

"Hey, you," I say.

We high-five. I sit down and unwrap our sandwiches, then set them on the china plates Karen has placed on the checkered tablecloth. We have a routine, she and I. We make our picnic lunches as country club as possible with china, glasses, cloth napkins, salt-and-pepper shakers her grandmother handed down to her, sterling-silver knives and forks and spoons. The whole setup shouts high society. As a surgical nurse assisting some of the most renowned surgeons in the San Francisco Bay Area, Karen earns top dollar. And being single, she has money to spend, as do I. We are well matched in that regard, but also in so many others.

My stomach is roiling with anticipation of our talk, heavily peppered with a good dose of fear. I'm afraid I'm going to lose my best friend. Which means no more lunches at Golden Gate Park, no more gabbing on the phone when Steven's at the hospital. No more Sunday dinners with Joy (though she's half interested) in attendance. But maybe all this worrying is for nothing. I plop down across from her and pick up my plate, set it between my crossed legs.

Karen unwraps her sandwich with a smile. "This looks delicious. Smoked turkey on rye?"

"Hold the tomatoes and jalapeños."

She laughs out loud. "We're like a couple of ninety-year-old ladies, I swear. When Steven and my whoever-I-marry passes away, we'll still meet here in our wheelchairs and eat yogurt because we won't have any teeth to chew with. We'll talk about who won on Wheel of Fortune, then fall asleep, drooling."

I chuckle, but at the same time, my ears are ringing. I swear, my tinnitus flairs up whenever I'm stressed. I'm hoping when things calm down, it'll go away. But from what I've read, that's probably not going to happen.

"So how's Joy doing?"

I take a bite of my sandwich and chew. "I love avocado and tomato and Swiss cheese. Maybe I really ought to become vegetarian." After swallowing, I continue. "The doctor put her on Prozac and Abilify. I pick her up tomorrow, if all continues to go well with the meds. The doctor said any bad reactions should occur within the first three days, so he's pretty sure she's almost out of the woods by now, after her initial stomach upset. I've already set up an appointment with a new psychiatrist."

"Dr. Simbulan is pretty well-known in the community as the best."

What? This is odd. "How do you know about Dr. Simbulan?"

Karen doesn't miss a beat and continues eating her sandwich. She picks up a Coke and pours it into a glass. "Steven told me while we were prepping for surgery yesterday."

"Oh, right. Of course." I shrug. "I'm sure we'll have to take it one day at a time, see how she does with regard to her depression."

"Well, you did the right thing, having her taken to Langley Porter, as I'm sure Steven already told you. And he and Dr. Simbulan go way back."

I take a sip of my Dr Pepper and stare at my best friend. "Steven never mentioned to me that he actually knew Dr. Simbulan. He said he spoke with a colleague who referred us to him. When did Steven tell you all that?"

"Like I said, Leena. Yesterday. Why?"

"What have you been up to lately? Any hot dates?"

"Oh, great segue." She pauses and dabs at her mouth with a beautiful, white, starched napkin. "No, I haven't had a date in a while. It takes so much energy to meet someone and get to the point where you can talk past the inane chitchat of how are you, oh, I'm fine, how are you bullshit. It's exhausting. I'd rather have sex with my best friend than a stranger. And I don't have any male best friends."

I quirk an eyebrow. "Steven's a good friend, isn't he?"

She sets her glass on the tablecloth. "Well, sure, he and I are friends, but I don't wanna fuck him, Leena."

"Where were you last night?"

She lays her plate on the grass next to her glass and wipes her lips. "Why do you want to know? You're acting weird."

"Oh, I'm sorry. I was just asking my BFF if she was on a date last night at the St. Croix. Were you?"

Karen licks her lips, leans back in her chair, and slides her sunglasses down from the top of her head to cover her eyes. "What are you talking about?"

I pause for a considerable amount of time, watching my reflection in her sunglasses. "What were you doing at the St. Croix?"

"If you're implying something, I'd appreciate it if you'd just spit it out and not beat around the proverbial bush."

"I'm not implying anything, Karen. I asked if you were at the St. Croix last night. Simple question. Either you were, or you weren't. Yes or no."

"Yes, I was. So what?"

"Steven was there, too. You arrived exactly eleven minutes after he did."

"You're following him?"

"He didn't come home last night, again, because he said he had a meeting. I went for a drive, and when I passed the St. Croix, I noticed his car. I pulled to the curb and saw him enter the hotel."

"Just because he and I were at the same hotel doesn't mean we met up, Leena. I resent your implying otherwise."

"So you were at the St. Croix. Why?"

She clears her throat. I believe she's thinking of an excuse that I'll believe. One that won't implicate her or Steven.

"I met up with an old friend from high school. I may have told you about him once upon a time. Duane. Duane Faulhaber."

"Yes, I recall you mentioning him once."

"We had drinks. I went home. Alone. End of story."

"I don't believe you, Karen."

She laughs out loud, but to my ears, it sounds forced. I've known Karen for years, and she doesn't look like she's having a good time. In fact, she appears irritated, angry even.

"You think I'm having an affair with your husband? After all these years of me being a part of your family, you think I'm fucking Steven behind your back at the St. Croix? Oh, that's rich, Leena."

My heart is pounding so hard I lay my hand on my chest to minimize hearing the thrumming in my ears. "That's exactly what I'm thinking."

"Well, thank you very much, Leena. I've told you hundreds of times, I don't fuck around with my coworkers." She kneels and begins emptying the Coke and Dr Pepper out of our glasses onto the lawn, putting plates in the picnic basket, returning all the rest of the paraphernalia as well.

All the while, she refuses to look at me. Oh, she's angry all right. Her teeth are clenched so tightly, her lips look like a pink slash in the middle of her jaw. Karen and I have never had a fight and rarely argue about anything. I don't know whether she's lying or not, and now I feel bad if she's telling the truth. Have I just crossed a line? Have I lost my BFF because of my speculations about her and my husband?

"Karen, please."

"Don't 'Karen, please' me, Leena. You just accused your best friend of screwing your husband behind your back! How would you feel if the tables were turned, huh?" She grabs the edge of the tablecloth and looks at me with a hateful expression.

I stand and fold the chair I'm sitting on, so she can pull the tablecloth off the grass. After she folds it into a compact square, she places it in the basket and closes the lid.

Without another word, she glides across the lawn toward her car.

I don't know what to think. Or what to do. I don't believe her. I think the whole thing is not coincidental, that she did not just so happen to be at the St. Croix at the same time as Steven. There was something about the way she reacted. She looked guilty. She was being too angry. It was as if her vehement denial was just a cover-up for the glaring truth of the situation. I caught her in a lie, and she didn't like it. Probably because she thought she'd outsmart me and get away with it. I don't know. She seemed more perturbed that I was "stalking" Steven.

At this point, my only recourse is to confront Steven. I guess my best bet would be to do that before Karen talks to him. I could have him paged and talk to him on the phone, but this is something best done face-to-face. I think it best to confront him when he least expects it, before he has time to think up an excuse. But I realize that's not going to happen. I can't have a one-on-one conversation with Steven before he talks to Karen. I know her, and she'll get to him immediately. Shit!

If I've just lost the best friend I've ever had for nothing, at least it will mean Steven hasn't been screwing her.

But what about the woman Michael said he saw him with?

STEVEN

I'm scrubbing up for surgery and look up at the wall clock. I have four minutes left to go before I can enter the surgical arena. Karen walks up to the sink next to me and presses the foot lever for the hot water.

"Good morning," I say as I scrub my fingernails with a brush.

"She knows," she whispers.

"Who knows what?"

"Leena." She sighs. "She saw you and me walk into the St. Croix the other night."

"She talked to you about this?"

"We went on a picnic yesterday afternoon. She said she went on a drive that night and saw you there, and then she told me I arrived eleven minutes later."

I turn to look at her, but she's intent on scrubbing her hands and forearms. "She's following me? Why would she go on a drive past the St. Croix at night anyway?"

"I have no idea, Steven," she practically hisses. "The point is, she saw us, put two and two together, and guessed we're meeting there."

"What did you tell her?"

"Obviously, I denied it. I told her I was meeting up with an old high school friend."

"Did she believe you?"

"I got really angry. Told her she was crazy if she thinks I'm fucking my best friend's husband. I picked up my shit and left her standing there. She knows I'm pissed off."

"She hasn't mentioned it to me, but I haven't seen her. We're supposed to pick up Joy at around five today. I don't know whether to say anything or not."

"If she truly believes we're having an affair, she's not going to let this go, Steven. She'll either talk to you about it, straight up, like tonight or something, or she'll stew about it until she blows a gasket, and it becomes a huge argument."

"She can't prove a thing. The St. Croix is very discreet. Even if she digs around and asks questions, the staff won't say a thing."

"So don't ask, don't tell? You're not going to bring it up first?"

"If it were true, you would have told me. If it's not true, then you might not ever mention it to me. So perhaps I should feign ignorance."

"So you're not going to bring it up, right?"

"I don't think so. If you and I aren't having an affair, it's totally likely you would never say anything to me about Leena's suspicions. It would be too embarrassing."

"If that's the way you want to play it." She pauses. "Are we still going to meet up tonight?"

I stop scrubbing, hold my hands up in front of me to drip-dry, and turn toward her. "Do you really think that's a good idea after what you just told me? If anything, I'll stay home with Joy and Leena tonight. I told you, I promised her I'd try to cut back on my hours at the hospital."

"After the Siamese twins' separation."

"I'm not going to risk my marriage and my daughter for—"

"For me. I get it." She steps back from the sink and turns to back into the surgical room for a gown.

I shake my head as I look at the clock. I don't have time right now to think about this. A patient is lying on the table, and Dr. Meisner has already opened the man's chest. Open-heart surgery requires my complete attention. I'm going to put this matter aside. If I worry about it, I'm not at the top of my game. Leena can't prove a thing anyway. If she brings it up, I'll deny it and move forward.

My biggest problem will be letting Karen go. She's become so damn clingy. It's been almost a year that she and I have been together. And it's the first time I haven't been screwing around with more than one woman at the same time. Other than my wife, of course. I realize I'm getting bored with Karen. I think it's time we parted ways.

Maybe being monogamous won't be such a bad thing.

For a while.

#

After another successful surgery, I refrain from taking the elevator and go down the stairs to the parking garage. This entire situation has devolved into me sneaking out the back door so I don't get waylaid by Karen or Stephanie or anyone else wanting a piece of my time.

I pull up in front of our house, and Leena's sitting on the front porch in the sun. It's a beautiful day to break our daughter out of Langley Porter. Leena doesn't smile as she walks to the car, and after sliding into the passenger seat, she doesn't lean over and give me a peck on the cheek as usual.

"How are you doing?" I ask.

"I'm fine. Just nervous about having Joy home again."

I reach over and cover her hand with mine. "Don't stress yourself out. Dr. Peterson has her on the appropriate medication. She'll start therapy this week, right?"

"Yes. I've already scheduled an appointment with Dr. Simbulan."

"Good. He has a great reputation for working with teens."

"Karen says you and he go way back. That's not what you told me."

I glance at Joy for a quick second. "Didn't I? Huh. I guess I forgot to tell you that."

"You forgot to tell me you've known Dr. Simbulan for years? You said one of your colleagues referred him to you."

"I'm sorry. My mind has been all over the place lately, Leena. What with the twins' surgery and Stephanie calling meetings at all hours of the day. I just lost my train of thought, I guess."

"Anyway, this whole thing is just…"

"What are you referring to exactly?"

"You know, Steven. Well, actually, no, you don't know, because we don't see each other."

"Leena, let's not turn this into an argument again. I told you I plan to cut back on my hours after the separation surgery."

"I know that. But that's months from now. And in the meantime, I'm on suicide watch until and if the meds kick in. The doctor said Joy might have to try different antidepressants until they find the right one. It could take months and months. Meanwhile, our daughter is suffering. And hopefully, she doesn't try to kill herself."

I notice her pull a tissue out of her purse. She's crying, but silently. I feel guilty for not being able to help out much with Joy, but my hours at the hospital will increase before the separation surgery.

"Leena, I'm sorry I can't help out more with Joy right now. But I promise, after the twins' surgery, I'll cut back on my hours at the hospital."

"What about stepping down as chief of surgery? You said you—"

"About that." I pause, and she doesn't fill the silence. "They won't be able to fill the position for several months."

"When were you going to tell me?"

"I just found out yesterday."

"Whatever."

"There's also a slight glitch in the timing of the surgery."

"Oh, my God! Are you kidding me? Don't tell me. They're pushing it ahead due to some unforeseen bullshit. My God, Steven. We'll be lucky if this family makes it until then."

"And what exactly do you mean by that? We're talking months, Leena. Not years. We'll be just fine."

"The bottom line is I don't believe anything you say anyway. Dates are constantly changing. You promise this and that, but you can't deliver because it's out of your hands."

"I'm doing the best I can. I'm not heading up this surgery for the twins. It's completely out of my hands."

"So what's the reason for pushing the twins' surgery to a later date?"

"Dr. Jordan, the surgeon from Stanford who we wanted to join the team, finally said yes, but he couldn't make the date he originally promised, so we had to move the surgery forward a month. Now he tells us he has to back out entirely. He himself has to have heart surgery. Obviously, he's in no condition to join us."

"So now what? The twins have to wait another few months for him to recuperate, or are you filling the position with someone else?"

We arrive at Langley Porter, and I grab a ticket for parking in the underground garage. As Leena and I walk to the elevators, I continue. "Actually, Stephanie has her mind set on a particular physician. And you know Stephanie. Not one blade of grass grows beneath her spike heels."

"She's relentless. But good at what she does, right?"

"This time, I think she's lost her mind." I push the button for the top floor, and the doors close. "The surgeon she wants on the team? He's getting out of prison soon. She's determined to add him to the team, but it'll involve some legal machinations I can't begin to understand. I actually worked with him once back in the day. You remember, the Siamese twins' surgery involving two little Russian girls who shared a heart? He was the head cardiac surgeon on that one. So I understand why Stephanie wants him. But I don't know if she's going to be able to pull this one off. But if she gets her way, Michael Casspi will be one happy fellow to have his license reinstated, let me tell you."

The elevator doors whoosh open, and I exit. After walking a few steps, I notice Leena isn't beside me. I turn, and she's standing in the middle of the elevator, and the doors are about to shut.

"Leena! What's wrong?" I stretch my arm between the doors, and they automatically open again. Leena looks pale, and her eyes are closed.

I curl my arm around her shoulders, and she leans into me. "Are you ill?" We step off the elevator and walk to the nearest chair. She sits down, and I kneel in front of her, grasping her wrist to take her pulse.

She looks me in the eyes, but it's as if she's not seeing me. Her stare is vacant, expressionless.

"Leena, talk to me." I grasp her hands and squeeze. Her pulse is normal, and the color's coming back into her cheeks.

"I just got a little lightheaded. I was so anxious, I didn't eat today." She stands and glances down the hallway. "Let's go get our daughter. I'm fine."

LEENA

What is the statistical probability that Michael is the surgeon Stephanie Yates wants on the team for the surgical separation? He's in jail, for God's sake. Yes, he was well-known in his field, but after five years, one would think another surgeon would have taken his place. But what do I know about cardiac surgery or Siamese twins' separation surgery? Observing my own husband's meteoric rise to fame, I figured another surgeon would have filled Michael's slot. Obviously not.

I'd be thrilled for Michael if his medical license were to be reinstated. But that isn't the nucleus of the story here. If, and I'm sure it's a big if, Stephanie's able to reinstate Michael and get him up to speed on the protocols, then Michael and Steven will be working together. And the team will be socializing together before, during, and after meetings and any other gatherings involved in a surgery televised around the world.

Does Michael already know about this? Is he keeping it a secret until he knows the final outcome concerning his reinstatement? Perhaps he didn't have time to discuss it with me during our last conversation. We were talking mostly about Joy and my feelings of guilt surrounding her depression and suicidality. We were cut off due to time constraints on prisoner-to-outsider phone calls. Maybe he wants to talk to me about it in person. I thought of asking Steven if this Michael Casspi has spoken with Stephanie yet, but I was so shocked at the time, it was the closest I've ever come to fainting.

Then we had to meet with Joy and Dr. Peterson before Joy's release from Langley Porter, while all thoughts of Michael working side by side with Steven lingered in the back of my mind. Joy is still depressed. Thus far, after four days, the Prozac and Abilify are not working, but the doctor insists it could take four to six weeks, and we have to be patient. Additionally, it's crucial that Joy begin outpatient therapy with Dr. Darryl Simbulan. Hence, Joy's appointment with him this week.

When Joy and Steven and I get into the car, Steven immediately asks if Joy wants to go to her favorite restaurant for dinner. She politely declines, says she just wants to go home, take a long bath, then watch Netflix on her computer. Same old, same old, as far as I can tell. And I guess that, until she works out some of her issues with regard to Steven's time away from home, she'll give Steven a wide berth. She's angry and hurt, and he knows it, because I explained it all to him after the meeting he missed at Langley Porter.

And it has yet to be known how or if her attitude will change about me and the role I've played in her feeling rejected and worthless. I vow to myself to be there for her no matter what, especially since I'll be on suicide watch until she feels prepared to go it alone.

After we return home, Steven takes off his suit jacket, and his phone chirps. I know what that means. All his promises to be around more are lies. Our daughter's mental health and her care will not be a shared endeavor. Unfortunately for Joy, Steven will not take this as an opportunity to get closer to his daughter. And that makes me sad.

I might not have known what it was going to be like to be a famous surgeon's wife, but I no longer can play the ignorance card. I know exactly what it's like to live with someone of Steven's stature. I've learned to go with the flow, accepting he'll be an absent husband and father. However, after the last several years of actually living the reality of it, I've come to resent him, and I want it to stop. And now, realizing it's likely a hopeless dream that he'll bond once again with his daughter, I resent him even more.

I need to see Michael and wonder how I'll pull that off when Joy needs me to be around for her. Steven puts his jacket back on, kisses Joy's forehead after explaining he has to leave, and after she rolls her eyes and remains silent, he throws a wave in our direction and runs out the front door.

I'm desperate to talk to Michael, and the time limit imposed on a phone call won't allow me to discuss this situation with him. Plus, I need to see his face, to know why he hid the fact St. John's wants him back. It's a huge secret, if indeed he knows about it and didn't say anything to me.

I rack my brain to think of a way I can be gone for at least three hours: one hour to drive to Balmoral, a half-hour visit, then another hour or more in traffic to get back home. There's no way Steven can return home and stay with Joy. And though I am active socially in the hospital community, the women I speak with at various functions are acquaintances. I would not feel comfortable inviting any of them to my home to hang out with my daughter. Joy doesn't even know those women. Not only would it be unusual to ask them to my house to sit with Joy, Joy would balk at having them here.

I was an only child, and my mother died of ovarian cancer at fifty-five years old. My father is in a nursing home for Alzheimer's patients in San Diego. I visit him several times a year, but since that's where we lived until I was a teenager, I'm comforted that his friends visit him on a regular basis.

Steven has a brother whom I've never met. He's from New York, and his brother still lives there with his wife and two kids. Steven and he are close in age, but don't get along. They talk on the phone at Christmas, but that's the extent of his involvement with his only sibling. His parents drowned while in their forties in a tragic boat accident. A barge ran into them at dusk because his father didn't turn on the running lights on their yacht.

When Steven and I met, after he graduated from medical school at UC San Francisco, and I was there at the same time studying archaeology, we gravitated to each other like magnets and spent every waking moment in each other's company. Steven had many more friends than I, but that's how I met Karen. She was my best friend for years, and when Joy came along, I spent my time taking care of her, and Karen often babysat so I could still do volunteer work and accompany Steven to the St. John's social functions.

I realize now that my only real friend is Karen. If I throw my pride aside, phone her, grovel my apologies, and ask if she can come over and visit with Joy, I can accomplish what I need to. I will be able to leave. But I have to make up an excuse for my absence that sounds urgent as well as believable.

My mind stalls. What the hell will appear plausible to

my once upon a time best friend? I call her cell and wait, hoping not to delay everything by having to leave a message and waiting for her to call me back, if she decides to do so.

"Hello, Leena."

"Karen, I'm sorry for what I said the other day, insinuating you and Steven are having an affair. I don't want to make up excuses for my behavior, but this whole thing with Joy and her attempted suicide and the depression and psychiatric hospital, I—"

"Stop, Leena. I mean it. I apologize for going off on you. Granted, I'm angry you would suspect me, but I understand you're under a tremendous amount of stress. And I apologize for leaving our picnic so abruptly. But I was hurt."

"And rightfully so. I accused you of acting like a shitty friend, when you've always been there for me to cheer me up through Steven's absences and now Joy's problems. You've been a good friend. And I'm sorry I hurt you." I was saying the words, but my heart wasn't behind them.

I still think Karen and Steven are having an affair, but I have no proof. Yet. So I have to go along, pretending she's telling me the truth, because I need her right now. And I have no one else I can rely on when it comes to my daughter. Karen not only has known Joy for years, but she's a nurse and can deal with any problems that might arise in my absence.

"We've both apologized, Leena. I forgive you, you forgive me."

"I do. Of course I do."

"Then let's do lunch. Tomorrow, if that's possible."

"I truly am sorry, Karen. But I have another reason

for calling, though it wasn't the original reason, believe me."

"What are you talking about?"

"Can you stay with Joy for several hours tomorrow? Like from ten in the morning until around one, one thirty?"

"What's up? Are you okay?"

"I'm fine. It's just… I have my own appointment. With a therapist."

"Of course. But shouldn't you and Steven be going together?"

"That might happen down the road, but right now, I need to talk to someone alone. About my feelings surrounding Joy's depression and how I contributed to that. You know what I mean?"

"I do. And yes, I'll be there tomorrow. It'll also give me time to talk with Joy. Maybe she'll open up a bit."

"Well, she sure as hell isn't talking to me very much. And not to Steven at all. But Dr. Peterson warned me Joy's resentment may take a long time to subside. It'll depend on her working it out in her mind, to accept that her father and I love her as much as we always have, but life got in the way. He's a famous surgeon. I thought she didn't need me anymore because she's a teenager. Both understandable reasons, but they come out sounding like excuses for our negligent behavior."

"It's hard being a parent, Leena, no matter what happens with your kid. And you've done a great job with Joy, because she's a great kid. I love her to death. She's smart and quirky and, even though she's pulled back into her shell since becoming a teenager, she's not some drug-dealing, smart-mouthed, asshole teen like you see in the movies."

"Well, thank you for saying that. And I love you, Karen." I say the words, and inside my heart, I miss my friend and feel like a liar for apologizing for accusing her of having an affair with Steven. Because, in all honesty, I think they are having an affair. But right now, I need to make sure my daughter's taken care of, and I need to see Michael. Those are my prime objectives.

"I love you, too, Leena."

I end the call and immediately phone Balmoral to leave a message with the administrative office. Twenty minutes later, the operator phones, I accept the collect call, and I hear Michael's voice.

"Leena, are you all right?"

"I'm sorry to bother you—"

"Bother me? I'm in prison, Leena. What else do I have going on in my life that's more important than talking to you?"

"I need to see you. Can I visit tomorrow? Is that too soon to get permission?"

"Not anymore it isn't. I have lots to tell you."

"And I think I know what you're referring to, but let's not get into that right now. I think we should talk, too. In person. So, tomorrow?"

"I'll clear it with the administrative office. If they will not allow it, I'll call you at eight tomorrow morning. Is that okay?"

"It's fine. And thank you."

"I can't wait to see you. I've missed you, Leena. Letters will never cut it for me. Not after seeing you in person."

"I feel the same way. Tomorrow, then."

We end the call, and I take an ohming breath, trying to settle my nerves. Though my mother died of ovarian cancer, my father has Alzheimer's, and I'm an only child with no one to lean on, this time in my life has been the most stressful I've ever experienced. I'm hoping everything gets resolved, but it's a lot to hope for.

I'm overwhelmed by life right now. And I've decided to hire a private investigator to find out about Steven and Karen. I don't have time to play private investigator. If what I suspect turns out to be true, I want a divorce. And if I can prove his infidelity, then Joy and I can live peacefully in this house without Steven. He can visit her any time he wants, which means never. Whether Joy is here or not, his schedule is never going to change, no matter what promises he makes to appease me.

And what do I want for me and Michael? He and I will have to talk about it, because right now, I have no clue.

MICHAEL

When I enter the visitors' room, Leena has her head turned slightly toward the window. She's as beautiful as the first time I saw her. Her hair is pulled up at the sides with what looks like a set of diamond-encrusted clips. With her hair up and off her neck, her profile reminds me of some of the paintings I've seen at galleries in Europe, where Heather and I often vacationed.

She's dressed in a pale pink long-sleeved angora sweater with pink pants and black ballet slippers. She's a classy lady, for sure. I've seen many surgeon's wives in my time, but Leena has something about her. She doesn't exude the snooty, country-club air I was accustomed to in the past.

The door slams shut behind me, and Leena jerks her head in my direction. She doesn't smile, which worries me. If she's found out about the impending possible reinstatement of my medical license and introduction to the team performing the Siamese twins' surgery, she's probably wondering why I didn't say anything before this. But I just got the call from Dr. Stephanie Yates yesterday and was waiting to talk to Leena in person.

I sit, and we stare at each other for a moment. Her eyes look bloodshot, and I hope she isn't losing sleep over my situation. Nothing has been decided, and I actually doubt any judge is going to reinstate my medical license, considering the crime they believe I've committed. Murder and surgeons are not accepted bedfellows.

"I've missed you, Leena. And it hasn't been that long since we saw each other the first time."

"That's true. But a lot has happened in a very short time."

"How's Joy doing?"

"The meds aren't working, and I'm afraid for her. What if she tries to kill herself again?"

"I'm sure the doctor already explained how long it takes for antidepressants to kick in."

She nods. "Yes, he told me."

"Who's with her now?"

"My friend," she begins, then shakes her head. "Karen, my best friend."

"What's wrong? I think you wrote me that she's a surgical nurse at St. John's, and you've known her for years. She's like a part of your family."

She smiles, but it doesn't reach her eyes, which have a faraway look to them, as if she's thinking of something besides this subject.

"I think she and Steven are having an affair."

"What? Are you sure? How do you know?"

"Long story short, I saw Steven park in front of the St. Croix the other night, so I parked on the street and waited. And watched. A few minutes later, Karen arrived. When I confronted her, she got very defensive and denied the entire thing. I needed to talk to you today, so I called her and apologized, and now she thinks everything's fine between us. I needed someone to stay with Joy. I was desperate. Desperate enough to lie about being sorry, that is. I don't believe her, and I'm not sorry for what I said. I think she and Steven are screwing around."

I clasp her hands in mine and look into her eyes. "What are you going to do?"

"I'm thinking of hiring a private detective. I don't have the time nor the skills to follow either of them. I have Joy to look after. I'm essentially on suicide watch 24/7, until the meds kick in and she's doing better. I won't risk my daughter's life to play private eye on my cheating husband and my… best friend."

Her voice hitches on the last two words.

"This must be really hard for you. I can't imagine, so I won't say any inane words of wisdom. I haven't experienced the infidelity of a spouse. And I never cheated on Heather. I loved her."

"And Steven supposedly loves me. And Karen loves me, too. She always said she never mixes sex with work. What a bunch of crap. But hey, I guess that didn't keep either of them from sleeping together, right?"

"Wait for proof of that, Leena. Don't tie yourself up in knots over something that, though seemingly possible, remains only probable at the moment. Maybe they were both there for other reasons, and it really was a coincidence."

Her lips curve up in a mock smile. "Playing devil's advocate, are you?"

I smile and lift her hands, then kiss her knuckles. "I just don't want you to stop eating or stop enjoying your daughter or stop having any fun in your life over something that might turn out to be false. But I think hiring a private detective is a good thing. I know someone, though after five years, he may not be in business any longer."

"Why would you know a PI?"

"I met him when a friend of mine's son was accused

of murdering his girlfriend. He's an ex-attorney, believe it or not. He found practicing law boring and useless. He didn't believe he was helping anyone as a lawyer and changed careers at a fairly young age."

"What happened to your friend's son?"

"Found innocent, based on what Grayson discovered. His name's Grayson Randall. He used to be in Tiburon. Don't know if he's still there, but you can try. Tell him I referred you."

"Thank you for that, Michael."

"Is that all that's bothering you? Not that that isn't enough to fill anyone's plate. But you said you had to talk to me."

"Have you heard from Dr. Stephanie Yates?"

I nod. "Yesterday. I wanted to talk to you about that in person, not over the phone and certainly not via a letter."

"What do you think you're going to do?"

"There's much to be done, but it's completely out of my hands. Dr. Yates is coordinating everything. She plans to meet with me tomorrow, as a matter of fact. At that time, she said, she'll map out her plan of action. She said she'll be bringing an attorney along with her as well. She seems to think she can get my medical license reinstated, and if she can do that, she's a miracle worker."

"I know her. We're not friends or anything, but after all these years of talking to her at functions and parties, along with what Steven's told me, she's a firecracker. One of the most intelligent people I've ever met, and Steven concurs. She was an attorney before becoming a doctor. The woman is amazing. If anyone can pull this off, Stephanie can. She's brilliant. And actually very sweet."

"Good to hear. That raises my hopes."

"Then you want to be on the team at St. John's?"

"Absolutely. I never dreamed I'd be allowed to practice medicine again." I pause. "Why do you ask? You want me to decline Dr. Yates' offer?"

She shakes her head. "No. I would never expect you to do that just because you'll be working side by side with my husband." She laughs under her breath. "What an odd situation."

"He doesn't have to know anything, Leena. There's no reason to tell him we already know each other when he introduces us, which I'm sure will eventually happen. We can pretend we've never met."

"That's true. And that would be advisable. It's just…"

"It's just, where do we go from here?"

She purses her lips and looks down at our clasped hands. "Yes. Where do we go from here, Michael?"

"I've been thinking about that. I have a lot of time, too much time, to think about you. I want there to be an us, Leena. I love you. I know it's early days in what is a very odd relationship that started via letters between a prisoner and an outsider. But we became friends through our letters. And now that we've met, you're exactly who I thought you were from reading your letters. I want to continue seeing you.

"I mean, when I get out of here. Whether they reinstate my medical license and I'm working at St. John's or not, I want to keep seeing you. But that's totally up to you. You're married, and you have a daughter, and if you find out Steven hasn't been cheating on you, you might want to work it out, save your marriage. It's all up to you. I'll accept whatever you decide. But I want to let you know, I care about you… very much. I'll be sad if you don't want to pursue a relationship with me, but I'll certainly understand."

She looks as if she's going to cry, then I notice a tear slide down her cheek. I swipe it away gently with my thumb and lift her chin to look her in the eyes. "No pressure. You don't have to decide right now. Nothing may come of this thing with Dr. Yates and St. John's. But I will be getting out of here, and I want to move back to my house in San Francisco eventually. It's currently rented out. But, again, whatever you decide."

"I want to find out if Steven's cheating, but whether he's cheating or not, Michael, I'm in love with you. What Steven and I once had is over. I don't believe he'll cut back on his hours and spend more time at home with me and Joy. It's a thankless marriage, although Steven thinks I should bow down and kiss his feet for all the material possessions he's given me. That's not what makes a marriage."

"But what if, whether he's cheating or not, he wants to work on your marriage, and he does cut back on his hours, and you're able to save what you once had? It's possible, Leena."

She shakes her head and takes a deep breath. "What I feel for Steven, despite all these years of neglect, is admiration for what he's accomplished and pride at how well he's done and for what he does every day. He works miracles. But for him to essentially leave me and Joy by the wayside is just... I don't know. It's something I'd never do. To anyone. Least of all, my husband.

"I feel guilty for not paying enough attention to Joy when she needed me, like I told you before, but Steven's actions are outright neglect. He doesn't want to change, though he said he will. But there's just no way, Michael. If anything, he'll be even busier after the twins' surgery.

He's well-known now. He'll be even more famous in the future. He's a doctor first and foremost, not a husband and father first. Do you understand what I mean?"

"I do. However, I know I'd fight for someone I loved. If Heather had cheated on me, I'd want to at least try to work it out."

"You can't be subjective about it, because that never happened to you. If you'd ever been in my position with your wife, perhaps then you would have felt what I'm feeling. And remember, Michael, Steven was cheating years ago. You saw it with your own eyes."

"Okay, let's say he's not cheating now, Leena, and perhaps he's been faithful since then. If you wait, maybe he really will cut back on his hours, and you and Joy and Steven can be a family again. I don't want to be the reason to break apart anyone's family."

"We haven't been a family in a long, long time, Michael. Don't tell me you've never met a surgeon who lived, ate, and breathed his career. Tell me you don't know what I'm talking about. And I can't just forget what you told me about seeing him with another woman."

I close my eyes momentarily, then open them to see her sad eyes staring at me out of that gorgeous face. All I want to do is pull her close and tell her how much I love her. "Yes, I know exactly what you're saying. He was probably cheating years ago, and sadly, it's likely he still is. And having little free time outside the hospital? That part, the lack of free time… often comes with the territory. It's unfortunate for the wife and family, but very fortunate for the patients and hospitals."

"And you know what? If you and I have a relationship, Michael, and you're part of the team for that surgery, you'll become even more famous, perhaps, than

Steven. Can you see the headlines? Ex-con Exits Prison to Fortune and Fame." She puts her head in her hands, eyes closed, tears dripping onto the Formica tabletop.

I gently pull her hands away and look into her eyes, bloodshot from either crying or lack of sleep, it doesn't matter. She's having a hard time of it right now.

"Please don't cry. I want you to know something, Leena. I love you. I loved Heather, and I was in the limelight then. Remember the surgery I performed that blasted me to the top of fame and fortune? I kept my hours reasonable, so Heather and I could vacation, and our marriage always came first. I'll understand if you change your mind and decide to work it out with Steven, whether he's having an affair or not, or if he cuts back on his hours and does everything he's promised.

"But if you decide you're divorcing him, I want to have a relationship with you. Whenever you're available. It'll take time to find out if he's having an affair, and it'll take time before the twins' surgery is complete, and Steven can step down as chief of surgery and reduce his hours. Everything will take more than a few days.

"But if my license is reinstated when I get out of here, I'll be busy as well, but never, ever too busy for you and Joy. I can promise you that. I'm not Steven. And I don't mean to slander Steven in any way, because I understand how he got to the place where there are only so many hours in a day, and what he does is so incredible— saving lives that only he has the skills to save. I get it. But I've been there, too, Leena. And you'll always come first."

Leena opens her arms and reaches for me, so I straddle the bench seat and scoot toward her, glance up at the guard, and our eyes meet. He nods and turns around, so I cling to Leena, and she hugs me so tightly, it's as if she's drowning and I'm her life jacket.

I pull away and look in her eyes, then kiss away her tears. She leans in and kisses me, deeply and completely. The kiss goes on and on, until I feel myself wanting so much more, I can hardly contain what's going on below my waistline. And we're in the visitors' room, though we're the only ones here. The guard's in the corner, pretending the view out the window—a yard full of rough-looking dudes shooting hoops and yelling at each other—is magnificent.

Leena touches my knee with her hand and slides it upward. At this point, I'm ready to blow. Her tongue glides like a silk ribbon along my bottom lip, and my erection hardens. It's been so long. So very, very long. Months before Heather passed away. Years in prison. My mind is no longer in this room. I'm picturing Leena and me in a king-size bed in the twilight of another day to come, and I'm inside her.

A low moan reaches my ears, but it could have been either of us. I don't care. I'm hoping the guard won't try to stop us now, because I'm already past the point of holding back. Leena's hand caresses my hard-as-concrete erection, and I let go. The mind-blowing pulsing seems to go on forever while our hot breaths mingle in a final kiss.

She whispers that she loves me. I look into her eyes and I believe her. And the hope is overwhelming that we can be together forever, though there are so many obstacles to overcome before that can happen.

I lay my hand on top of her fingers as she continues to caress me until the pulsing subsides. But I'm already getting hard again, so I pull her hand away.

"Next time, it will be your turn," I whisper in her ear.

She pulls away and smiles. "I can't wait."

LEENA

Now I'm vacillating on whether to hire a private investigator to follow Steven, because I've already made up my mind to leave him whether he's having an affair with Karen or not. So does it matter if I have him investigated? Isn't it a waste of money? I chuckle as I'm driving home. A waste of money? We have more money than we know what to do with. Spending Steven's money on a PI to find out if he's cheating on me? Oh, that's rich.

Though I know California is a no-fault state, and I believe I'll get half of whatever Steven and I have made together, I'm unsure of the legalities with regard to alimony and child support. I'll need to hire an attorney. Perhaps Michael can refer me to an attorney friend, so I'm not worried about that… yet.

I find Grayson Randall's number on my iPhone and wait for him to answer. We make an appointment for the next day, and I'm scrambling in my head—again—for a way to get someone to stay with Joy.

So, once again, if I can't get Karen to stay with Joy, I have no relatives and no friends to help me out. Dare I leave Joy home alone for the hour or so it will take me to meet with Grayson Randall? I have no one else to turn to. When I return home, Karen and Joy are sitting in front of the TV in the theater room.

"What're you guys watching?"

Karen turns to me with a smile as she holds out a bowl of popcorn.

I shake my head. "Not hungry, but thank you."

"Alien. Aliens, plural. Return of the Alien. Return of the Alien Squared. And Uh Oh, There's Another Alien."

"Stop it," Joy says, laughing.

It is the first time I've seen Joy laugh since before she went into the psychiatric hospital. This is a good thing, Joy having a good time. Is it Karen or the Prozac? I don't know which is responsible for the change in my daughter's mood, but I am so happy that Joy's happy. I smile. Right now, I feel like a traitor, after having set up an appointment with Grayson Randall to investigate Karen and Steven sleeping together.

Karen pats the couch next to her. "Come join us. We were just talking about going to the Planetarium tomorrow afternoon. Like to join us?"

"I'd love to, but I have another appointment at two o'clock."

"Oh, Mom."

Joy sounds truly disappointed, and my heart clenches.

"You're as bad as Daddy. He never has time for me." She stands and walks out of the room.

"Wait, Joy," I yell after her, but she keeps walking up the stairs. "What about after I get back?" I shout.

Joy pops her head around the corner. "For real?"

I grin. "Of course. The meeting is a quick one, with my new gynecologist. I'll be back in an hour."

Joy gives me the peace sign and disappears around the corner.

"Female problems?" Karen says.

"Just my yearly, but I keep putting it off, and I swore

I wouldn't cancel again. You can stay with Joy again tomorrow, then?"

"Of course. Don't worry about it. Who's your new gynecologist?"

I wasn't prepared for this, and my mind goes completely blank.

"Leena? I said who's your gyno?"

A name appears in my mind from the many colleagues of Steven's I've met. "Dr. Brent Martin."

"Brent Martin? Never heard of him. Where does he practice?"

It isn't unusual for Karen to ask questions. We've known each other for years, but I want to get off this subject. All this deceit is making me uncomfortable. Granted, she's obviously used to it, if she's sleeping with my husband. I am not.

I shrug. "He's new to the area. I have to look up the address before I leave. Hey, thank you again for staying with Joy today. Do you mind waiting until I get back tomorrow, so the three of us can go to the Planetarium?"

"Fine with me. Joy would probably rather go see a movie. We can always do that instead."

"Whatever she wants, Karen. I'm happy I can join you two."

"How was the counselor? What's her or his name?"

I wasn't ready for this either and can't think of a single name of any therapists I've seen in the past or heard of through the grapevine. So I decide to just make one up. At least Dr. Brent Martin is a real gynecologist! "Bradley. Bradley Silverstein." Inwardly, I'm rolling my eyes. Bradley Silverstein? Sounds plausible, I guess. Doesn't matter anyway.

"Is he a marriage and family therapist or a psychiatrist or…"

"Uh, I think he has an MFC or something like that beneath his name, so a marriage and family therapist, I guess."

Karen shrugs, grabs her sweater, and stands. "I should go. I forgot I need to get to the hospital a little early to read the report on a surgery. I traded someone for the night shift."

I have the feeling she's uncomfortable being alone with me. Whether because of our previous conversation while on our picnic at Golden Gate Park, or maybe she feels guilty having an affair with Steven, which would make for an awkwardness only she could feel. I don't know anything for sure anyway.

Be that as it may, we say goodbye, and she says she'll be at our house tomorrow at one thirty in the afternoon, giving me plenty of time to get to Grayson Randall's office in Tiburon.

At noon the next day, Joy and I have lunch together for the first time in forever. She doesn't say much, besides the fact that she isn't as depressed as she's been for the last several years. When I ask her if she's still having suicidal thoughts, she says she isn't. I guess I'll just have to take her word for it, but I still don't want her home alone, and I'm grateful when Karen shows up. I leave, promising to return in time to visit the Planetarium or go to the movies with them later.

Grayson Randall's office is located on the fourth floor of a beautiful all-glass building in the middle of Tiburon. When I enter, a perfectly coiffed secretary escorts me to his office and asks me if I want tea or coffee. I decline both, then turn to meet Mr. Randall.

Grayson Randall is not the stereotypical private investigator you see on television. He's wearing a dark blue Hugo Boss Italian suit with cuff links at his wrists and a maroon tie. He comes around to the front of his desk, shakes my hand while looking me in the eyes, and introduces himself. Strikingly handsome, he's polite and soft-spoken. He takes considerable notes on a yellow legal pad, then says he'll get back to me within a day or two. I pay him his five-thousand-dollar retainer and speed home in time to meet Karen and Joy.

I'm sitting in the Planetarium with my daughter and Karen, leaning back, watching the stars skim across the domed ceiling. All the while, I'm thinking about whether Steven and Karen are sleeping together in between reliving the explosive (literally) kiss between Michael and me. The next few days will be nerve-racking while I wait for Grayson Randall to get in touch with me, as well as Michael to write to me about what Stephanie Yates finds out about reinstating his license. My life is truly hanging in the air, based on what Grayson discovers and what Stephanie can pull off in Michael's favor.

In the meantime, Steven comes home late every night for the next three nights, slipping into bed at two or three in the morning. He invariably turns to me, pressing himself against my side, his erection smashed against my leg. I've been feigning sleep, making sure to let out a tiny snore.

To my logical mind it sounds ridiculous, but I'd feel traitorous if I had sex with my own husband. That makes no sense on an intellectual level, but deep down, I'm in love with Michael, and I want to know the truth about Steven's fidelity before I let him touch me again. No, that's a bald-faced lie. I don't want to have sex with Steven ever again. My heart's not in it, and he never pleasures me anyway. So why bother?

Joy and I spend a good deal of quiet time together. She's working on catching up with her college classes, and they've made an exception, allowing her to do that online. Midterms are on the horizon. I try to read a book, but my mind is all over the place as I wonder what I'll be doing a month from now. Will I still be with Steven? Will I be dating Michael?

More important, how will all of this impact Joy? She's fragile right now. Actually, if I'm honest with myself, she's probably been fragile for years. And I never knew. How will she react if I divorce Steven? What will she think of Steven if she finds out he's been having an affair with Karen? Would integrating Michael into our lives 'cause her more anguish and pain? Would she ever accept him as her stepfather?

My mind whirls round and round as I imagine different scenarios. I awake exhausted, having fallen asleep with a book in my hand. Joy's working on her laptop.

We have dinner together in front of the TV, while we watch a movie of her choice. I zone out, thinking and imagining again and again, over and over, until I fall asleep for the second time. When I awaken this time, Joy has left the room, and when I pass her door, her lights are off. She's sleeping more, which the doctor said is normal while her body gets accustomed to the medication. And I still haven't heard from Michael.

So I wait.

STEVEN

"Dr. Arlington, you can close, please."

I walk out of the surgery room and rip off my mask. I've been sweating under the lights, and I'm just flat-out exhausted. I need to blow off some steam and plan to head to the gym on the top floor and use the rowing machine for thirty minutes. I've had four open-heart surgeries in four days, and my brain is fatigued.

When I come home to Leena at night, she's out like a light for some reason. She usually feels me slip in next to her and wakes up. Then we can at least have sex. So, unless her sleep patterns have suddenly changed, I have a gut feeling she simply isn't interested in what she's labeled my slam-bam-thank-you-ma'am way of making love. I can't blame her. Not many people are wide awake at two or three in the morning.

But she's my wife. I'm not going to waken her to talk about open-heart surgeries or Joy's depression. Isn't it her marital obligation to please me? I work hard to give Leena and Joy all they want or would ever need in life. Leena knew what she was getting into when she married a cardiac surgeon. She wasn't hoping I'd do a terrible job at St. John's. Granted, it was a surprising rocket to the top once I arrived at the hospital. But I hoped that would make Leena proud of me, not resentful.

She hasn't had to work outside the home since she

gave birth to Joy. Most wives would love the fancy dinners, hours every week to play tennis, country-club lunches and dinners, expensive clothes and shoes. She can have whatever she wants. And my credit card bill proves she takes full advantage of it.

So when I come home and need some relief from the stress, she can at least pretend to be grateful and not turn her back to me or snore when I join her in bed. Is it too much to ask? It's not as if I ignore her needs. But lately, she says she's too tired to do anything. She doesn't want to get off nor help me do the same. It's not as if I'm a sex addict or something. Yes, I have sex with Karen, and she's the only other woman I've been with for almost a year now. I used to have multiple female partners, but Karen's the first woman I've ever met who's willing to do anything, and I mean anything, with me.

When we get into one of our arguments, Leena constantly brings up the fact I'm never home, that when I do come home late at night, all I want to do is screw her. That's not the way I look at having sex with my wife. She's not a prostitute. But she owes me a little attention for everything I do for this family. Is it too much to ask that she just open her legs and let me slide in?

I'm in the elevator, headed for the top floor where the cafeteria and gymnasium are located, when the elevator stops at the third floor and Karen steps in. We nod to each other, then wait for several others to exit at various floors until we reach the top.

"We need to talk," she whispers. "Let's have coffee."

"I don't have time," I tell her. "I'm exhausted, and I need to work out. Then I'm going home."

"You'll want to hear what I have to say, Steven. This isn't some romantic interlude. It's the cafeteria."

I let out a breath to show my irritation and follow her. We order two coffees, and she takes a seat next to the window at the farthest table from the entrance.

I take a sip, waiting for her to talk. If she doesn't say something soon, I'm leaving.

"She knows, Steven."

"Who knows what, Karen? I don't have time for fooling around."

"Leena knows about us. I swear to God, I'm not fucking around. She knows."

"That's impossible. No one knows about us, Karen. Unless you've told one of your friends, Leena has no idea."

She lets out a protracted sigh, treating me like a disobedient teenager, which I find irritating.

She waits until I look her in the eyes, something she does often when she wants my full attention. God forbid I have more important things on my mind than playing these games with her. She's constantly asking if I think Leena knows about us. It's annoying.

I look in her eyes and wait.

"She asked me to babysit Joy, for lack of a better word. To stay with her while she went to see a therapist."

"She's seeing a therapist? News to me. So what?"

"So what?"

I take a second to calm myself, but I'd like to throw my hot cup of coffee in her face. She's being paranoid. Again. I'm finding her to be extraordinarily irritating. Probably because I'm so tired.

"What the hell does you hanging out with Joy, or Leena going to a therapist, have to do with Leena knowing about us? Could you just get to the point, so I can get out of here, please?"

She sighs so exaggeratedly, I push back my chair to stand.

"Are we done?" I ask.

I can tell I've made her angry. Her nostrils flare, and she's gripping her coffee cup so tightly, her fingers are turning white.

"Hell no, we're not done. And if you don't sit down and talk to me—" She stops when her voice gets a bit too loud.

Several nurses sitting near us turn their heads in our direction.

I scooch my chair forward and take hold of her forearm and squeeze, hard, knowing it's too hard, knowing she'll get the point. "Don't you ever raise your voice to me again, either here or anywhere. Do you understand me?" I smile and tighten my grip, and she gasps. I widen my smile and chuckle, raise my hand and pat her arm. "Now, why don't you explain to me what you're worried about, and believe me, I can hear you perfectly fine from where I'm sitting."

She pulls her hand inward, as if she's touched a flame, then rubs her arm up and down. There are unshed tears in her eyes. She understands my meaning. There's a part of her that's scared of me. I see it in her eyes.

"Leena called me and apologized for asking if you and I are having an affair. But she was being way too conciliatory, given how angry she was at our picnic. I can just feel it. It's just not like her to give up so easily."

"Thanks for the heads-up," I say in a monotone.

A tear slides down her cheek, and she swipes at it with a fierce movement of her hand. "There's more."

"Jesus Christ, Karen. Get to the goddamn point, will you?"

"All right." She takes in a deep breath, letting it out slowly. "She told me she went to see a therapist. Bradley Silverstein in the Bay Area. He doesn't exist. Then she said she saw her gynecologist, Dr. Brent Martin. I called his office, too, and he's in the Cayman Islands and has been gone for three weeks. She's lying, Steven. Why would she lie?"

"I have no idea, Karen. Even if she knows about us, what the hell does her making up doctor's appointments have to do with you and me?"

"That's just it. I have no idea. She's your wife. Why don't you ask her?" She leans back in her chair and smirks. "Better yet, why don't I just come clean with her? Tell her all about us. How about that?"

I push my chair back and stand. I knew Karen was becoming more attached than I wanted. We're having an affair. I'm not leaving my wife for her. It's sex, plain and simple. But Karen's turning into a shrew, always wanting to know my whereabouts, when we can next meet, asking how I feel about her. I evade her questions, but lately she's gotten worse. She's becoming possessive and controlling. And now this. I've had enough.

"Are you threatening me?"

She raises her eyes to meet mine, then slowly stands so we are almost at eye level. "I'd never threaten you, Steven. I'm asking you what we're going to do about Leena. Maybe she's meeting with a private investigator. Did you ever think of that? Should we start meeting somewhere else in case she's having us followed?"

"I don't know what the hell Leena's doing, Karen, but what I do know is that the cafeteria is not the place to get into this. But since you insist… maybe we should put this on hold for a while."

Her mouth drops open. I was right. She's in love with me. I should have addressed this issue long ago. This is all my fault. I should never have allowed our affair to go on as long as it has. Usually, I'm with a woman, or two women, for a couple of months, then I end it. But Karen's made it so easy. She's always been amenable to meeting at my convenience. But this new behavior, threatening me and making a public scene? She's gone too far. My back's against the wall. This has to end.

Karen's face flushes when she's upset, and right now, it's fire-engine red. And we're in the middle of the hospital cafeteria. I should never have allowed us to discuss anything here. And I shouldn't have hinted at dissolving our relationship. What's that expression, never shit where you eat? In other words, do not have romantic relationships with co-workers. This could get ugly.

"Maybe we should put this on hold for a while? This?" She steps toward me, then stops only inches from my face. "This, Steven, is my life you're talking about. This, Steven? I'm a human being. Not a thing you just throw away like a piece of trash off your cafeteria tray." She turns, grasps the nearest dirty tray on the table next to ours, and throws it at me.

The tray smashes into my stomach, then falls to the floor. What looks like vomit, but is actually cafeteria-style porridge, drips down the front of my pants. Lucky (or not) for me, the prune juice missed me by inches.

Karen flies past me toward the exit. Everyone around me is mumbling, and when I look up, several of my colleagues are smirking. They probably know Karen and I are having an affair, since most of them frequent The Drunken Ball. Or perhaps Karen hasn't been as discreet as she purports to be. Is it possible Leena found out and told a few of the wives? But Leena's never been that close with any of my colleagues' spouses. At least, that's what she's always told me.

I swipe at my pants with a clump of napkins and slowly walk to the stairway. If I have to, I'll take the stairs all the way to the basement. Anything to avoid running into anyone else, especially Karen. Lord knows, if she's capable of making a scene like the one in the cafeteria, I can't be sure of what she'll do next.

I should have waited until we were alone to bring up a possible breakup. No wonder she threw the tray at me. She didn't know what hit her when I suggested putting our liaisons on hold. And now, I don't trust her to keep our affair under wraps. If she was so vocal in front of everyone in the hospital, I can no longer count on her being discreet. And threatening she'd confess to Leena? Oh-ho-ho. That goes way beyond the pale.

It's too late to go to the gym, and now I have to change clothes. By the time I burst through the door on the garage level, I've gotten my exercise for the day running down so many flights of stairs. The Porsche revs to life, and I press the pedal to the metal, as the expression goes, and zoom toward home to grab another suit for tonight's meeting.

On the drive, I phone Karen. I think it best to be prepared if she's thinking of doing something stupid, such as revealing everything to Leena. I'm sure when she cools down, I can talk to her, explain I wasn't thinking clearly. Then, over the course of the next few months, I'll taper off our evenings together. Then she won't be so surprised when I put an end to "us" completely. At least, I'm hoping that's a viable plan.

"What do you want, Steven?"

"I'm sorry, Karen. I didn't mean what I said. Let's meet tonight."

"You're scared I'm going to tell Leena, aren't you? That's the only reason the almighty Dr. Steven Coughlin would ever apologize. It benefits you to make nice with the woman you're banging behind your wife's back. Otherwise, I might open my big, fat mouth and tell all. You forget, Steven. I know you."

"That's not why I'm calling. You know for a fact you're the only woman I've ever been with for this long."

"Other than Leena."

"Stop it, Karen. I've told you over and over again, you and I… we're good together."

"Yeah, I've heard those words. Usually when you're just about to come."

"Stop it, Karen. That's not true. Can we please meet tonight? After my meeting? Ten o'clock?"

"You said you want to end this."

"I was angry. You can understand that, can't you? You scared me when you threatened to tell Leena about us. That would definitely be the end of us, Karen, and you know it. And I don't want to end it."

A few seconds of silence ensues, then she whispers, "You're telling me the truth?"

"Believe me, I don't want to lose you, Karen. We both enjoy our time together, right?"

"Of course. But, Steven, she knows."

"There's no way Leena knows anything. She's fishing, Karen. And you didn't take the bait. Now, meet me. Please. And stop worrying about Leena. She's my wife. That's my job, not yours. Trust me on this."

"Okay. But we can't meet at the St. Croix anymore, Steven."

I've got her just where I want her, and I inwardly sigh. "I've already picked a new venue. The fancy hotel four or five blocks from The Drunken Ball. The Orchid Inn. You've heard of it?"

"It just opened. But can you be assured of the privacy and discretion you need so Leena doesn't find out?"

This last sentence she says sarcastically. But I'm wise to the games Karen plays. The only reason she cares if Leena finds out is because she hopes that, with time, I'll divorce Leena and marry her. I shake my head, wishing I'd never started this thing with her in the first place, yet knowing why I did. It's all about the sex, and she's great at giving me what I need, kinky as it is to most people.

"They're discreet. I'll make a reservation for tonight, okay?"

I envision her pouting and hold my breath, though I know what she'll say. I know her too well. It's become almost like a marriage between us.

Definitely time to end it.

"Will you be wanting the usual, baby?" she asks.

She usually talks to me like that only when we're in bed together, and my groin clenches in anticipation of everything tonight will bring.

"You know it, sugar. I love you."

I've said the words before to get what I want, and dammit, I have to shut her up with whatever means available. Right now, all I have are my words, since we're talking on the phone.

"I love you, too, babe," she says. "See you tonight."

I don't love Karen and never have, but I placate her to get what I want in the end. And I will end this thing between us, though it may take longer by necessity. I'm not about to ruin my future at St. John's with a sexual-harassment lawsuit. This breakup must be handled with the proverbial kid gloves. Dammit all to hell! I knew this had gone on for too long. Now look at the mess I've created.

I change clothes at The Drunken Ball and have one drink then head home. I suddenly realize three things. One, the dashboard clock tells me it's already seven thirty. Two, I have to shower and change before meeting Karen at ten o'clock. Three, tomorrow is chock full of surgeries and another after-dinner meeting, then I'm sure I'll have to meet Karen at The Orchid Inn again, just to keep her mouth shut and appease her for a few weeks. Fourth and final, Leena's birthday is in a few days, and if I don't get her something soon, it'll never happen.

I have no idea what to buy her, and I can't go shopping now. I don't have time. I head for home, all the while racking my brain for the perfect gift. Leena always has a book in her hands. When I come home late at night, a book is always lying on her stomach, as she's sound asleep. I have no clue who her favorite authors are. If that makes me an awful person and husband, then I'm terrible. I haven't read a book just for fun since high school.

I'll go home, check in her bedside drawer where she puts the book she's currently reading, then I'll head for the mall for a few minutes to the Barnes & Noble and ask for advice on similar authors, buy her some new novels.

LEENA

I wake up and have no idea what time it is. Joy never goes to bed until late at night, but when I glance at the grandfather clock in the hallway, it's only eight o'clock. Steven told me he'll be having team meetings almost every night until the twins have their surgery, so it looks as if I'll have to pretend to be sound asleep for quite a while.

I imagine he'll get the hint eventually, or I'll finally acquiesce, so as not to have to listen to him sighing and mumbling at my constant rebuffs. Or I could make believe he's Michael, but that idea doesn't appeal to me. When, or if, that ever happens with Michael, I want it to be unique and special and not a re-creation of my nighttime imaginings while I'm having sex with Steven.

After grabbing a glass of sparkling water from the fridge downstairs, I head to the second floor. Along the way, I glance out the windows that line the stairway that look out onto the front porch and curved driveway. Steven's car is in the driveway, but I didn't hear him come inside. Then again, I've been under so much stress, I've been sleeping like the dead. Where is he?

The door to our bedroom is cracked open, as it always is. But a light is on inside, and I didn't leave it on. I'm compulsive about saving electricity. I push the door open slowly with one hand, feeling like I'm in a horror movie, waiting for a monster to jump out. Steven is sitting on my side of the bed. The book I'm currently reading lies next to him on the comforter. He's reading a letter. I suddenly realize it must be the last letter from Michael. Steven has never gone into my bedside table. Ever.

He looks up at me, his face void of expression. "You know Michael Casspi?"

I am gobsmacked. It's the only word that describes my shock. I never dreamed in a million years that Steven would not only look in that drawer, but then take out my book where I placed Michael's letter in the inside cover. It must have slid out, because I had it tucked under the flap at the back of the book.

The look on my face must make it obvious that I have no words. I am so stunned, I stagger to the side and smack into the doorjamb.

"You've been writing to him while he's in prison?"

I open my mouth to answer, but nothing comes out. Do I tell him the truth? Does it matter if I do? If I find out he's sleeping with Karen… well, I've already made up my mind to leave him anyway, even if he'd want to reconcile. I'm tired of being single. A woman alone, with no husband around, is considered single. So I fit that description.

There truly is no need to make up a story to get out of this. I've been writing a friend I made while he's in prison. Is that so wrong? However, I believe Michael signed that letter with I love you, Leena, which makes it nearly impossible for me to tell Steven a story of mere friendship between Michael and me.

I've been found out, and I'm sure my face reveals that anyway.

"What can I say, Steven?"

He stands, raising the letter in his hand, waving it at me. "You've been writing a fucking con at Balmoral State Penitentiary? Have you known this guy from before he was convicted of murdering his wife?"

"Of course not. I'd never heard of him before."

He waves the letter back and forth, again and again. "Then what the hell is going on here, Leena?"

"Long story short, I—"

"I want the entire story. Not the abbreviated version."

"Okay." I suddenly feel as if all the energy in my body has seeped out of every single pore. I slide my back down the wall until I'm sitting on the carpet with my knees bent under my chin. "A few months ago, I discovered a website called PrisonersNeedFriendsToo through Joy's high school. One of the students got caught selling marijuana, and there was a gun in the trunk of his car. He was eighteen and ready to graduate, and they tried him as an adult. Joy and I both made it a point to find out where they took him. I felt sorry for him, a young kid in such a community with hard-core prisoners. The PrisonersNeedFriendsToo website cited that research shows inmates who have contacts outside of prison are less likely to return to prison. We got his inmate number from his mom, and Joy and I sent him a Christmas card."

"What the hell does that have to do with Michael Casspi?"

I take in a huge breath to calm my nerves. "I was lonely, Steven, okay? I have no other excuse. I'm sick of being lonely. I wanted someone to communicate with. And it sounded like a safe way to do that with another adult. It's not as if I went to a bar to find some man to have sex with.

"The Balmoral State Penitentiary website hadn't been completely integrated into the ProsonersNeedFriendsToo system, so there were no details regarding the prisoners except their first name and whether the prisoner was interested in receiving correspondence from an outsider who wanted to be their pen pal. There was no other information from my end either. I signed my letters with an A for Annaleena."

He walks toward me and wafts the letter in front of my face. "Then why does it say Michael Casspi on the corner? And why is it addressed to Leena Coughlin? And why does he say at the bottom that he loves you? It's obvious you know each other pretty intimately."

"After we started writing letters, the two computer systems finally became integrated, but that wasn't until recently."

He smirks, and goose bumps pop up along my arms. He looks like a madman, and he's scaring me. I've seen Steven angry before, but nothing like this.

"You know he's getting out soon, don't you, Leena?"

I nod.

"Very soon." He chuckles, and he sounds like a crazy person.

"And I told you about Casspi's involvement in the twins' surgery. I demand to know why you didn't say something then that you knew him, if it's all so innocent."

I shake my head, back and forth, back and forth. "Steven, please." I push my back even harder against the wall. I look through his legs at the bed. I don't want to look at his face, see his eyes. I know it will scare me, and I don't want to show fear.

"You're awfully quiet, Leena. You're not saying much. Cat got your tongue?"

"I believe his release date is coming up in four weeks."

He grins. "Ah, she speaks. The cat hasn't gotten your tongue. Or are you saving your tongue for other things when you're not here, Leena?"

There's no way Steven could have found out I visited Michael. Twice. I told no one. "What are you talking about?"

"You remember who I called to help us find Joy?"

I suddenly recall Steven is friends with San Francisco's police commissioner. A freezing coldness begins in my chest and spreads down my arms and legs. I know what he's going to say before he speaks the words.

"One phone call to Mark, Leena, and I can find out if you've visited Balmoral State Penitentiary."

My hands are so very cold, and I rub them up and down my legs to warm them. I don't know if I should lie or tell the truth. I realize I'm being ridiculous. Of course Steven will find out about my visits. It's useless to deny it now, when he'll discover the truth soon enough. He's resourceful and relentless, both qualities that have served him well in his quest to be the best cardiac surgeon in California and perhaps around the world.

I look him in the eyes, not wanting to appear afraid of his reaction. What I'd like to do is throw his affair with Karen in his face, but I don't know the truth about that yet. Grayson Randall hasn't gotten back to me.

"Yes, I visited him."

"How many times, Leena?"

I shake my head. This is ridiculous. How dare he interrogate me about my whereabouts when I am absolutely sure he's cheating on me, if not with Karen then someone else? There have been too many nights when he arrives home at two or three in the morning for me not to be suspicious. And it irks me that he thinks I'm that gullible and stupid to fall for his incessant excuses. That he's been at meetings that run far into the night.

"Twice. I visited him two times. We're friends, Steven. I'm not having sexual intercourse in the visiting room at Balmoral Penitentiary, for God's sake."

"Still cheating in my book, Leena. What else do you call seeing another man behind your husband's back?"

I'm gritting my teeth so hard, my temples throb, trying my best to keep my mouth shut. Not only do I not want to incite more of his anger, I want proof before I reveal my hand. If he knows I'm having him watched, he'll change his behavior. If I confront him now about Karen, he'll deny it. Steven is a master manipulator. He'll definitely concoct some story about what he does during his free time, and it will not be an admission of being guilty of infidelity. Until I have solid proof of Steven's infidelity, I am not going to accuse him right now of fucking around behind my back with my best friend.

"I told you, I was lonely. I am lonely. I have no one to talk to. I need companionship, Steven, and I haven't gotten that from you in years."

"There are plenty of women you've met at various functions. You could go to lunch, dinner, play tennis, do whatever you choose. You're gregarious enough, Leena. You could have many female friends to fill all the free time you have on your hands."

"That's not what I'm talking about, and you know it."

"So you don't deny you're looking for male companionship. I can read between the lines, Leena. You're wanting an affair. It's just that it hasn't progressed that far yet. Deny it. I dare you."

I remain silent, refusing to take the bait. Somehow,

he's managed to make me out to be the bad guy here. Talk about the pot calling the kettle black. No, I don't have proof of his continual infidelity, but I'm sure of it. The clock is ticking. I just have to wait to sound the alarm.

"Deny it!" he shouts.

Steven never raises his voice. He always speaks in a controlled, subdued manner. But for some reason, this time, he's as angry as I've ever seen him. He obviously doesn't feel guilty about anything he's done behind my back. Can he really be taking his vows seriously? Maybe he's not having an affair after all. Which would make his anger at my behavior completely understandable. But I don't believe that for a second.

"Steven, please lower your voice. Joy's sleeping."

He grabs my forearm and yanks me into a standing position.

The look on his face is frightening. His eyes are wide, and he's staring at me as if he doesn't know who I am, like I'm an alien.

"You're hurting me. Let me go. What's gotten into you?"

"Mom?"

I whip around. Joy is standing outside the door to our bedroom, which has been open the entire time. Did she hear our entire discussion or just a part of it? Joy is going through enough emotional turmoil right now. She doesn't need this added stress and worry. She already thinks she's the cause of her parents' arguments and that if she weren't around, Steven and I would either work out our problems or divorce and be happier apart. I need to diffuse this situation immediately, before Joy tumbles into a more depressive state than she is now.

I walk to her and curl my arm around her shoulders,

look her in the eyes. "I'm sorry, honey. Your father and I didn't mean to wake you up."

"I wasn't asleep."

I pull her along with me down the hall to her room.

She stops and turns toward me, eyes glistening. "What's going on, Mom?"

"I—"

"Are you having an affair?"

"No, of course I'm not having an affair. But your father—"

She's shaking her head. "I'm not a baby, Mom. I heard Dad say he can read between the lines. That you're wanting an affair, but it hasn't progressed that far. He yelled, 'Deny it.' I heard him, Mom."

Now tears are streaming down her face, and she looks so bereft, as if her world is coming to an end.

And it's in my hands to fix this. I'm her mother, and I will not let Steven's shouting nor his angry words tear my baby's world apart when it's not true. I am not having an affair, yet. It's highly likely it will happen eventually, but right now I've fallen out of love with Steven and in love with another man. However, until I hear from Grayson and sit down and discuss our marriage with Steven, it's all speculation.

"I am not having an affair, Joy."

"Then why'd he say that? You must have done something to make him think that."

I grasp Joy's hand, bring her into her bedroom, and we sit on the edge of her bed. I turn to her and take both her hands in mine, look her in the eyes. "Joy, I'm going to be honest with you. I was writing to a man in prison through PrisonersNeedFriendsToo. Remember when we did that for your friend at school?"

She nods.

"I thought it would be a nice thing to do. This man, Michael, and I have become friends. That's all. I am not having an affair. But your father doesn't believe me."

"Why would you do that? Why would you write to another man like that?"

I close my eyes for a few seconds, vacillating. Should I tell her more of the story? Would it be fair to her to be that honest, given all she's dealing with right now? She hates being treated like a baby. I get that. But right now she's just as fragile as an infant. I must be a responsible parent. At this time, Joy needs to be treated carefully, even delicately, so she can make it through this difficult time in her life and come out on the other side, alive and strong.

"Joy, I want you to listen to me. I wrote to Michael for the exact same reason you wrote to that young boy from your school. Remember how on the PrisonersNeedFriendsToo website it said that research showed inmates who establish and maintain positive contacts outside of prison walls are less likely to return to prison? That they're less likely to return to crime and substance abuse and are more likely to find employment and remain productive members of society? I wanted to help someone, just like you wanted to help your friend, feel connected to his normal life. That is exactly why I wrote Michael. We're friends. That's all we are."

"So what Dad says can't be true, right? 'Cause this guy's in prison."

I nod. "That's right, honey. I cannot have an affair with a man who's locked up in prison far, far away from here. I don't blame your father for being jealous. Not to sound too sexist, but it's a typical male response. And your father didn't know all the facts. I was trying to make him understand, and he—"

"He wasn't listening to you." Joy pauses. "Typical," she whispers, her head angled down. She's shaking her head.

I tip her chin up with my finger. "Please don't worry about your father and me, Joy. As soon as I straighten this whole thing out with him, he'll understand. He's tired, and he's stressed out." I smile, stare into her eyes. "Everything will work out, don't worry. Okay?"

She nods again.

"I want to get back to your father, finish up our discussion. You're going to be all right?"

"I'm okay. Go. I'm really tired."

I take her face in my hands and kiss her on the forehead. "I love you, Joy."

"Love you, too, Mom," she mutters.

JOY

I guess I believe Mom. I mean, I've heard them arguing a gazillion times before. Mostly about how he's never home and shit. Mom yells at him about how he doesn't spend any time with me. He mumbles that he works all the time to support his family, yada, yada. Nothing I haven't heard since I was in high school.

Daddy never yells, though. But I mean, they're married. Parents yell at each other all the time. It's not that weird. Mom's usually the one who raises her voice. Dad's quiet, and most of the time, Mom's shouting at him to please talk to her 'cause he doesn't say anything.

What pisses me off most is, how can he be all angry at Mom even if she is having an affair? He's probably been fucking around on her for years. Since that time I saw him with that chick. He probably never stopped. Why should he? Mom obviously didn't know about that, so he must be hella good at keeping that shit a secret. He's always telling her that his hours are so long, and he makes up this shit about surgeries and meetings. But, come on! Surgeries in the middle of the night? Meetings at two in the morning? What a crock.

So what if Mom's writing to some dude in prison? It sure as hell isn't as bad as what Dad's done. Nothing wrong with trying to help out somebody who probably won't ever

217

see the outside of the prison walls. Getting a letter from the outside probably makes him feel more human.

Which isn't how I feel anymore. Like a human, that is. These drugs make me so tired all the time and kinda lethargic. I don't wanna do homework, and when I open a book, it's like I can't read the print. I mean, I can read it, but the meaning of every sentence is kinda fuzzy. I feel like jumping off the bridge, but I don't have the energy to even drive there right now. I really don't give a shit about anything anymore.

I don't care if I go to school. I don't care if I make friends. Nothing's that important. I watch TV and fall asleep. I pick up a book, then I realize I have no idea what's going on in the story. My brain feels like it's filled with that pink cotton candy they sell at the fairgrounds.

Whatever's happening right now with Mom and Daddy, it's all bullshit. Should I go back to bed? Has Daddy gone maniac, thinking he can have affairs but Mom's a piece of shit because she's sending letters to some dude in prison? Talk about a sexist pig. But Mom said it's nothing for me to worry about, and as far as I know, she's never lied to me. Maybe she's writing to this guy because she's sick of arguing with Daddy about me and my problems.

I don't know what to do, but whatever's going on, it isn't good. Daddy yelling? Then Mom's being all nicey-nicey? I'm so damn tired I can't keep my eyes open.

But Mom wasn't screaming this time. So maybe it isn't as bad as all that. Just like she said. Maybe this shit goes on in every marriage. All I know is every fight I've ever heard coming from their bedroom is about me and how Daddy doesn't spend enough time with me... or Mom. No matter what the shrink says about them loving me and that they'd do anything for me and that they want me to be happy and shit, the reality is, I'm the root of the problem in this family. Mom worries about me and what I'm going to do with my life. Daddy ignores me, then gets yelled at by Mom that he's never around for me. Now they're arguing about Mom having a prison pen pal. Argue, argue, argue. And it all stems from them arguing about me in the first place.

Shit. I really am the cause of all the problems in this family.

If I wasn't around, maybe they'd get along. Or hell, maybe they'd get divorced and find somebody else who makes them happy. If I wasn't around, for damn sure they wouldn't have to worry about me anymore. If I wasn't here, they wouldn't be disappointed at how I've turned out to be a boring nobody with no friends and no boyfriend, who can't cut it at freaking junior college and will never be a doctor like Daddy, or beautiful and likable like Mom.

Fuck it!

I check my phone for the BART and bus schedules. It would be easier to sneak out tomorrow morning, when I'm supposedly sleeping or doing computer work in my bedroom. I keep telling Mom I'm feeling better, so she won't have to sit at home all day babysitting her nineteen-year-old daughter. But I don't feel better. In fact, I feel worse than I have in months. Too much shit is going on inside me and all around me. I hate it. I hate me. I hate life.

I jump into bed and pull the covers over my head. I am so, so, so sick of feeling this way. I just want it to stop. And all these meds do is make me slow and fuzzy. I don't wanna be here.

Whatever.

LEENA

I shut Joy's bedroom door, and when I return to our bedroom, Steven is gone. To be honest, it would be easy for him never to come home. There are rooms for surgeons to sleep in at the hospital, because they often have back-to-back surgeries and need to rest. He had a newly pressed suit hanging over a chair in our bedroom. He eats either at the hospital cafeteria or at nearby restaurants. He doesn't need to come home to shower or dress. They have staff facilities for that.

I realize I have no one to talk to about what just happened. Steven is so angry about me corresponding with Michael. I'm hoping he doesn't do anything to sabotage Michael's release from Balmoral. It's too late to phone the prison today. And I'm just so exhausted from this argument. I don't want Steven to ruin Michael's future reputation at the hospital because Michael will save hundreds of lives each year. I pray Steven doesn't take his anger out on Michael because I befriended him while he was in prison.

I feel as if I've been working out in the weight room at the gym, and I'm exhausted. I grab my book and a second comforter. I'm freezing, and my teeth are chattering. It must be the stress. And now Joy's heard Steven accusing me of having an affair. Naturally, she's wondering what's going on between her parents.

I snuggle under the covers with my knees cocked and my book pressed against my legs. But all I can think of is Joy's reaction to what she's heard.

The words blur before my eyes, because I'm crying again. This is all so, so wrong. I can tell when Steven's pissed off by his eyes. His eyes get so intense, as if he can see right through me. He knew every question to ask to get the truth out of me, too. But he didn't look hurt. He was just horribly angry. Livid. He'd always exhibited jealousy since I'd known him, but this… this was rage caused by jealousy that I was "seeing" another man. Not that I slept with him, but that I wrote to him and visited him two times. In Steven's mind, I was unfaithful. Period.

Which reminds me of a line in one of Shakespeare's plays: Ay, there's the rub. Is a person unfaithful simply by wanting another man? Or is someone unfaithful only if they've had some sort of physical contact with someone other than their husband? And by physical contact, does that include kissing and touching each other with your clothes still on? Or is a person unfaithful only if you have sex with a person other than your spouse?

If I found out that Steven kissed another woman, I would be upset, and we'd have quite an argument, perhaps see a therapist, work on why he did it. But if I discover he's been sleeping with another woman? That… that I cannot forgive. There's no way I'd get past the fact if Steven's had intercourse with someone other than me, if Grayson discovers that is what's been going on.

But for Steven? Perhaps he draws a different line. I have no idea what his thoughts are regarding infidelity. Now I realize it's a discussion every couple should have before they say I do. It's similar to whether you want to have children. It should be talked about beforehand. You shouldn't wait until one or the other of you does something outside the realm of what is typically "normal" married behavior to have a discussion about the meaning of infidelity.

All this pondering has made me dizzy. I place my book on the bedside table and am about to turn off the lamp when my phone beeps.

A text from Grayson Randall.

If you're awake, call me. If you get this in the morning, call me.

On one hand, I am completely drained after what just happened, and the only person I want to talk to is Michael. But I know I can't turn off my speculation about Grayson's text, so I phone him immediately.

"Mr. Randall? It's Leena Coughlin."

"Please call me Grayson, Leena. Considering I'm investigating the intimate details of your personal life, I'm comfortable with you calling me by my first name."

"You're right. Did you find out anything?"

"My first request? Don't shoot the messenger."

My chest feels as if someone's pressing down on it with a brick. Even though Steven and I just had a huge, unresolved argument, I guess my subconscious knows I still care about him. I'll be hurt and disappointed if he's been leading a double life that doesn't include me. I've stood by that man's side since we met.

"I don't own a gun, Grayson, so don't worry about me shooting you."

"Good to know. It just so happens I followed your husband from the hospital to your house. I saw him leave a little while ago. I'm parked in front of The Orchid Inn right now. He entered the inn about ten minutes ago. Right now, I'm watching your friend Karen get out of her car. She's walking into the lobby of the inn. Hold on."

I hear him shuffling around.

"Sorry, had to get my binoculars. I saw your husband check in after he arrived. Karen's at the front desk now. Wait. She's walking to the elevators. She didn't get anything out of her purse, so she didn't pay any money for a room. The restaurant and bar are on the first floor, so she must be going up to someone's room."

I close my eyes, and disappointment seeps out of my pores. At least, that's what it feels like. Disappointment. I'm sweating now. A moment ago, I was freezing to death.

"Are you still there, Leena?"

"Yes, I'm still here. I want proof, Grayson. I want pictures."

"So you told me. And I'll get them. Trust me. You paid for proof of his infidelity, and I'll get that for you. I promise. But as soon as I find anything out, I always call my clients to make sure they want me to continue the investigation. For some clients, what I just told you is enough. But don't worry, if the two of them have any pattern at all to their meeting up, I'll find out. And I'll provide you with pictures to back it up."

"That's what I want. And thank you for being so diligent. I appreciate it. You're fast."

"I aim to please. Your husband made it easy. And like I said, I'll get you your proof."

"I can't wait. Good night, Grayson. And thank you."

I end the call and stare at the wall across from me. I quit my job to support Steven in his career. I've been the perfect surgeon's wife. I've attended all the functions and parties and meetings. I've volunteered on hospital committees, opened my house to other surgeons' wives. I changed my life to suit his.

And this is what I get in return for supporting him and standing by his side all these years?

He is not getting away with a slap on the wrist.
I will make him pay.

MICHAEL

The clanging metal of the door to my cell wakes me from a dead sleep. It can't be seven thirty yet, because outside the tiny window across from me, it's pitch black.

"Wake up, Casspi."

I sit up, a bit disoriented. Nothing goes on around here when it's dark. Not in the early morning nor in the evening. I've always thought it has something to do with the ease of escape or hiding something that could be construed as a weapon. The lyrics "darkness, darkness, be my pillow" by the Youngbloods hovers in the recesses of my brain.

"I said, get up. Gotta get going."

I stand and run my hands through my hair, blink several times. "What's going on? What time is it?"

Gifford, the guard nearest me, has always treated me like a human being. He's asked me questions about his wife, who has heart disease. I've been happy to answer them. We're not friends, of course, but we have a connection.

Gifford smiles. "Time for you to get the hell outta this shithole." He dangles a pair of handcuffs in front of me.

I automatically turn and clasp my hands behind my back. He places the cuffs around my wrists, squeezes them to make sure they're locked, then turns me around by my shoulders, looks me in the eyes.

"Don't think for a minute the guards are ignorant. We

know what's goin' on in this place, even if the warden tries to keep it a secret."

"What're you talking about? What did I do wrong? I'm a model prisoner, Gifford, and you know it."

"Yup, tha's true, buddy boy. Tha's true." He smiles.

The other guard, whom I've seen only a few times in the cafeteria, grabs my right arm and pulls me out of the cell, then gives me a light push.

I start walking in the opposite direction of the cafeteria. They must be taking me to the administration building. But at this hour of the morning? This whole thing is making me suspicious. Guys have disappeared around here, never to be heard from again. And the guards are so uncommunicative. Mostly, they don't talk to us, only to other employees.

I turn my head, and Gifford remains standing in front of my cell, still with that smile on his face. I don't get it. Something's going on, and there's no good reason for me to see the warden at this time of the morning.

After passing through numerous locked doors and walking through endless hallways, the guard brings me to, yep, the warden's chambers, shoves me down in the chair near the door to the warden's office, then stands across the room, watching me.

The warden's secretary, Annette, glances at me and nods, then continues typing on her computer. Why the heck is she here at this time? I'm sure office hours are eight to five.

Her phone buzzes, and she picks it up, listens for a second, then replaces the receiver. "He'll see you now, Mr. Casspi."

I glance up at the guard, who is already crossing the room toward me. He grasps my upper arm as I stand, then he opens the warden's office door and pulls me along with him, leading me to the front of the warden's desk.

Warden Shiffman is sitting in his swivel chair behind a huge oak desk that looks to be eight feet wide. He's a pleasant but plain-looking man, not intimidating in looks or demeanor. But from what I've heard from other inmates, he carries a big stick and knows how to use it. At least that's the scuttlebutt in this place. He's a by-the-books kind of guy, and rules are not to be broken, ever, or in Warden Shiffman's exact words, "There will be hell to pay."

I stand, until I'm told to do otherwise. I'm a model prisoner. The moment I arrived at Balmoral, I was told, "Don't give 'em anything to bitch about and keep your trap shut." And so I have.

"You may be seated, Mr. Casspi."

I lower myself into a hard wooden chair with no cushion, keeping my back straight and tall. "Thank you, Warden Shiffman." They also said to always be polite and address the warden as if he's the president of the United States. So I do.

He leans back, elbows on the arms of his chair, fingertips touching the underside of his chin. He swivels the chair side to side.

"Know why you're here, Mr. Casspi?" he says with a smile, though it looks more like a smirk.

I clear my throat and sit up straighter. "No, Warden Shiffman. I have no idea."

His right eyebrow twitches upward. "Really."

"Is this about my release date? Has it been changed?" My stomach churns, though it's empty. No snacks allowed in your cell, and it's almost breakfast time.

He nods and keeps on nodding while he says, "Yes, the date's been changed, Mr. Casspi."

I remain silent. He'll tell me what's going on when he's damn good and ready, and I don't want to antagonize him by pushing for an answer.

"It's today," he says, lowering his hands to the desk blotter, then he folds them, looking like a kid in first grade.

"What is today, sir?"

Once again, that same eyebrow shifts upward. "Don't play dumb with me, Mr. Casspi."

"I'm not playing dumb, Warden Shiffman. I'll admit I spoke with a Dr. Stephanie Yates. She said she wants to reinstate my medical license for a surgery at St. John's Hospital in San Francisco. But I haven't heard anything. I know the wheels of the law turn slowly, so I'm not expecting to hear anything until after my release."

He shakes his head, then pulls a file from the stack lying on the desk, places it in front of him, and opens it. After he looks down at it, he reads, "It has been adjudicated that as of this day," he glances up at me, "today, Mr. Casspi," then he returns to reading the file, "Mr. Michael J. Casspi shall herein be released under the supervision of Dr. Stephanie A. Yates of St. John's Hospital in San Francisco, California. Michael J. Casspi has from this day forward been reinstated by the Medical Board of the state of California to practice medicine in the state of California as adjudicated by His Honor Judge Bartholomew Hillyard. Said medical license is formally and absolutely valid as of this day, and Michael J. Casspi may begin the practice of a medical doctor immediately and forthwith. In addition, Michael J. Casspi shall as of this day be released from Balmoral State Penitentiary to Dr. Stephanie A. Yates and is heretofore a free man."

He closes the file and leans back in his chair.

Tears creep behind my eyelids, and I want to burst out crying. She did it. Dr. Stephanie Yates did everything she told me she'd do. I thought at first it was possibly all a scam, though she sounded serious enough. When I looked her up in the library, she turned out to be real. Then Leena verified her as an important person at St. John's, and that's when I let a teensy bit of hope pop into my heart. Still, I didn't imagine this ever happening.

There was a part of me that believed her and hoped and prayed this would happen. The other part thought it was all a terrible hoax. There are a lot of people out there who were outraged at my act of assisted suicide, and I wouldn't have put it past any of them to pull a sick prank by dangling the possibility of an early release with a reinstated medical license in front of my face, then pull it away as a huge joke.

He starts swiveling back and forth in his chair again. "Don't you have anything to say, Mr. Casspi?"

I swallow past the lump in my throat and open my mouth, but I don't know what to say. Do I thank him? He seems displeased at this chain of events. Does he have any say in what is happening to me right now, or are his hands tied? My guess is he's against it, but was voted down.

"Thank you, Warden Shiffman. I appreciate you telling me this. I'm happy about this, naturally."

He looks me straight in the eyes. "I would imagine you are." He stands and lifts his chin toward the guard standing at the side of the room.

The guard takes hold of my upper arm again and guides me out of the room, down an extremely long, dimly lit hallway with nothing but closed doors. We are alone, and the sound of our feet on the buffed linoleum echoes off the walls.

At the end of the hall is a set of double doors. When we reach them, he stops, and still holding tightly to my upper arm, I notice him look up at a camera hanging from a corner in the ceiling. The doors whoosh open, and I am met by two guards I've never seen before.

One guard hands me a bag and points to a room across the way. "You can get dressed in there. Leave all prison garb, including shoes, socks, and underwear in the bin inside the room. We'll wait for you."

I do as she says and go into what appears to be a dressing room in any store I've been in. There's a mirror on one wall. I open the plastic bag and take out a folded pair of jeans, a white T-shirt, a pair of boxers, a pair of black socks, and a pair of shoes in my size. After I dress, I throw my prison clothes into the bin and stare at myself in the mirror.

I close my eyes for a few seconds.

If this is a two-way mirror, I'm sure they've seen this many times before. I am being released. And the elation I feel, I will hold inside until I pass through the prison gates, and this place is truly and literally behind me.

After returning to the other room, a guard points me in the direction of another door. He walks behind me, down an extremely long hallway to another set of double doors. They whoosh open when we get within a few feet of them, and he escorts me down an outdoor tunnel made of cyclone fencing, at the end of which is a multi-bolted door that opens after the guard keys in numerous numbers on a keypad. Outside this door, there is nothing but a desolate-looking, dirt-covered area about one hundred feet wide and one hundred feet across. On the far side is a parking lot. Several cars line the side facing me.

I hear the door close behind me and turn. The guard

has left me with not one word having been spoken between us. I look back at the cars, and a tall, graceful woman of about forty years old, dressed in a prim and proper dark blue suit and white blouse, walks over to me and stretches out her hand.

"I'm Dr. Stephanie Yates. You must be Dr. Michael Casspi."

I want to hug her and cry for everything she must have done to orchestrate my release. But I have to remember who I am now and who I'm going to be—Dr. Michael Casspi, cardiac surgeon at St. John's Hospital of San Francisco.

I smile and reach out and shake her hand. "It's a pleasure to meet you, Dr. Yates."

LEENA

It took me forever to fall asleep. My heart continued to beat erratically for about an hour. At one point, I contemplated driving myself to the ER, but then I recalled when Jack Nicholson in the movie Something's Gotta Give thinks he's having a heart attack, but it's actually a panic attack brought on by stress. I try to ohm myself into a calm state.

The next I know, I am awake, and it's nine o'clock in the morning. I never sleep this late. When I walk downstairs, Joy isn't in the kitchen, so she's either still sleeping, which isn't that odd, given the new meds she's taking, or she's on her computer doing homework.

I need to shower and wake up, because my mind is fuzzy. My hands are still shaking, my ears ringing. After standing under the shower head with the hot spray prickling my skin for thirty minutes, I exit and wrap myself in a fluffy towel. I'm feeling more awake and ready to face the day.

Though I don't have the physical proof of Steven's infidelity, I have complete faith in Grayson Randall. He'll get me the photos of Steven and Karen. I just have to wait it out for, hopefully, only a few more days. Then I'll confront Steven, tell him I want a divorce. I'm equally sure Grayson Randall has the name of an attorney who handles divorces, since he told me a majority of his clients are just like me. What a sad state of affairs. And what a sad pun on marriage in America.

My phone beeps while I'm dressing, but I don't recognize the number. My brain is still a bit muddled, so I press the talk button and answer the call.

"Leena? It's Michael."

Dropping down onto the bed, I shut my eyes, relieved to hear from someone I know who cares about what I'm going through. Michael's been the only person with whom I've shared the loneliness of my marriage as well as my deepest fears concerning Joy's suicidal tendencies. He's probably the closest person I have in my life right now.

"I thought an operator had to call and ask if I'll accept a collect call. What's going on?"

"I'm at St. John's Hospital right now. I'd like to see you. Is there somewhere we can meet?"

"Wait. What are you talking about?" I stand and begin pacing the room. "Are you out of prison? What the hell is happening?"

He chuckles, and I can see him in my mind's eye, and I smile.

"Stephanie Yates is a miracle worker. I got out early this morning. She found me a place to stay for a month, a rental house near the hospital. I met up with her for an hour or so, but she wants to integrate me into today's meeting on the twins' surgery. So I'm free until I meet up with her and the team after lunch."

"Oh, my God. Are you on cloud nine? Michael, you're free! And you get to practice medicine! I'm so happy for you. Congratulations!"

"Thank you. But, Leena, the best part is, you and I can meet. And we won't have to sit across from each other in the prison visiting room with a guard watching our every move." He pauses for a few seconds.

A wall of silence separates us, and I don't know how to fill it.

"I'm sorry," he says. "I've just made the biggest assumption in the world, and I apologize. I want to see you, Leena, but that doesn't mean you feel the same way. I should never have assumed—"

"Stop, Michael. It's just… something happened with Steven that… that I want to talk to you about. And I also heard from Grayson Randall."

"Oh. Wow. Well, can you come to my house? We can have breakfast, talk. Stephanie made sure the refrigerator is fully stocked, and there's a great espresso machine. I might not know how to use it, but—"

I burst out laughing. He sounds like a little kid in a candy store.

"What's so funny?" he says.

"I can't imagine how you must feel after being in prison for five years. It must be an overwhelming high point in your life. You sound so excited."

"The high point will be seeing you, Leena. Do you want to come over?"

"Uh." Suddenly, I start crying. Then I'm sobbing. What the hell will Michael think, hearing me break down on the phone when this is one of the happiest days of his life? He doesn't know what I'm feeling. He has no clue Steven found the letter Michael wrote in which he declared his love for me. He doesn't know my daughter heard her parents arguing and Steven accusing me of having an affair. Joy's living on the edge of disaster already, and last night could contribute to another downward spiral.

Of course I want to see Michael, but at the same time, a part of me wants to curl up in bed and sleep. It's taking all my inner strength to move forward, erase the night like chalk from a blackboard. But it's so fresh, and it's so hard. I'm so disappointed to find out Steven's been cheating, disappointed that my husband of all these years has turned into someone I want to divorce. Who the hell have I been married to and sleeping with for twenty years?

"Leena, what's wrong? Is it me? Am I pushing too hard? Because we can wait to see each other. Take all the time you need. I know you weren't expecting me to get out so soon. I'll understand if—"

"It has nothing to do with you, Michael. I do want to see you. I'll explain it all then."

"But you're crying. You don't sound like it's because you're happy to see me."

"I'm sorry. I don't want to put a damper on this day for you." I swipe the tears from my cheeks and take a big, deep breath. "You know what? It'll be refreshing to not be inside that dreadfully depressing visitors' room at the prison. I want to help you celebrate your freedom."

"Are you sure?"

"Yes. Seeing you will make me feel better. Talking to you will do me a lot of good. So text me your address."

"Okay. If you're sure. We'll talk about whatever's bothering you at that time. So, when can you be here?"

I glance at the clock. "Give me a half hour? I have to talk to Joy first. I think it will probably be okay to leave her here alone for just a short while. She keeps telling me not to be such a helicopter mom, that she's feeling better and that she and her therapist have actually Skyped a few times when Joy was feeling bad. The medication is making her so tired, all she wants to do is sleep. And last night didn't do her any good. But let me talk to her first. Make sure she's okay this morning. If I can't come see you, I'll call you right back."

"Totally understandable. Go talk to Joy. I'm not going anywhere. And, Leena?"

"Yes?"

"I can't wait to see you."

"Me, too, Michael. Let me talk to Joy first."

"And, Leena?"

"Yes?" I can hear it in his voice. He's smiling.

"I love you."

I take a shuddering breath and smile. "I love you, too." I disconnect the call and finish dressing, then take a look at myself in the mirror and realize that if I can leave and visit with Michael, I want to look special. I had to observe strict prison rules for attire when I went to Balmoral. But that's behind us.

Did I just think us? I stare out the bedroom window at the bright blue San Francisco sky, trying to keep in mind that what happened last night is over. I have to put it away for now and enjoy Michael's freedom. Just for a little while. I want to share that with him. He's been there for me. Something that's been sorely lacking in my relationship with my husband.

"Michael is not Steven," I whisper.

Turning to my clothes, I flip through the hangers, sliding them along the rail until I find the perfect outfit: a pastel pink, cap-sleeve chemise with a slim gold belt. Matching pink, open-toed, sling-back heels complete the look I'm going for—casual yet sophisticated. I don't want to wear pants and a T-shirt to our first meeting outside the prison walls.

I turn this way and that in front of the mirror, checking to see if I'm presentable. Definitely presentable.

I spray a bit of perfume on my wrists and chest, fluff up my hair, then scoot down the hall to Joy's bedroom.

I knock lightly on the door, but she doesn't answer. She's probably asleep, so I gently turn the knob and open the door, popping my head around the side to see if she's still in bed.

She's not in her bedroom.

I check the attached bathroom. Empty. I'm standing in the middle of her room, looking out the window, wondering where she could be. That's when I notice a yellow piece of paper taped to the screen of her computer.

Grabbing the note, I sit and begin reading.

Mom,

I love you. I want you to know that. But I'm so, so tired of fighting this thing. The constant thoughts of wanting to die. Of being a disappointment to you and Daddy. I have no friends. No one will really miss me, but you and maybe Dad. I'm not normal, Mom. Who cries over their father not spending time with them when they're my age? There's obviously something wrong with me. And I can't follow in either of your footsteps. You graduated from UCSF. Daddy's a famous heart surgeon. And I'm flunking out of fucking junior college? And I'm still living at home? I have no one to be my roommate anyway, so I'd have to live alone. And how would I pay for that? I can't find a job. Who'd hire me? Some days I can't even get out of bed. I'd be fired within a week. Isn't this supposed to be the happiest and most exciting time of my life? I'm nineteen. I'm on the precipice of a fantastic future,

Dr. Simbulan tells me. That's what you keep telling me, too. But you know what? How I feel is I'm standing on a precipice, but I just want to jump off so I don't have to feel all this… nothingness. My days are a black void of nothingness. I don't look forward to waking up in the morning. I just want this to be over. It's not your fault, so please don't blame yourself. You've tried to help me out. But I feel I'm a burden to you, and I don't exist for Daddy. What's the point? I don't see a point in staying here. I believe a person has a spirit, so I'll be around, Mom. You just won't be able to see me.

Love you forever, and I'll see you later, just not here,
Joy

I stand up so fast, the chair topples to the floor, but I'm halfway out the door already, running to my bedroom to find my phone.

I press 9-1-2, tears blurring my vision. I delete the numbers and pound in 9-1-1 with my index finger. My hand is shaking so badly, the phone slips to the floor. As I'm reaching to pick it up off the carpet, I hear a female voice.

"911. What's your emergency?"

"I just found a suicide note. My daughter wrote it, but I'm not sure if it was last night or this morning. She's not here and—"

"Ma'am, if at all possible, can you take a deep breath? Can you do that for me?"

"Yes. Yes." I take a breath. "Okay."

"Can you tell me if you know where she's gone?"

"She doesn't say in the letter, but last time, she went

to the Golden Gate Bridge. You've got to send someone there to look for her before she—" I burst into tears and can't talk. They're not going to find her. It's already too late. She probably left in the middle of the night. I should have set an alarm reminder on my phone and checked on her every hour during the night.

"Ma'am, someone is already on the way to the Golden Gate Bridge. I've dispatched police and an ambulance. They should be there within ten minutes."

I'm frantically searching the room, looking for… what?

"My keys. Where's my purse?"

"Ma'am, can you stay on the line, please? I'd like a description of your daughter."

My purse is downstairs on the dining room table, and I race down the stairs, holding the phone to my ear.

"Long, dark brown hair, past her shoulders. Five feet tall. One hundred pounds. Round face with a dimple in her right cheek. I don't know what she's wearing."

I find my purse, grab it, and fly out the door to my car.

"She's done this before?"

"Yes, but I have to go. I'm driving there right now."

"What's your name?"

"Leena. Leena Coughlin. I have to call my husband."

I jump in the Mercedes, and my iPhone syncs with the car. The woman's voice blares through the speakers.

"Ma'am, please stay on the line while I—"

I press the end-call button, then press the Contacts number for Steven's cell phone. It rings and rings until it goes to voice mail.

"Steven, call me immediately. I think Joy's on the way to the Golden Gate Bridge. I'm headed there now. I've already called 911." I end the call.

By now, I'm halfway to the bridge, driving way over the

speed limit. Holding my phone next to the steering wheel so I can see the list of recent calls, I press the number that I didn't recognize this morning when Michael phoned me.

He answers after one ring.

"Leena, are you on your way?"

I'm sobbing and can barely talk, but manage to force out a frantic jumble of words. "I think Joy went to the Golden Gate Bridge. She left me a suicide note. I'm driving there now. Oh, my God, Michael."

"On my way. Park in the lot next to the entrance. I'll meet you."

I cannot believe his words. I can't fucking get in touch with my husband, but Michael's going to drive to the bridge to be there for me.

Flashing lights flicker in my rearview mirror.

"Shit!"

I know I'm driving faster than the twenty-five miles-per-hour speed limit.

"I don't have time for this shit!" I scream.

I slow down, pull to the side of the road. As I open my door to talk to the officer, "Stay inside your vehicle," blares through the noise of cars and trucks passing by.

I slide back into the driver's seat and shut the car door, then look in the side mirror. The officer is walking slowly toward my car, his hand resting on the butt of the gun on his belt.

When he reaches my window, I'm already trying to explain.

"My daughter might be on the Golden Gate Bridge. She's suicidal—"

"License and registration, please."

"Officer, I don't have time for this. My daughter—"

"If you would please hand me your license and

registration, then you can be on your way after I give you a ticket for going seventy miles an hour in a fifty-five miles-an-hour neighborhood."

"You're not listening to me," I shout. "My daughter—"

"Please step out of the car," he says in a monotone.

"What? Why?" I reach my hand toward the glove box for the registration.

He draws his gun with one hand. "Ma'am, please keep your hands on the steering wheel," he says, then presses the finger of his other hand on what looks like a small cell phone attached to his shoulder. "Call for immediate backup. Presidio and Highway 101."

I place my hands on the steering wheel, then press my forehead on the top of my hands and breathe. This is not going well. In fact, this is a goddamn nightmare. Joy may be standing at the railing of the bridge, ready to jump, and I'm dealing with a cop who won't listen to me, and he's now calling for backup. Fuck!

My car is still idling. I put it in gear, then slam my foot on the gas pedal. As the car blasts away, I can hear the officer yelling for me to stop. I swerve out of my lane, hear a honk, then swerve back into my lane and press down harder on the gas pedal.

I'm almost there, but there's so much traffic. I should never have taken this street, but now I'm stuck, waiting, and I can hear a siren behind me and surmise it's the officer I left standing in the street.

The traffic is stop-and-go for blocks and blocks, and it seems as if time has stopped. My heart is pounding in my ears. My mouth is so dry, I can't swallow. My stomach aches. My arms and shoulders and neck are on fire. The tinnitus in my ears is ringing so deafeningly loud, it matches the screaming siren from the police car.

The traffic coming in the opposite direction is minimal, and I swerve into the empty lane, going the wrong way, hoping to find an opening to reenter the lane I should be driving in. Suddenly, several cars are coming toward me, and I hear horns honking, and they swerve around me. I see an opening and cut back into the right lane. The light is yellow, and I slam down on the gas pedal and run it.

I can see the bridge. I can see the parking lot on the right side. I'm almost there, but traffic has come to a dead stop. Flashing lights swirl on five or six police cars parked two hundred or three hundred feet from the entrance to the bridge, which explains the massive pileup of cars.

"Joy!" I scream. "Joy!"

I jam the gear shift into park, leave the car idling, open the car door, and run toward the bridge.

"Joy! Joy!" I'm out of my mind. I know I'm acting like a crazy woman, but my daughter must be on the bridge. Or she's already jumped off.

"Oh, my God! Joy!" I'm running as fast as I can, screaming her name, hoping I'm not too late, knowing I'm too late, praying I'm not.

I get as far as the first police car, and an officer steps toward me, arms outstretched. "You can't be here, ma'am. Please turn around and go back."

"My daughter," I say between gasps. I lean over, hands on my knees, struggling to take in a breath. I look up. That's when I see her. She's straddling the railing of the bridge. "Oh, my God. That's my daughter."

He frowns, turns his head to look behind him, then looks back at me. "What's your daughter's name?"

"Joy. Joy Coughlin. Please. Let me talk to her."

He grasps my forearm and pulls me toward the other police cars.

That's when I see a man, not a police officer, but a man dressed in plain clothes reaching out to Joy.

"Joy!" I shout.

The man holding on to Joy's arm turns in my direction.

It's Michael.

JOY

The water is so freaking far away, but it's beautiful. I always loved the ocean. Mom and Daddy and I used to go to Ocean Beach when I was, like, eight or something. I don't remember. But it was so much fun. Just the three of us.

Before Daddy got all famous. If he wasn't at the hospital, he was probably at that stupid bar with that stupid name with some stupid bimbo, when he could have been home with Mom and me. Mom is so beautiful. Way prettier than I'll ever be. And that time I saw Daddy with that girl, she looked like a fucking skank. Why would he do something like that? He spends his time with some ho-bag, and when he comes home, it's like two or three in the morning and him and Mom end up arguing.

And why was he accusing Mom of having an affair last night? After what he's done at least once and probably hundreds of times? That's such a double standard and so wrong. He's probably been boinking a bunch of lowlifes since the time I saw him with that chick.

So screw him. Spend your free time with someone you just met in a bar instead of coming home to your gorgeous wife and your daughter who you used to say was the light of your life. Now you won't have to worry about a fucking thing about me, 'cause I won't be here.

When I look around, there are people all over the place. There's a line of tourists on this side of the bridge. They aren't speaking English, and everybody's taking pictures of everybody else. I'm freaking having a panic attack. My heart is racing so fast it feels like a hummingbird's inside my chest flapping its wings a million miles an hour. Another bus turns into the parking lot next to the bridge. I'm not too far from the start of the walkway, and people are pouring out of all these buses, marching this way. Unbelievable how many people visit this place.

They're talking and laughing, and the wind is blowing so hard my eyes are watering. When I look around, nobody looks me in the eyes. I'm invisible. Just like I'm invisible everywhere. No difference. No one cares what's going on in my life. And none of these people even notice I'm standing here.

I lean over the railing, and the water looks black. One of my teachers in high school explained it looks like that because it has something to do with the clouds and the light and the bottom of the bay, or something. I don't really remember. It looks like what hell would look like, except it wouldn't be cold in hell. I read that the water under the bridge is fifty-four degrees. Our swimming pool is set at eighty degrees, and sometimes I'm still cold when I'm in the pool.

I wonder if I'm going to hell for jumping off the bridge. When I was in Catholic grammar school, the nuns told us that committing suicide is a mortal sin in the eyes of God. How do they know that? Did someone actually talk to God? Did God appear to somebody once and tell them that killing yourself is a mortal sin? But I don't believe that it is. I'm not a bad person. God wouldn't want me to be sad all the time. It says in the Bible over and over about how happy everyone is who's with God in heaven. If everyone's so happy up there, then why would they begrudge anyone joining them? That would be a pretty selfish thing, right? To let only the people in heaven be happy when lots of us down here are sad? And being selfish is a sin, too. So none of this makes sense.

I look up and see these huge-ass orange metal poles and stuff that make up the bridge. I don't know how high up they go, but there are clouds covering some at the top of the bridge. I guess it's fog. Oh, spires. That's what I think the orange poles are called. So it must be hella high up. What I read is that people who jump off the bridge almost never survive. That's a good thing. I wouldn't wanna be in a coma for the rest of my life, listening to people cry at my bedside, if I could hear them at all, and not being able to move and shit.

It's hard to get my leg over the railing, but I do it as fast as I can, so no one will really notice. When I'm on the other side, I still have to get over to another place where I can stand farther away from the railing. I grab on to this cable thing that's above my head and stretch my foot over to where I can stand up and not bash my head on the metal pole that goes sideways at eye level. Once I get to that place, then I can see pretty easily down to the water, and when I jump, I won't slam into this other steel walkway running lengthwise along the side of the bridge.

That's when I hear the sirens. And people start talking really loud and yelling, "Stop," and too many voices are screaming shit at me, and it just sounds like a bunch of chitchat when you're at a party and the music's too loud and everyone's talking to each other. None of their words makes sense, so I concentrate on looking down at the bay.

I dreamed of this. I mean, I dreamed of the day I'd be standing here. I won't have to ever, ever again feel like I've been feeling for years. It's like the blackness of the Pacific Ocean wants me to join it. The waves are calling to me, but I can't really hear them in my ears. I hear them in my head. They're whispering, "Joy. Joy." And I smile. I want to go there. I want to be where I won't be me anymore. I'll be Not Me. And I've dreamed of being Not Me for a long time.

"Joy!" someone says. It sounds like a man's voice.

The voice didn't come from below me, so I look up.

Everyone's gone. No one's standing on the walkway or near the railing anymore. I can see the undersides of a bunch of police cars, and the lights look like strobe lights at a concert at the Fillmore. Cool.

It's bright out, and I cover my eyes with one hand so I can see. There's a shift in the sun's rays, and that's when I see a man leaning over the railing. It's pretty quiet now, except for the whistling of the wind. But no more tourists are speaking languages I don't understand.

"Joy! Joy!" He's calling my name and waving his hand.

He's a good-looking guy with dark hair and a mustache. But what I see most are his eyes. They remind me of those marbles I used to collect when I was a little girl, sort of a pale blue, sky color.

"You a cop?" I ask him.

He shakes his head and smiles. He's actually a beautiful man. Maybe he's like an angel or something, trying to talk to me about what it's like after I jump off.

"No, I'm not a cop. But I'm a friend of your mom's. My name's Michael."

"You're Michael?"

"You know who I am?"

"My mom and dad were talking about you last night."

"They were?"

"Actually, they were arguing. I should say my dad was yelling and my mom was trying to explain. Wait a minute. Mom said you're in prison."

He laughs. "Your mom wrote to me through PrisonersNeedFriendsToo. Ever heard of that website?"

"Oh, sure. Mom told me all about writing to you. A guy at my school, Buffalo, got busted for selling weed. They put him in jail, and my mom and I wrote him through that website."

"Buffalo? Are you serious? That's his name? Did he ever get out?"

"Yeah. They called him that 'cause he had all this brown, furry-like hair sticking out of the sides of his head, like a buffalo. But he was a cool dude. One of the… no… the only guy who was ever nice to me. He goes to the same jc I go to now. He talks to me sometimes, but I'm not in any of his classes or anything."

"Did he ask you out? You smiled when you said his name."

I laugh for the first time today. "How did you know?"

He shakes his head. "As your generation says all the time, duhhh. You're a beautiful young lady, Joy. Your mom told me what you looked like, and she described you perfectly. You look just like her, as a matter of fact."

As cold as it is standing on this bridge, my face feels hot, and I know I'm blushing. Something I hate to do, but it happens, and I can't stop it. "I'm not near as pretty as Mom. She used to be a model for a while, but she says that was back in the day."

"Well, she's still a beautiful woman, and you look just like her."

"Thanks. So you were in prison, too. What for?"

"My wife was very sick with cancer, and she was going to die in a few weeks. I'm a doctor. I gave her a drug to help her go to sleep forever. So I went to prison for assisting her suicide. Your mom wrote to me, and we became friends through our letters."

"So, you two a couple now or something?"

"Your mom's married."

"That never stopped my dad from… oh, never mind."

"Does your dad have girlfriends on the side?"

I nod.

"And you know this how?"

"I saw him once outside a bar with some chick, making out against the side of her car."

"Did you tell your mom this?"

I shake my head.

"Why not?"

"I didn't want to hurt her feelings. She'd be really sad if she found out Dad's cheating on her. She'd never cheat on him. That's why she was yelling at Daddy last night. 'Cause he thinks she's having an affair with you. She told me all about you. About writing you and stuff. She said you're just friends. Just like you say."

"So you wouldn't want to hurt your mom's feelings, would you?"

"Never. She's a good person. I think she felt sort of neglected all the years Daddy and I were close. But she never said anything. Then when she got busy with committees and stuff, I was pissed off that she wasn't around for me. Then I thought about it and realized I wasn't there for her either. I never asked her to go with me on school trips or whatever. When my dad didn't have the time anymore, I never asked Mom to take his place."

"She would have gone with you, you know."

"Yeah, she probably would have."

"Joy, you know your mom's told me you're her life. Do you know that?"

I shake my head.

"She said she wouldn't want to live if something happened to you."

"No, she didn't."

"Yes, she did. I swear on my own life she did. She loves you. And you know something else, Joy? When you become a mother yourself, you'll understand what it means to have a child. You change your entire life to spend time with your kid and raise her, giving her everything you might not have had as a child yourself, trying your best to make sure your child is always happy and never sad. She wants you to be happy. When you're happy, she's happy. If anything happened to you, Joy, your mom would never live another day without being sad. Believe me, I know."

"How would you know?"

"Because not only did your mom tell me, but I lost my brother. He was depressed, wouldn't take his medication, and he killed himself."

"How'd he do it?"

"He shot himself in the head with a rifle. I found him. And not a day goes by that I don't think about him, and I cry about it, wondering if I could have done something to help him not be so depressed. And my mom killed herself two years later. She couldn't live with the grief. She blamed herself for not knowing my brother was as depressed and suicidal as he turned out to be."

"Are you telling me Mom might kill herself if I jump?"

"Joy, I haven't known your mom that long. We're kind of like acquaintances and not yet friends like she is with, who is it, Karen?"

"Yeah."

"I know you think what's going on in your life now is going to be like this forever. But I promise you, it will change, Joy. With the right meds and the right therapist, you'll look back on today and wonder how you ever decided you wanted to jump into that water. I wish I would have been able to tell my brother that, but it was too late by the time I found him. He could have gotten through it. And so can you."

"But I've been depressed for years. I'm tired of it. And Mom should have a daughter who doesn't make her worry all the time, and now she has to stay home to make sure I don't kill myself."

"It won't be that way forever, Joy. Think of the future. You can have a good life, when you get past this point that now seems like forever. When you're twenty or thirty or forty years old, you'll look back and think, 'God, that was so long ago. I was really sad back then.' You'll be glad you stuck it out. You'll have a husband and kids and a dog. Your life is waiting, Joy. And your mom wants to share your life with you, too. Do this for yourself and your mom... and your dad, Joy." He stretches out his hand. "Please, trust me. And I promise, if you ever feel this bad again, all you have to do is call me. Any time. Any hour of the day."

"You love her, don't you?"

"Your mom?"

I nod.

"I love your mom. We're just friends, but I love her. She's a kind, generous, thoughtful, bright woman. And you're just like her, Joy. And someday you'll find someone who'll love you for all the wonderful qualities that make you Joy. And I promise you'll look back on this day and you'll be glad you didn't jump. Here." He reaches out even farther, stretching his torso over the railing until his fingertips are right in front of my face.

I love my mom. And Daddy, too. In philosophy class, the teacher talked about how everything in life is ephemeral and that when you think life is going to be a certain way, if you wait a few seconds or days or months, it's pretty much guaranteed it'll change. Maybe this guy Michael is right. If I look at my life as ever changing, there's no reason to expect that it'll remain the same, because nothing's static.

And if I jump and Mom kills herself 'cause she feels like she's to blame? I wouldn't want that to happen. Since Daddy's been cheating on her, she deserves better than suddenly having no husband and no daughter. And this guy Michael could be my stepdad someday, for all I know. And he promised me, to my face, that he'd be there for me if I need him, something Daddy's never said before. Daddy breaks all his promises, to me and to Mom, because I hear what he tells her, and none of it ever happens.

I shut my eyes and suddenly feel dizzy and sway.

Then someone grabs my hand, and that steadies me.

I open my eyes and see the blue marbles from when I was a kid. Michael's eyes. They're so beautiful. They look like the sky.

Michael smiles at me, and I squeeze his hand.

He reaches down and grabs my other hand.

He pulls me toward him so I can step up over the metal bar to the platform under the railing, then I put my arms around his neck, and he walks backward and pulls me over the railing to solid ground.

I hear clapping in the distance, but I'm clinging to him so tightly, my ear is plastered against his chest and the wind is blowing, so the clapping seems far, far away. With my eyes closed, I wish like when I'm blowing out a birthday candle that my life will be better soon. Or someday at least.

Someone else wraps their arms around me and leans their chest on my back, then Mom whispers in my ear, "You're alive. My baby, I love you. You're alive."

LEENA

Before I have time to talk to Joy, a man dressed in a suit, his sunglasses propped on his head, approaches us.

"I'm sorry to interrupt, but are you Joy Coughlin?"

Joy nods, tears running down her cheeks, mascara smudged beneath her eyes. She looks like one of those Goth chicks running around the campus at Cal-Berkeley.

"I'm Detective Ramsey. We have to escort you to the ambulance located just behind me." He turns and points to the bright red San Francisco Fire Department ambulance, flashing lights pulsing on the top and sides.

I curl my arm around Joy's shoulders and bring her body as close to mine as possible. "What for? She's not hurt."

"Your daughter, right?"

I nod. "Yes."

"It's been determined that Joy is a harm to herself. Have you heard of a 51/50?"

"Yes. She was in a psychiatric hospital under a 51/50 not too long ago."

He glances at Joy, then at Michael, then at me. "Then you understand that under the California Legislative Code 5150, when a person, as a result of a mental health disorder, is a danger to herself or others, we are designated by the county to take your daughter into custody for a period of up to seventy-two hours for assessment, evaluation, and crisis intervention in a facility approved by the State Department of Health Care Services."

"I know the drill, Detective. It's just that—"

The detective touches Joy on the shoulder. "You have to come with me, Joy."

"Where are you taking her?" I ask, my heart in my throat, making me feel as if I'll vomit. Lord, this is all too much.

"It'll depend on where there's a bed available, ma'am. You can call County General. That's where the ambulance is headed. Call 'em in a couple of hours. See what psychiatric hospital your daughter goes to, after they do the intake."

"Can I go with her in the ambulance?"

The officer shakes his head. "Sorry, ma'am. First your daughter has to have an intake evaluation. No friends or relatives allowed during that time. After that, depending on when a bed's available, you might be able to see her later, depending on the time frame. Might be too late by the time she's actually in a hospital. Like I said, call and check. That'd be your best bet."

Joy turns her head toward me. I grasp her face between my hands and look her in the eyes. "I'll talk to you soon, honey, " I say, then kiss her on both cheeks.

She turns to Michael. And smiles.

I am so taken aback, my mouth drops open.

She flings herself at him in a bear hug, and he wraps his arms ever so slowly around her back, his chin resting on the top of her head. He stares at me. "It'll be okay, Joy," he whispers. "You're going to be all right."

"Joy!"

As if in slow motion, I watch Steven shove himself

past an officer standing about three feet away from us. Joy turns around, and Steven pushes her aside with his left arm and, at the same time, raises his right fist and punches Michael in the jaw, knocking him to the ground.

I don't have time to think, plan, or even speak. I didn't see this coming, nor did Michael or Joy. I throw myself at Steven and shove him as hard as I can with outstretched arms. He stumbles backward and falls to the ground. Instantly, three officers are on top of him, holding him down, turning him over, cuffing him.

I swing around to see several people helping Michael up. He stands, blinking, looking dazed.

I cover my mouth with the fingertips of both my hands. "My God. I can't believe Steven would do such a thing."

"I'm fine, Leena. I'm fine," he says, rubbing his chin.

Joy is standing next to me, looking as dazed as Michael.

Detective Ramsey rushes over to her and grasps her upper arm. "We have to go, Joy."

I kiss her one last time on the cheek, and she walks next to the detective toward the back of the ambulance.

She turns her head to look at me. I've joined Michael, and he has his arm around my shoulders, and I'm leaning my head on his chest. Joy is crying, and I smile and wave. Michael gives her the peace sign. Two officers escort Steven into the back of a police car.

Michael pulls away, turns me toward him, and tenderly touches the side of my face. "I think she'll be okay, Leena."

"Excuse me," the officer says. "We'll need statements from both of you." He nods at a second officer next to him then looks at me. "And you'll need to talk to Officer Renton here about your speeding ticket."

With everything that's just happened, I didn't recognize the second officer right away. I feel my face suffuse with heat. "Uh, sure," I answer. They both walk with me toward an empty police car.

Michael nods at me, then walks with another officer to that officer's vehicle. It takes about thirty minutes for both Michael and me to give statements, then we're allowed to leave.

Michael grasps my hand. "What happened to Steven?"

I shrug. "I'm assuming he was taken to the station. I really don't care."

"Where's your car?"

I gasp, close my eyes, and shake my head. "I left it in the middle of the street." I open my eyes and point toward where I recall leaving my car. "I'm sure it will have been towed by now. Shoot!"

"It'll be okay, Leena. Let's go see if it's still there," he says.

We half walk, half run for about two blocks, and lo and behold, my car, still idling, is sitting in the middle of the street. Cars honk and zoom past it, some flipping off the nonexistent driver.

"I don't believe it," I whisper.

Both of us burst out laughing, then I suddenly begin crying, shoulders shaking while I sob.

Michael pulls me toward his chest, and I wrap my arms around his waist. We stand on the sidewalk for several minutes, clutching each other. We've never had this freedom before, to be together without a guard watching our every move.

"Are you going to tell me what happened, Leena?"

"Yes, I promise. But not here, not right now." I look up at him, tears pouring down my cheeks.

"Joy will be fine, Leena. I can feel it. I'm not going to tell you not to worry about her, because you're her mother, and of course you'll worry."

"What did you say to her? How did you stop her from jumping?"

"I spoke about my brother, who committed suicide."

"What? I never—"

"Leena, let's move your car first. Then we can talk. Or better yet, let's go to my house."

"Let me get my car. I already have the address. I'll meet you there. We'll talk."

He gives me a quick kiss on the lips, and we part ways.

San Francisco isn't a large city—only seven miles long and seven miles wide. After entering Michael's address in my iPhone, I notice the address is not that far from mine. He's near Alta Plaza Park in the Pacific Heights neighborhood, both upscale and classy. Stephanie Yates obviously has connections, since she was able to secure a place for Michael to live on such short notice.

After I drive to the top of a very steep hill, Siri notifies me I have reached my destination. At the same time, I notice Michael leaning against the trunk of a car parked in front of a mansion. He walks over to me as I click the key fob to lock my car.

"At last," he says, opening his arms wide.

After snuggling into his embrace, I look up into his gorgeous blue eyes. "Welcome home, Michael."

"It sure feels good to be outside of Balmoral. And you should see the inside of the place Stephanie secured for me for the next six months."

"Do you know I live only about ten blocks away?"

"I did not. But that's a good thing."

"Stephanie pulled out all the stops to get you this place, believe me. It's hard to find homes to rent here."

He lifts his chin in the direction of the mansion I noted when I parked. "I have the entire top third floor to myself. The owners converted it into a flat for their son, but he moved out. It has perfect views of Alcatraz and the Golden Gate Bridge."

"Yes, the bridge."

He gently pulls me away from him and looks me in the eyes. "I'm sorry I mentioned the bridge. It was insensitive of me. Should we call someone to see where they've taken Joy?"

"Let's go up to your place and sit down and relax for a few minutes. I'm absolutely exhausted. Physically and emotionally drained."

"Sounds good. We can take a short break, sit on the couch, enjoy the view. Then you can check to see where they took Joy. Sometimes it can take hours to find a bed on a psych ward."

I nod. "That's a good idea. I'm just so worried about her. I can't think straight. I need to take my mind off seeing you… pulling her away from the side of the bridge. God, Michael." I close my eyes and shake my head. "What if you hadn't been there?"

He tips my chin up with gentle fingers. "I'm glad I was able to help Joy. And I think you should take a short break, relax for a bit. Maybe you have time for a couple of short kisses?"

I push away from him and close my eyes. "Hold on, Michael." I stick out my hand like a stop sign, shaking my head. I know where a few kisses can lead with Michael. He just got out of prison. We're both physically attracted to each other. But first, we need to talk about Steven finding the letter. Now that Steven knows about Michael and Michael's declaration of love for me, things could get uglier. And I don't want that to happen. We, Michael and I, have to talk about us, if there's going to be an us, and the ramifications of that for both Michael and me and Joy.

And I can't be stupid or selfish. I just found out for sure that Steven's having an affair with Karen. I surmise it's been going on for a while. And I know Karen's been around the block a few times. Actually, I know she's been around the block many, many times. In fact, I'd call her fairly promiscuous. But her sex life has never been any of my business.

Well, now it is. Who she's screwed is totally my business, because Steven and I have been having sex, too. Which means I should be checked for STDs. I'm a doctor's wife. And a teenager's mother, for God's sake. I know all about sexually transmitted diseases.

I stare into Michael's blue, blue eyes. "We need to talk first, okay?"

"Of course. Let's continue this inside."

He grasps my hand, and we walk through the front gate to the side of the house where outdoor stairs lead to the top floor.

He stops at the bottom. "It'll certainly keep me fit, walking up these stairs every day."

I nod. "But the view is going to be fantastic."

We climb two very long flights of stairs, and by the time we reach the top, I'm exhausted. The last few weeks have been especially difficult. I just want to find a comfortable place to relax and talk to Michael about what happened last night.

He opens the door leading inside, and as I pass through, the view takes my breath away. Windows line all four walls, and the entire flat is bright and cheerful and tastefully decorated.

"Oh, man, this is great, Michael. I bet you'll enjoying looking at this instead of the sky through the tiny window of your cell."

He comes up behind me and wraps me in his arms, his hands joined at my waist, his chin atop my head. He sways side to side, and I go with the flow. It's so quiet and we're alone, like we've been transported to our own private island.

"This is so peaceful," I whisper, my lips trembling. I take a quick breath, trying to stifle a sob.

Michael slowly turns me around, and I look up into his eyes.

"What is it, Leena? Please talk to me. You said something happened with Steven, and that you'd tell me about it later. I don't want to push you, but—"

"Let's sit down, Michael. I have to sit down."

"Of course." He guides me to the couch, and I sit, scooching into the corner amongst the pillows.

Michael sits a few feet away.

"Steven found one of your letters."

"Oh, my God. Are you serious?"

"The one where you told me you love me."

"Shit. He thinks there's something going on between us, because you've kept our letters and visits a secret."

"He was very angry. He thinks you and I are having an affair."

"While I was in prison?"

"I tried to explain to him that I only wrote letters to you, but he knows about the two visits."

"You told him about visiting me?"

I shake my head. "He's friends with the San

Francisco police commissioner. He said with one phone call, he'd be able to find out. So I didn't bother to lie."

"Did he hurt you? Do you feel safe living in the same house with him? You can stay with me, Leena. You'd be safe here. You and Joy."

"Thank you for the offer, but I have to go home. I don't know anything about what I should and shouldn't do in a divorce case. I don't want to leave our home, in case that makes a difference in the judge's ruling. This is all new to me, Michael."

"But—"

"No, seriously. I won't be alone with him ever again. I won't leave Joy's side."

"Joy's not home, Leena. She'll be in the psychiatric hospital for at least several days."

"Oh, you're right. Okay, then. While Joy's gone, I'll stay here with you. I'll stop by the house later and pick up a few things."

"Just make sure he's not there."

"I will."

"But you've already decided to divorce him?"

"I got in touch with Grayson Randall. He phoned last night and told me, even though he has no pictures yet, that Steven and Karen meet at The Orchid Inn. I'm sure, when he finishes his investigation, he'll have all the proof I need to show Steven why I want a divorce. California being a 50/50 state, we'll split everything right down the middle anyway, I suppose, but I don't want to hear Steven's denials and lies for why he's always gone, all his reasons and excuses for never being around. I want to be able to show him all the proof he'll need to admit he's a cheating son-of-a-bitch. And I want this over as soon as possible.

"Steven makes promises, but at the same time he

believes he's allowed to break those promises just because of who he is. He's shown signs of thinking he's God's gift to everyone for years now. I just don't think I took much notice. I'm sure he feels I've wronged him by communicating with you, but he can screw anyone he wants, and I bet, in his mind, he'll have a valid excuse for doing so."

"I don't usually use this term, Leena, but the man's a prick. You're a good person. You care."

"Yes, I do care, but maybe too much in this case."

"What do you mean, too much?"

"On the one hand, I'm so angry that he's cheating on me, I'd like to keep him away from Joy because he's the type of man I don't want my daughter to admire. On the other hand, a part of me doesn't want to be that type of ex-wife, you know? I'm sure he'll pay for Joy's education, and I'd like to keep the house, mostly to maintain stability in Joy's life. But sometimes divorce cases don't go the way you want them to. I don't know. I guess I'm just worried about the future."

He reaches out and takes my hand in his. "Don't worry about the particulars right now. You've had something very traumatic happen to you. Take a little time to breathe. You'll figure it all out."

I pause to gather my thoughts. "On top of all this, I'm worried he may have given me an STD. While he was having sex with Karen, who isn't terribly particular about who she has sex with, Steven and I were also having sex." I pull my hands away and clasp them so tightly, my knuckles are white. "I have to get tested immediately." I glance up, and Michael's eyes are glistening, as if he's about to cry.

"I want to have a relationship with you, Leena.

Whether you have an STD or not, we'll deal with it. Together. Okay?"

I nod. "I hate him. Not only for cheating on me with my best friend, but how all of this, all of this, will impact Joy and you, too. The ramifications are more than I even want to think about right now."

"Then let's take a little time to relax. Just enjoy being together alone like this for the first time. Just talk."

I move closer to his side, and he reaches around and pulls me toward him. I lay my head on his shoulder and sigh. "You have a meeting at the hospital later, right?"

"One o'clock."

I can feel the tension in his arm around my shoulders. "I wonder if Steven will be there."

"I told the officer I wouldn't press charges, so I'm sure they released him. He's supposed to be at the meeting as well."

"I'm so sorry he hit you. That was totally uncalled for."

He chuckles. "Five years in prison and no one touched me. Less than a day here, and I get a fist to the jaw by my co-worker."

I turn in his arms to face him. "No doubt you two are going to have to make amends somehow. The surgery is the most important thing right now, not the jealousy he's holding on to about you and me, nor the anger I know you're feeling against him in my defense."

"Now that I know about the argument you had last night with Steven, I'm getting a glimpse into just how angry he must be. Then he comes to the bridge, probably terrified his daughter may have jumped, and he finds me hugging Joy and whispering everything's going to be all right. And you're standing next to me, and I'm sure that just added fuel to the fire. I'm afraid his actions might escalate."

"All this time, he's been having an affair with my best friend. Unbelievable."

"And he must have been totally taken by surprise when he read my letter to you."

"He sees me as his possession. He has the gall to be angry at me for writing to you, when all along he's screwing my best friend?"

"Then he sees the three of us on the bridge, and we probably looked like the perfect little family. Instead of him talking his daughter down from the bridge, it was me. The ex-con who he thinks is having an affair with his wife, and I'm hugging his daughter. Plus, he obviously came late to the party, as they say. The entire episode was over. His daughter was already safe. I understand why he punched me in the face."

I let out a deep breath. "I'm so exhausted. My husband is having an affair. Joy almost jumps off the bridge. Jesus."

There is a moment of pure silence. A foghorn blares, bringing me back to the present. "I can't believe we're sitting here together."

"I know. I'm out of prison. I'm free."

"And you're a doctor again." I lean in and kiss him gently on the lips. "Welcome home, Michael."

We both lean back into the puffy pillows lining the couch.

"This view is so gorgeous," I say. "I never get tired of it."

"I won't either," he says. "Though, starting tonight, I don't know how much time I'll have to enjoy it."

"Meetings for the twins' surgery?"

"Yes. After today, I'm hoping Steven will maintain a professional attitude around me. After finding out he's been having an affair all this time, I'd like to throttle him for you."

"You'd never do anything like that, would you? I mean, get physical?"

He lets out a long breath. "Of course not. I don't have it in me to be violent. I've spent most of my life saving lives. I'm not going to jeopardize my medical practice because of him."

"You know, I've seen Steven around surgeons he despises, and you'd never know. Honestly, you'd think he was their best friend. I don't think he will ruin his reputation by acting unprofessionally. His reputation means everything to him. Without it, he's nothing. In his mind, that is. Above everything else, he's a surgeon. Not a father and not a husband. Steven Coughlin is a cardiac surgeon."

"He doesn't want to ruin his fabulous reputation, and I'm the newbie on the team, trying to create a new reputation for myself after being in prison. If anyone's going to be let go, it would be me."

"That's ridiculous! Stephanie didn't go through all this to even think of letting you go. If Steven acts out in any way, or starts spreading rumors about you and me, I wouldn't be surprised if she takes him off the team. What she did for you is huge, Michael."

"You may be right. Stephanie told me the surgery can't be done without me. I performed a similar heart procedure on a set of twins the year before Heather died. And there's not enough time for me to teach that particular procedure to Steven. Of course, he could learn, but the time to learn is past. But Stephanie wants him by my side, and she expects me to teach Steven as much as I can, before the surgery takes place."

"Then there will be two of you who know how to do that surgery at St. John's. There's always a plan behind Stephanie's decisions, and she means to make St. John's the premier hospital for all Siamese-twins surgeries in the future."

He chuckles. "Surgeons' wives know more than the rest of us, I guess."

My phone's ringtone chimes, and I look at the screen. "It's Grayson. I should answer this." I pick up my cell phone, and my hands are shaking, I am so stressed out. I hope Grayson has the proof I'm waiting for. "Grayson, thanks for calling."

"I have some additional information for you. Is this a good time to talk?"

"Yes, it is. What did you find out?"

"I got a hold of footage from The Orchid Inn showing your husband and Karen entering the hotel, checking in, then heading into the elevator. Then there's footage of them exiting the elevator on the third floor, walking down the hall, and entering a room together."

"How in the world did you do that?"

He laughs. "That's for me to know and you never to find out. I'm not actually going to be able to get pictures of them, uh, doing their thing in the room."

"Yes, I understand that. I appreciate everything you've accomplished in such a short time."

"My pleasure. I'll drop all of this off at your house at your convenience, or I can have my secretary send it to you by Priority Mail."

"I'll come by your office and pick it up, if you don't mind."

"I'll leave it with my secretary, and you can drop by at your leisure. It's been a pleasure working with you."

I end the call, then turn to Michael. "He got video footage of Steven and Karen. Once I have it in my hands, I'll put it in my safe-deposit box, and then when Steven and I talk, I'll have some ammunition."

"Congratulations. I guess. I'm not one to be happy over anyone's loss. And the end of any marriage is a loss, I would guess, in some way."

I gaze out at Alcatraz and think of all the good memories of when Steven and I were in love. "Yes, it's sad. Though having met you, I now have a good friend. It takes the edge off the loss of my relationship with my husband."

Michael places his fingertips under my chin and turns my face toward him. "Is that all I am to you, Leena? A friend?"

My heart starts to pound as I look into his eyes. "No, that's not all you are to me. I consider you a friend and…" I shrug. "Well, we've kissed."

"Yes, we've kissed, Leena. And we both know what happened the last time I saw you in the visitors' room."

I have a hard time looking straight at him, feeling embarrassed about our minor sexual encounter in the visitors' room at Balmoral.

"Do you regret kissing me, Leena? Do you want to stop this right now? There's no pressure on my end. You're a married woman. I have no claim on your affections. Even now, if you want to try to work it out with Steven—"

I lay a hand on his chest. "Stop. I am not working anything out with Steven. He's been cheating on me. Probably for years. I'd be willing to bet if I hired Grayson to dig deeper into Steven's past, he'd find other women Steven's been with. Karen is just the tip of the iceberg, I'm afraid. Don't forget, you saw him with another woman years ago, Michael."

He nods.

"What are you thinking, Michael?"

"I'd like to ask you out on a date."

"I'd like that."

"How's tomorrow night? Oh, wait, I have to make sure we don't have a team meeting. It may end too late or go until some ungodly hour."

"Hey, I'm used to this, Michael."

"But this isn't how I want to begin a relationship with you."

"You said you and Heather spent a lot of time together, because you kept your hours manageable."

"And that's true. I promise you, Leena, after the twins' surgery, I will not be working the hours Steven has apparently been working."

"You know what? I don't think his hours at the hospital are probably all that bad. He's obviously had time for plenty of trysts with my best friend. All the hours he's been spending with her, he could have been home with me and Joy. He just chose not to be. Does that hurt? Yes, it does, but—"

"That won't happen with us, Leena. You haven't known me for long, but I'm a man of my word. I want to start a relationship with you, but for the next few months, if you agree, we'll work on seeing each other as often as you have time, when I'm free. Then after the twins' surgery, I'm all yours. If you want me."

I lean in until our lips almost touch, and I whisper, "I do want you."

"I have to go," he whispers as he touches his forehead to mine. "I love you, Leena."

"And I love you, Michael."

STEVEN

I have to sit in the back of a police car for thirty minutes before the detective talks to me from the front seat, treating me like a common criminal. It's humiliating. Even after I explain I'm a cardiac surgeon at St. John's Hospital, give him my address in Pacific Heights, explain it's my daughter who almost jumped off the Golden Gate Bridge, and I was only trying to make sure she was okay, because Michael Casspi had Joy in his arms... he still keeps asking me inane questions.

Why did you punch the other man in the face? What's your relationship to Dr. Michael Casspi? What's your relationship to Leena Coughlin? Where was I when I found out Joy was threatening to jump off the Golden Gate Bridge? On and on, endless grilling, until he finally tells me Dr. Casspi does not plan on filing assault charges, and I'm free to leave.

I don't thank him for his public service nor say goodbye. I am royally pissed off. Who does he think he is, querying me about my life? He should have ended the investigation once he found out who I am and my relationship to both the young girl as well as the woman standing beside Dr. Casspi.

During the drive home, I call and leave a message on Stephanie's voice mail. Tell her I've had a family emergency, won't be able to make the meeting. No way am I going to sit across the table from that bastard, Dr. Casspi, now. Besides, I'm sure as shit going to finish the talk Leena and I were having. I could feel myself losing control last night, so I left. Just the thought of Leena and that ex-con fucking their brains out makes me want to kill Dr. Casspi… and Leena.

The drive home takes me half as much time as usual. I've never driven the Porsche this fast in my life, up and down the hills, until I reach home, expecting to see Leena's car, but she's not home. So I park in her spot in the garage. Surprise the bitch when she gets home and sees my car in there. Make her wonder what I'm up to. And she sure as hell better not have her fucking boyfriend with her when she walks in the goddamn door.

I don't even know where they took Joy, so I call my friend Mark, the police commissioner. His office tells me he's on vacation for another three days. Doesn't do me much good now.

When I phone the San Francisco Police and give them the name of the officer I spoke with at the scene, then ask which hospital they took my daughter to, the woman puts me on hold for fifteen minutes. I finally hang up, grab the bottle of Scotch behind the bar, and pour myself a generous glass of the golden-brown liquid, sit on the couch, and wait for Leena to come home.

I've just knocked back the last of my second drink when my phone beeps. A reminder of the team meeting. Stephanie apparently didn't get my message. Not my fucking fault. I'm supposed to meet privately and talk to Dr. Casspi about a particular step in the procedure he performed in a previous Siamese-twins surgery several years ago. Instead, I pour myself a third (or is it a fourth?)

Scotch and swirl it round and round in the glass. I can see the Golden Gate Bridge through the glass, which brings back thoughts of Joy.

Why would my daughter want to kill herself? She has everything any young woman could want: a nice home, a caring mother and father, a car, opportunities to travel and enjoy life, to do whatever she wishes. I've never said no to her in my life.

All I ever hear from Leena is, You're never home. Joy needs you, not the things you buy her. Joy's depressed because she thinks she's worthless because of your continual absence in her life. Granted, Leena has accepted partial responsibility for leaving Joy on her own, thinking Joy is a typical teenager and needs her space and her cell phone.

But what comes through most in our arguments is, because Joy and I were so close until she was in high school and that changed when I became successful, then Joy's depression is on me! But Leena's the stay-at-home mom. She's the one I assumed was in charge of my daughter. I'm too busy dumping more and more money in the bank for all the expenses my family incurs. Is anyone grateful for my hard work and fame? Leena said she's proud of me. Joy never says a word. No Thank you, Dad.

The only thanks I expect from my wife doesn't come in words anyway. If Leena showed the least bit of interest in thanking me, she could express herself in a physical way. I've told her over and over again that I enjoy having sex with her. But she needs to feel connected, she says. We've grown apart, she says. What a crock! Anything to get out of lying on her back and spreading her legs for a few minutes. Bitch! Maybe she's not into me any longer, because she's getting boinked by that ex-con.

My phone chirps again. Stephanie. Not going to answer that. She doesn't know anything about Joy, though I'm sure she'd understand. But I don't take my personal issues to the workplace. Stephanie doesn't need to know my home life is a mess. That this morning my daughter was on the Golden Gate Bridge, ready to jump into the abyss. That my wife has a boyfriend who was just released from prison, who just so happens to be my colleague! Stephanie would expect me to act like a professional. "Leave the personal stuff at home," she always says.

But right now I feel like I don't have any personal life. I'm home. Alone. No wife. Where the hell is she anyway? No daughter. Don't know where the hell she is either.

I'm just tired. So very, very tired. I can hardly hold on to my glass, but there's only a few more sips left. Don't want to waste good liquor. Shutting my eyes for just a second, I envision Karen, naked, waiting for me. Of course, I don't want a future with her, but she's about the only one around who pays any attention to me. I should call her. See if she can meet me tonight at The Orchid Inn. But I can't reach my phone. It's so far away. Far, far away, on the coffee table in front of me.

LEENA

I call the San Francisco Police Department. Michael was right—Steven's been released. I don't want to talk to Steven on his cell, because I have to make sure he's not at the house. So I call the home phone several times. He doesn't pick up. By the time I get home, he'll be at the same meeting Michael's going to at St. John's.

When I call County General Hospital, they tell me Joy's back at Langley Porter. I get in touch with Langley Porter, and they say it would be best if I wait until tomorrow to visit. Joy will be meeting with her psychiatrist either before or after dinner, then they'll be having group therapy.

Steven always parks in front of the house, and his car is nowhere in sight. I'll just be a few minutes picking up some things, so I quickly park in the driveway and rush into the house. That's when I hear a sound coming from the family room. I grasp my cell phone in one hand, then walking backward, I reach behind me and grasp the door handle leading to the garage and twist. A quick glance shows me Steven's car is parked inside. But he never parks in the garage. That's my designated parking spot. My stomach plummets.

"Leena."

I whip around, and Steven is standing in the doorway

leading to the family room. He has an empty glass in his hand, but I suspect, by the ragged look on his face and his bloodshot eyes, the glass has probably been full several times.

I slip my hand in my purse to make sure my cell phone is inside. Just in case. "Hello, Steven."

He leans against the doorjamb and stares at me. An eerie feeling seeps through me. Steven drinks, yes, but I've seen him drunk only a couple of times, and then all that happened was, he'd become überamorous, and we'd fool around in a closet before we left a party. One time, we were in a jet, high over the ocean on the way to Hawaii, and had sex in one of those terribly claustrophobic bathrooms. Now, those random thoughts make me want to puke. I swallow several times, feeling hot bile rise in my throat.

This Steven I don't recognize. This Steven scares me. Normally, he always has to be on the move and constantly doing something, be it reading, typing on his computer, attending meetings. Steven is always on the go. But this Steven is holding his empty glass, standing absolutely still, watching me with the most unusual look on his face. I can't tell if he's been crying or sweating. And his face is pale. Usually when he drinks, his face reddens from the alcohol. I don't recognize this Steven. This is not normal.

Before I let it go any further, I say, "I'll be right back. I have to use the restroom."

He's silent, nonreactive. Another oddity.

When I reach the bathroom next to the family room, I text Michael.

Just got home. Steven's here. Thought he'd be at meeting with you. He's drunk and acting strange. I think I need help.

After I press send, I hear something outside the door. It must be Steven, and I don't know why he's following me. I told him I'd be right back.

After patting my face with a bit of cold water, I dab it dry with a towel, take a deep breath, and open the door.

Steven grabs me by the wrist and tugs me out of the bathroom, dragging me behind him down the hall into the family room, flings me toward the nearest couch, and lets go.

I land on my back amidst the pillows lining the couch. Now I'm afraid.

MICHAEL

At the team meeting, I'm introduced to everyone involved in the twins' surgery, except Steven. I explain my background and experience as it impacts the surgery. Stephanie expects me to meet up with Steven in order to go over the details of the twins' hearts, but he never shows up. Stephanie is livid. Every hour is precious and necessary in order to pull this off without a hitch.

After I receive Leena's text, I surmise what must have happened. Steven is angry at being arrested, furious at seeing his daughter in my embrace, outraged that Leena has been communicating with a convict. It's understandable he might blow off this particular meeting with yours truly. Pair that mind-set with alcohol, and it's possible he's become violent.

Without a word to anyone, I exit the hospital, and phone 911 on my way down the stairs, then jump in the car Stephanie lent me and head for Leena's house. The Jaguar lives up to its capabilities. As I drive up the steep hills to Pacific Heights, the engine roars to life.

LEENA

Steven's standing next to the couch, looming over me. "How long have you—" He stops and blinks several times, then is silent.

I have no idea what he's asking me. Does he want to know how long I've known about him and Karen, or is he searching for information concerning my relationship with Michael?

I take the easier of the two. "I had you followed. The PI found out you and Karen meet at The Orchid Inn. I know you've been having an affair with her for quite some time."

He closes his eyes and sways. I'm afraid he's going to fall down in a heap right in front of me, then he opens his eyes and focuses on me. He shakes his head. "Wrong answer. That wasn't my question. How long have you been fucking Michael Casspi?"

I laugh out loud. "You have the audacity to ask me that? I'm not, as you call it, fucking anyone. I honored my marriage vows, Steven. Something I can't say about you. How long, exactly, have you been fucking my best friend?"

He lunges toward the couch.

I bolt up and scramble several feet away. Now he's sitting on the couch, looking livid, his face so red and sweaty, he looks like he's just run a marathon. I'm afraid he's gone over the edge and will assault me. And the weapons are Steven's hands and arms and legs and torso. He's much bigger than I am, and I wouldn't stand a chance if he pinned me beneath him.

"Steven, please. Let's talk like civil human beings. There's no need to get violent."

"You're still my wife, Leena. I want you. But this time, we're going to do it my way." He stands.

Instantly, I move farther away from him, around the table. We're facing each other, him on one side of the coffee table near the couch and me halfway around on the other side.

He fumbles for something in his pants pocket and extricates a knife. With a flick of his thumb, the blade bursts out, and he waves it back and forth.

"You might like it rough, Leena. Ever tried that with Dr. Casspi?"

He's staring me in the eyes, smiling. He looks demented.

I am so angry, I refuse to be in this position with my own husband. I'm feeling helpless, trapped. He moves a bit closer around the side of the table and waggles his tongue.

"I've always loved your breasts," he says in a raspy voice, inching a few more inches closer.

With every move he makes, I slide a bit to my right, away from him, toward the couch. Round and round we'll go if that's what it takes, because it's obvious Steven has no intention of sitting quietly and discussing our marriage.

He reminds me of one of those pirates from the movies with Johnny Depp. Even this far away, with the coffee table between us, which probably measures six feet across, I can smell booze, and his face is a combination of a sickly shade of gray mottled with red patches. A wisp of a thought flits through my mind. I've actually never seen Steven totally blitzed out of his mind. Drunk? Yes. Blitzed? Never. I have absolutely no idea how much he's drunk, perhaps on an empty stomach, too. That would explain his sickly countenance.

I try to keep calm, though I am literally furious. How dare he wave a knife in front of my face, insinuating he'll assault me, perhaps rape me, in our home? It makes me wonder how many other women in seemingly "perfect" marriages are being assaulted by their husbands. I understand now the fear that keeps them from running and telling their stories to the police. When it's a husband and wife, it must be terribly hard to prove.

It is at that moment I wonder if it's possible he's not interested in raping me, but rather, he wants to kill me. He is so angry, and he looks so scary. His hair is plastered to the sides of his head, he's sweating so much. And his breathing is labored, perhaps the result of this entire day. It's been an emotional roller coaster for me. I can't imagine how upsetting it's been for him, too, as Michael said, finding his wife and daughter with another man after Joy's suicide attempt. Then I confront him with my knowledge of him and Karen, that I'm aware of his infidelity.

He's on emotional overload, and he can't get to me, unless he jumps on top of the table. But he knows I'll run away and probably reach the front door before he does. I am not intoxicated. He is. Suddenly, I realize he's missed the team meeting—something completely unlike Steven. My mind reels. His behavior is so erratic, so out of character.

Steven sidesteps quickly, and I do the same. We're still on opposite sides of the table.

"Stop!"

My eyes are so intensely focused on Steven and his movements that for a split second, the word stop doesn't register. I'm not sure if I actually heard a female voice shout that one syllable, I am so intensely focused on keeping out of Steven's reach, because I'm certain he wants to kill me.

I take a quick glance to the other side of the room.

Karen is standing in the doorway, feet spread apart, arms stuck straight out in front of her. In her clasped hands is a gun, pointed straight at me, then at Steven, back and forth, back and forth. I cannot tell which of us she's intending to aim at.

"Karen, put the gun down," I say slowly.

Karen laughs, but it doesn't sound like her typical guffaw, the one that makes me smile because it's so incongruent with her pretty face and petite body. This laugh sounds maniacal, hideous, like one of the patients in One Flew Over the Cuckoo's Nest.

"Don't worry, Leena. I have no intention of hurting you," she says.

She takes a few steps closer and points the gun directly at Steven.

He's looking at Karen, eyes wide, shaking his head. His Adam's apple bobs as he swallows. He gradually straightens his back, puffs out his chest.

"How——" he says, waving his arm about the room.

Karen takes a few more steps forward, eyes glistening, focused on Steven. It's as if I'm not in the room. She seems to not take notice of me at all.

"How did I know you were here?" she says to him. A

tear—one lonely tear—slides down her cheek, and she shuts her eyes for a second. She opens them and plants her feet firmly on the ground. "I asked Dr. Yates where you were. She said you told her there was a family emergency. I've been sitting in my car right down the street. Waiting. Then I see Leena drive up. What did you do, Steven? Come home for a nooner now that you've decided you don't want to get down and dirty with me anymore? I've been calling you. Texting you. You're ignoring me, Steven." She pauses, swipes at her tears with her fingers. "I will not be ignored," she screams.

Karen told me she carried a gun. A woman living alone. Not unusual. But for this? My heart splinters. She must be hurting terribly to think of shooting Steven. I reach out one hand toward her, palm facing up, fingers stretched out. "Give me the gun, Karen. Don't shoot him."

She shifts her eyes in my direction. "What the hell is wrong with you, Leena? After everything you know that's been going on with me and Steven, you want to save his life?"

"It's not so much that I want to save his life, Karen. I don't want you to ruin yours."

"Why do you care? After what I've done to you? Screwing my best friend's husband? You must hate my fucking guts."

"I don't hate you, Karen. I'm hurt, yes. More than you'll ever know. You were—you are my best friend." If anything, I want to defuse this situation. A gun? Karen killing Steven? It seems impossible. I know this woman. She's not capable of doing such a thing. Or is she?

More tears slide down Karen's cheeks, and she stifles a sob. "And you're the best friend I've ever had, Leena."

She glares at Steven. "I fucked over my best friend in

the world for this…" She pokes the gun in Steven's direction. "For this piece of shit. I actually thought he cared about me."

"I do care about you, Karen," Steven says in a monotone.

Even I can tell he's placating her. He doesn't give a shit about her. It's so obvious. And exactly what she wouldn't want to hear.

"You were planning on dumping my ass. You know it, and I know it."

"I never said I'd divorce Leena to marry you," he mumbles.

He sounds bored. He's saying the words, but they have no meaning, because it's so damn obvious he doesn't give a rat's ass about anyone but himself.

Karen is shaking her head. "No, you never said you'd marry me. I know that."

I actually feel sorry for her. She's hurting and she's… well, she was my best friend. A part of me hates her. But I still feel the part that has loved her for so many years. It's not so swiftly removed, just because she's sleeping with my husband.

"It's been over a year, Steven. I thought you loved me. But the only person you love is yourself. You're an egotistical bastard. You never had any intention of leaving Leena. I finally realize Leena probably loves… loved me more than you ever would."

Steven smirks. "You were an amazing fuck, all right?"

The gunshot is so loud, my ears feel as if they've been poked with hot sticks. Then, suddenly, the silence is even louder than the gunshot, and I turn toward Steven.

He lifts his hands to the area of his heart. Blood is

spurting through his fingers onto the coffee table. His mouth is half open, and he's gurgling, bright red blood seeping over his lips, dribbling down his chin onto his white shirt. He looks like a vampire, and I almost laugh, it so reminds me of the Twilight movies.

His knees crumple, and he falls face first. His head slams against the side of the coffee table, bounces up, then slams back down again, hitting the corner of the wood. Then his body collapses to the ground.

The silence hits me as hard as a fist to my gut.

Sirens wail in the distance.

I slump to the floor.

I hear a voice calling my name, getting closer and closer.

Three, four, five police officers run into the room, guns drawn. Two of the officers grab Karen's arm, wrenching the gun out of her hand, then twisting her arms behind her back, cuffing her wrists.

The officers part like the water before Moses as four paramedics rush toward Steven's lifeless body. A second later, one of the paramedics, his fingers lying on Steven's neck, shakes his head, and I know.

Steven is dead.

And someone is calling my name.

MICHAEL

I arrive at Leena's house in record time. My heart's beating triple time when I pull onto her street.

An ambulance, five police cruisers, and a firetruck are parked in front of her house. Praying to God I'm not too late, I bolt for the front door, which is wide open. No one's in sight, but I hear voices and rush inside.

No one's in the kitchen or the sitting room in front of me, though I notice the view is identical to mine. The light is waning. And so is my hope.

"Please don't let anything happen to Leena," I cry out loud. Not now. Not when we're so close to having a life together.

"Leena! Leena!" I shout.

When I round the corner, I see her slumped to the floor, hands covering her face. Police officers, paramedics, firefighters crowd the room. They're all looking down. Steven is on the floor next to the coffee table, his shirt covered in blood, eyes wide open. One of the paramedics is shaking his head.

Leena cries out, "Noooo."

And I go to her.

I cradle her in my arms. She sways back and forth as I hold her. And dammit, my thoughts are not kind.

I'm thinking, how lucky can a man be? Leena is free

from her neglectful husband. I am free to marry her, if she wants me. Joy will have an attentive and loving stepfather. She needs a father in her corner, especially given the precarious state of her mental health. Now Leena won't have to slog through what might have been a messy and bitter divorce.

Leena's staring at Steven's lifeless body, and I gently lay my hand on her chin and turn her head in my direction. Tears stream down her cheeks, and all I want to do is kiss them away.

She blinks several times before her eyes focus, and she opens her mouth, but doesn't speak. She's probably in shock. I take off my suit jacket and wrap it around her shoulders.

A paramedic kneels beside me. "I think she's in shock. Excuse me, I'd like to take her vitals."

"I'm a doctor." I take my penlight from my shirt pocket, flash it from side to side in front of her eyes, then reach for her wrist. "Pupils are fine. Pulse is within normal range, given what must have just happened." I stand. "Let's get her out of here, maybe to the other room, where she can lie on a couch."

He helps me as we each take hold of one of her arms and slowly walk to the sitting room adjoining the kitchen by the front door.

"She'll be okay," I tell the paramedic.

He nods and returns to the family room.

I guide Leena to the couch, where she slumps down into the cushions.

"I'll be right back. I'm getting you a cold drink of water."

After filling a glass from the refrigerator door, I sit next to her, then lift the glass to her lips. She takes a few sips and shifts her eyes in my direction.

"What happened, Leena? Did Steven attack you? Did you shoot him?"

Her eyes are glazed. She takes another few sips, holding the glass in two hands, staring over the rim at me. After a few swallows, she leans over and sets the glass on the table nearby.

"He was so drunk. And behaving strangely. His face was gray with red splotches. I don't know how much Scotch he must have had. I think he was blitzed out of his mind. And he was very angry. About me and you. He was furious because he thought we were having an affair, and he—he pulled out a knife. He was going to attack me or... or rape me. I don't know."

Her lips are trembling. I've never been able to relate to how it must feel for a woman to be assaulted, rendered helpless to move, trying to defend herself. I'm sure Leena did that today. Oh, my God. Did she kill Steven?

I take her in my arms and hold her while she sobs, not knowing what she must be feeling right now. Her husband is dead, and though she wanted to divorce him for his infidelity, Steven and she had once been in love. And there's Joy, suddenly without a father with whom she was close at one time. And I can't help wondering, if Leena killed Steven, how is she ever going to live with that? This is a family disaster, and I cannot fix it. But I'd like to try.

She pulls back, takes a deep breath, and stares over my shoulder, as if in a daze.

"I was able to keep away from him by standing on the far side of the coffee table. He was on the other side, waving a knife back and forth, taunting me. I didn't know what he was going to do. I was so afraid... of dying. Joy would be all alone. And you and I would never have a chance to—" She pauses, tears pour down her cheeks. "That's when Karen showed up."

"Karen? I didn't even see her."

She gasps and covers her face with both hands and sobs.

I know she has to get this out of her system, talk about it, so she can deal with it. Telling the story in her own words will allow her to come to terms with the reality that Steven is dead.

I grasp her hands. They're ice-cold, and I rub them between mine. She switches her gaze in my direction.

"Thank you. I don't know why I'm so cold."

I grab the blanket draped over the back of the couch and cover her legs with it, tucking it under her thighs.

She reaches for my hands and holds on to them tightly.

I squeeze her fingers. "What happened next?"

She looks me in the eyes. "She shot him. Straight in the heart." Her voice hitches. "She loved him." She pauses. "But he said she was just a good fuck. That's when she shot him."

She pulls her hands from mine and covers her face, elbows resting on her knees. "Karen killed him. Oh, my God, Karen killed him." She drops her hands and dangles them between her knees. "What's Joy going to think when she finds out her father's dead? That Karen killed him? I know she's angry at him right now, and he was having sex with my best friend, but he didn't deserve to die, Michael."

"Leena, listen to me."

She faces me, her eyes streaked with tiny red lines.

"He obviously turned violent, Leena. He was either going to rape you or kill you or both. He saw you and Joy and me on the bridge today. We must have looked like an actual family. He was furious. So he comes here, pulls out a knife. What did you think he was going to do, let you walk away from him? Who knows what he might have done if Karen hadn't arrived and shot him? You're lucky you're alive."

She nods slowly, then reaches for me. We hug for the longest time, until we're interrupted.

"Excuse me, but I'll need to take individual statements from you."

It's one of the officers from the bridge this morning. A morning that seems like days ago.

"I recognize you," he says.

"I was with Mrs. Coughlin and her daughter at the Golden Gate Bridge this morning."

"That's right."

He hitches his chin in Leena's direction. "Do you think she needs to go to the hospital?"

I shake my head. "She was just telling me what happened."

"You weren't here?"

"No, I was on my way over after she texted me that she needed help. I called 911. You guys arrived right before I did."

"Gotcha. Mind if I speak with her?"

I stand. "I'll be out on the deck, waiting."

LEENA

Everything is happening so fast. The officer takes my statement, while another speaks with Michael on the veranda. The coroner arrives, and after several minutes, Steven's body is taken out in a black body bag on a stretcher. Karen must have been taken away the moment the police officers arrived.

I have to tell Joy what happened. Her father is dead, and Karen is the one who killed him.

When the last of the crew shuts the door behind them, Michael and I are left alone, and the silence blares in my ears, like it does after a very loud concert when you step outside. Suddenly, my ears are ringing.

My discussion with the officer took longer than Michael's, so he's still on the balcony.

I open the French doors wide to let in the cool, fresh breeze. I feel as if I can't get enough air, after hours of being cooped up inside, first with Steven and then the cops and firefighters and paramedics.

I sit next to him on the porch swing and grasp his hand.

"I have to tell Joy her father's dead. Before she finds out some other way." I let out a loud sigh and lean my head back on the cushion of the swing.

A foghorn blares in the distance.

"I love that sound," I whisper. I am so mentally

exhausted, I close my eyes to listen to the deep bellow of the foghorn, comforting in its familiarity.

"I'm sure they'll let you in to see Joy even though it's late, considering the circumstances," Michael says.

I let out a huge sigh. "They'll let me in, though I'm not looking forward to that conversation."

"Do you want me to drive you there?" Michael says.

"If you wouldn't mind."

He starts to stand, and I set my hand on his forearm. "Let's take a few minutes to talk about anything other than the current state of my life."

"Okay," he says, then leans back into the cushion. "What would you like to talk about?"

"Did you and Heather live in Pacific Heights, too?"

"Yes. But after I was sentenced, I had to rent out our home to pay attorney fees. It was well worth it. My sentence wasn't as long as it might have been, and after the renters' lease expires, I can have my home back."

"And in the end, it was Dr. Stephanie Yates who sprung you from Balmoral earlier than expected."

"Yes, she did."

It feels so good to sit quietly like this with a man. A man who I know cares for me and seems to always show up when I need him. A man who was faithful to his wife until her dying day. A man who is not my husband. But now I don't have a husband.

Can I picture marrying Michael? It's early days, and we have yet to go on an actual date. But if I had to answer in less than ten seconds, I'd say, yes. I can see myself married to Michael. Is he an ex-con? Yes, he is. With the caveat that his crime is as controversial as abortion. Personally, I would have done the same thing that he did, but hopefully I'll never be in that position.

"Penny for your thoughts," he says.

"Oh, they're worth much more than that, Sir Galahad," I say, turning my head in his direction.

He chuckles and looks me in the eyes. "Why am I Sir Galahad?"

"Because you seem quite adept at coming to my rescue when I most need it."

"You're referring to Joy?"

"Yes. And you arriving just in time after Karen shot—" I swallow to release the tightness in my throat, visions whirling in my head of Karen with the gun in her hands, pointing it at Steven, then Steven lying on the floor, blood pooling out from the sides of his body. "You saved my daughter's life. And now that Steven's dead, you're saving mine."

I turn toward him and sit cross-legged. "You were telling me a story right before we found my car idling in the middle of the street, remember?"

"I do. My brother committed suicide with a shotgun. I found him. Two years later, my mother killed herself from grief." He shrugs. "I wasn't able to help either of them and have always felt horrible about that. Granted, I was young, not even out of college, but both deaths affected me deeply. I always told myself that one day I'd make amends, some way, somehow. And I think that's happened." His eyes are glassy with unshed tears.

"Thank you for making amends by saving Joy. I will forever be in your debt. And thank you for helping me through this. I loved Steven. Past tense. But I did love him once. Very, very much."

"Of course you did."

I let out a quick breath. "Okay. I think I'm ready to go."

"I'm at your service," he says, standing.

He reaches out and takes my hand.

I grasp his hand, and he pulls me out of the swing, then wraps his arms around me.

I am flush against his chest, and I can feel him breathing. It's comforting, and I lay my head over his heart. "I still can't believe Karen shot Steven."

"If she hadn't, it might have been you they took out in the body bag."

He rubs his hands up and down my back. "Do you think you'll be able to forgive Karen for what she did to you? Betrayed your friendship, had an affair with your husband?"

I lean back and look up into his face. "I think there's a part deep inside me that will always love her. I love the Karen I knew for so many years. The Karen who went with us on vacations when Joy was little. The Karen who listened to me when I was sad or happy. The Karen who could make me laugh. The Karen, dammit, that I could count on no matter what I needed or when."

"And the other part of you?"

"I'm not a saint, Michael. And if that disappoints you, I'm so sorry, but—"

"I have my own views on how I think I'd feel if I were you, Leena. Now tell me yours."

"I don't forgive her, no. I would never cheat with my best friend's husband. I'd never do it, period." I pause, wondering what Michael's answer will be. "And you?"

He stares out at the view behind me. "I am as faithful as the day is long." He chuckles. "That's what Heather always said about me."

"So you would never cheat."

He shakes his head, stares into my eyes. "Never."

"But we've gotten off-topic. Would you forgive Karen if you were in my place?"

He puckers his lips, moving them from side to side. "I don't know if I could, Leena. Here's the thing. I believe everyone, and I mean every human being, has a line that, if that line should be crossed, it's an unforgivable act and can't be forgiven. Now, everyone's line is going to be different. Which is what makes human beings so unique. There's no telling where anyone's line is, and sometimes you don't even know where it is yourself, until someone crosses it."

"Karen crossed my line, Michael."

"And I agree with you. You should be able to have at least one or two people in your life that you can trust unequivocally. One should be your partner, husband, wife, whoever. And one should be your best friend."

"That sums it up for me. I'm sad I lost my best friend, but I'd never have done such a thing to her."

Michael dips his head and kisses me gently on the lips. "Ready to go?"

"In so many ways, no. But it's something I have to do."

"I'll wait in the lobby for you while you talk to Joy."

"I'd like to have you there with me."

"I'm not family, Leena."

"I saw something this morning. Something between you and Joy. Something I used to see between Joy and Steven that I haven't witnessed in years. She trusted you, Michael. And that's so important, especially for Joy, who lost that when Steven allowed his work life to replace his home life."

He smiles, and when I see the look on his face, it makes my heart melt.

"I always wanted to have a daughter," he says with a smile.

"You can share mine with me."

He takes my hand and gently pulls me toward the sliding glass doors into the house. "I'll drive you there. Maybe you should call them beforehand. Tell them why you're coming by so late."

JOY

I think the meds have finally started to work. I felt horrible last night and this morning, which is why I went to the bridge. Duh. But after talking to Michael and seeing Mom and him together… I don't know, I started to feel better. After I got here and did the whole intake thing, I had lunch, and damn, I didn't take a nap. Usually, I can't keep my frickin' eyes open most of the day. Later, I went to a yoga class in the rec room and stretched in so many different ways, I felt like a pretzel. After that, some hippy lady tried to teach a group of us how to meditate. That shit's hella hard, 'cause my mind's going all over the place, all the time. I'd shut my eyes, and all I could see were a bunch of bright orange cables holding up the Golden Gate Bridge. I kept picturing the water way, way down. I got so scared. Then we had dinner, and I didn't fall asleep after that either.

Now it's like this video keeps going through my head, over and over, of taking that final step over the edge of the bridge into the water. Shit! What if I'd jumped? In group, the therapist always asks each of us why we tried to kill ourselves. I already know why I wanted to die, but now I'm thinkin' kinda different about the whole thing. Ever since my mom's friend Michael talked to me about how Mom might wanna kill herself like his mom did, after his brother shot himself, I've been feeling hella guilty. I mean, I can do whatever I wanna do with my life, but I love Mom, and it's bad enough she's married to a guy who's screwing around on her, but then, if I wasn't around? Who would she have? No one.

And that's a big thing I hate about my own life. I don't have anyone. No friends. No boyfriend, that's for sure. I have Karen, who's kinda like my aunt. But other than her, the main person in my life is my mom. Daddy hasn't paid any attention to me in years. I can't freaking believe he showed up yesterday morning at the bridge and socked Michael in the face. No matter what Mom told him about that guy in prison, Daddy doesn't trust her. How the hell would Mom have an affair with a guy in freaking prison? What are they gonna do, go at it in the visiting room in front of the guards and the other prisoners? That's hella messed up that he doesn't trust her. She's trusted him all these years and for what? The shit Mom doesn't know about Daddy is more than even I probably wanna know. I've lost all respect for him anyways.

But Michael seems like a cool guy. And he didn't talk down to me, or act like I'm some dumbass kid who can't think like an adult. He told me the truth. He loves Mom. But I bet he loves her loves her, ya know? I mean, who wouldn't? Except Daddy, of course. Mom's gorgeous, and she's got a good heart.

"Lights out, you guys."

I've just been staring out the window while I'm sitting on the couch in the rec room. Two guys are playing Ping-Pong, and a girl's watching a Lifetime movie.

I get up, and I'm walking to my room. I don't feel as much like a zombie as I did before. I'm more awake. I don't wanna go to bed either, but rules are rules, and if you don't follow 'em, then they don't let you do shit around here.

"Joy, could you come with me, please?"

The therapist lady, I think her name's Jill, is standing in the doorway of the rec room. She looks real serious. I didn't do anything wrong, so I have no idea what she wants.

"Okay," I say.

She turns and walks toward the visitors' lounge, then stops a few feet from the archway and turns to look at me, then gestures for me to go inside.

What the hell? It's my mom!

"Mom?" It's almost eleven o'clock. What the hell is she doing here?

"Joy," she says, then puts her arms around me.

Michael's standing behind her, and I look at him over Mom's shoulder, and he nods and smiles at me. Not a big toothy smile, but kind of a smile like he feels sorry for me or something. I don't know what's going on. It's not visiting time, so…

"What're you doing here, Mom?"

She pulls back and takes my hand, turns, and pulls me toward the couch, where we sit. Michael sits across from us on the other couch and folds his hands between his knees and stares at the floor.

"Joy, something happened tonight that I need to tell you," she says.

I look her in the eyes, and she's gonna cry. I can always tell, 'cause her lips get all weird and shaky. She reaches out and holds both my hands in hers and squeezes them.

It reminds me of when Mocha died. Mocha was our chocolate Lab when I was, like, eight years old. She got hit by a car while I was at school, and Mom had to tell me after I got home. She did the same thing then. She looked the same. Her lips were twitching, and she was squeezing my hands, staring me in the eyes. Just like she's doing now.

"Someone died, didn't they?" I say.

She nods, and a tear falls from her eye and goes down her face and drops off her chin. She lets go of one of my hands and swipes at another tear with her fingertips.

"Who?" I say. We don't have any pets. "Did Karen get in an accident?" I ask this 'cause I've seen the way Karen drives. Mom always uses the expression like a bat outta hell, which I think is funny 'cause bats get a freaking bad rap when they're actually kinda amazing creatures.

Mom shakes her head. "No, but she killed someone. She—"

I move my head left to right, left to right, trying to make sense of this. Karen's a nurse. She'd never kill anyone. Unless maybe some guy assaulted her or something. But Mom wouldn't come here at eleven o'clock at night to tell me Karen killed her assailant. She'd wait until tomorrow, 'cause I'm going home tomorrow anyways.

"So what's up with that, Mom? Who'd she kill? I don't under—"

Mom grasps me by the shoulders and stares in my eyes. I feel like she's trying to get into my brain or something, like she's trying to tell me something telepathically or some shit.

Then she takes in a big breath and says, "Your father. Karen killed your father."

"No fucking way." I know I shouldn't be swearing—or shouting—while I'm here. It's not allowed, and I could get into trouble. But this is just insane. "No fucking way is Daddy dead."

I run out of the room and realize I don't have anywhere to go. All the doors to our bedrooms are locked. The bathroom's even locked, 'cause you have to ask permission to go, and then someone stands outside and waits for you to finish.

I stop in the middle of the hallway leading to the electronically controlled big-ass doors that lead to the outside world. No one gets past those without permission from the staff behind the glass-walled room where they work.

I turn around, and Mom's suddenly right behind me. She opens her arms, and I collapse, taking her with me, onto the cold linoleum floor.

"He can't be dead, Mom. Why're you saying this shit? Karen wouldn't kill Daddy." Now I'm shaking and crying, and Mom's trying to hold me tightly against her, while she sits on the floor in front of me.

She pulls away a few inches and dabs at the tears running down my cheeks. "Karen was in love with your father, Joy. She killed him because she and he were sleeping together, and she wanted him to leave me, so they could be together. She was so angry at him, she shot him."

I'm shaking my head as if that'll make all of this go away. Yes, I've been pissed at Daddy for years now, but I don't want him dead. He can't be dead. Lately, I've been hoping that maybe when he's finished with that twins surgery Mom's always arguing with him about, he'll have more time. He and Mom and I will go back to the way it was. Maybe we'll go on a vacation together. Even take Karen with us.

"That can't be true," I say. "I don't believe you."

I look beyond Mom's shoulder, and Michael is slowly walking toward us. Why would he be with Mom right now anyways? I really think he's in love with her. To go with her so she can tell her daughter that her father's dead is something only someone who's really close to her would do.

The look on his face is the same one Daddy used to make when I'd fall and hurt myself when I was little. The same way he used to look at me when I knew I was the light of his life and meant something to him, though it's been so long since I've seen that look. That's exactly how Michael looks right now.

He bends down and helps my mom up, then reaches for my hands, takes them in his, and I let him pull me up, too. That look on his face is the same one. It is. I'd know it no matter whose face it was on.

He cares.

And I collapse onto his chest and cry so hard, I can't stop. I can hardly breathe, and I want this all to go away.

"He can't be dead, Michael. Daddy can't be dead."

Michael holds me like Daddy used to, and Mom rubs my back like she used to when I'd get sick and feel so awful, I couldn't feel any worse.

"I'm sorry, honey," Mom whispers.

I can hardly hear her words 'cause I'm sobbing. It doesn't matter anymore that Daddy's been a total shit to me for years. I was just starting to have hope that things might change. Just like I learned in school. Everything changes. Nothing's static. Like Michael told me, too, that I'd change my mind about jumping off the bridge. When he said after I get older, I'll wonder why the hell I wanted to jump, 'cause my mind will be in a different place than it is now.

But now things with Daddy won't be able to change, 'cause he's gone. That's a fucking hella permanent thing. He'll never come back so he and I can be close again.

"I'm so sorry, Joy," Michael says. "I know you love your father, and no matter what you might think about him being busy with work, he loved you. You're his daughter, and he loved you very much."

I pull away and look him in the face, then I glance at Mom, and she's still crying. I look up at Michael again. "Are you gonna be around?"

"Am I going to be around?" he says. "I'm here for good, Joy. I'm not going anywhere." He glances at my mom, and there's this look that passes between them. Damn, man. I know they're in love with each other. I can just tell.

Mom nods at Michael, then turns to me. "Neither of us is going anywhere, Joy. We're both here for you."

"I care about your mom, Joy." He pauses. "I love her, Joy. And even though I don't know you yet, your mom's told me a lot about you. You're a great kid. I don't want to see you hurting like this any more than your mom does. But I'm here, Joy. I'm a good listener. I'm a pretty good talker, too."

I nod. "You helped me when I was on the bridge," I whisper.

"And I'll help you through this, too." He glances at my mom again, then back at me. "I promise."

We stand there for a while together, doing the group-hug thing. My heart isn't pounding as fast as it was, and for the first time in a long time, I believe in someone. Other than my mom, that is. I want to believe Michael. Mom obviously believes him. I can tell by the way she looks in his eyes. Those baby-blue marble-like eyes that stared down at me from the railing of the Golden Gate Bridge.

He helped me not wanna jump.

I believe he'll help me if I feel like jumping again.

THE END

302

About the Author

Fascinated by broken-hearted couples and atypical families, Patricia writes women's fiction, weaving engaging tales of men and women who create cohesive families where love reigns supreme. She sprinkles her books with intriguing characters who struggle to find balance in life. Whether an unwed teenager, desperate widow, abandoned father, disconnected sisters, or a troubled couple, her characters form relationships impacted by their desire to create a family.

Patricia lives with her husband and two children on the island of Alameda, across the bay from San Francisco, along with three chocolate labs and a rescue terrier mix. When she's not writing or spending time with her family, Patricia enjoys riding her Friesian horse Maximus, who lives in the Oakland hills with a million dollar view.

Sign up for Patricia's newsletter at
www.PatriciaYagerDelagrange.com

Connect with her at:

Facebook: https://bit.ly/FB_PatriciaYagerDelagrange
Amazon: https://bit.ly/AZ_PatriciaYagerDelagrange
Bookbub: https://bit.ly/BB_PatriciaYagerDelagrange
Goodreads: https://bit.ly/GR_PatriciaYagerDelagrange
Twitter: https://bit.ly/TW_PatriciaYagerDelagrange

Other Books By Patricia Yager Delagrange:

Passing Through Brandiss
Moon Over Alcatraz
Taken Away
Maddy's Phoenix
Mending Fences